THE COPPER BOX

Suzanne J. Bratcher

Mantle Rock Publishing
www.MantleRockPublishing.com

Published by Mantle Rock Publishing LLC
2879 Palma Road
Benton, KY 42025
http://mantlerockpublishing.com

Printed in the United States of America

ISBN 978-1-945094-17-0 Print Book
ISBN 978-1-945094-18-7 Ebook

Cover by Diane Turpin, DianeTurpinDesigns.com

Published in association with Jim Hart of Hartline Literary Agency, Pittsburgh, PA

Dedication

In memory of my grandfather Jerry Schroeder who spun stories of gold from darkness.

"But this one thing I do, forgetting what lies behind and straining forward to what lies ahead, I press on toward the goal for the prize of the upward call of God in Christ Jesus."
(Philippians 3:13b-14)

Acknowledgments

On a first published novel it's hard to know where to begin with the thank-yous. With my mother, Marjie Bratcher, who not only read everything I wrote but also kept it in a box for me to find after she was gone? With my father, Ed Bratcher, who understood the long process of writing a book from his own experience? Or with my daughter Jorie Hoskins, cheerleader, brainstormer extraordinare, and fashion consultant to the characters?

Wherever I begin, my deepest gratitude goes out to the following people:

Mary Johnson, my writing buddy, who has walked this path with me from the very beginning. Thank you for talking about imagined characters and their lives as if they were flesh and blood people facing life-altering problems.

Marlene Lloyd, my faithful reader, who has read every draft of every book. You have the gifts of gentle critique and genuine encouragement.

Vaughn Delp, Marcia Coman, Beth Stroble, and the teachers of the Northern Arizona Writing Project. You helped me find my writing voice by listening and sharing.

The people who make up ACFW. Thank you for conferences, contests, online courses, recommended books, and so much more. Thank you for connecting me with Sandra

Orchard, Regina Smeltzer, Lori Beatty, and Linda Fulkerson, encouragers and teachers all.

My friends in the Village Writers' Club, especially Mary Lou Moran, Madelyn Young, and Jerry Davis. Thank you for your encouragement and your commitment to writing.

The professionals who took a chance on me. My agent, Jim Hart. Thank you for believing in my writing and finding the right publisher for this book. Mantle Rock Publisher Kathy Cretsinger, line editor Pam Harris, and cover designer Diane Cretsinger Turpin. Thank you for bringing my manuscript to life and guiding me cheerfully through the publishing maze.

How to express my gratitude to the enigmatic I AM we call God: Creator, Redeemer, Comforter? Thank You for the breath of life and for the life of story.

Chapter One

Beware the wolf in disguise.

The text message was nonsense. Marty dropped her cell phone in the pocket of her denim apron and glanced around the workshop. An armoire with a broken door loomed in the afternoon shadows. A harpsichord minus its strings languished beside a worm-damaged oak table. Dust motes floated across a stray shaft of sunlight. The mingled odors of beeswax and turpentine tickled her nose. Out in the parking lot, a car door slammed. But not a creature stirred, certainly not a wolf.

The text was a wrong number. It had to be.

Marty picked up the steel wool and went back to cleaning the 1850s blanket chest. It was a simple, six-board design, but the wood was cherry instead of the usual pine. The crack in the top looked worse than it was. As she worked, she let her imagination wander. She could envision the scene now. A middle-aged man with kind brown eyes and a beard streaked with gray working on a raw cherry board with a smoothing plane, joyful because his daughter was about to marry her young man or melancholy because his son was moving his family out West.

Her cell phone vibrated on the worktable. She ignored it. Probably not a good idea; the signal didn't have to mean another text. It could just as easily mean a call from a client.

Marty picked up the phone. Another text.

Take special care today. Beware the wolf in disguise.

A prank. A prank that was wasting time. She typed.

Wrong number.

But her reply bounced back.

Sender blocked.

She didn't have time for games. She powered off the phone. She would respond to missed calls, legitimate calls, after she finished work.

Marty dipped a slender brush in wood glue and began to spread it along the edges of the split. Easy to turn off the phone. Not so easy to get her mind off the text. Who would send her such a message? Wolf in disguise could mean only one thing. But after the fiasco with Ted, she had let her friends know she was taking a break from dating. From now on, she would wait on God for her soul mate.

The message had to be sarcastic. Could it be from Ted? Not a word for months and then this? Absurd. The grapevine had it he had moved on quickly, much more quickly than she had.

Vicki was more likely. Ticked because Marty had refused Saturday's invitation to meet Vicki's single cousin from Texas. After work she would go up front and explain to Vicki one more time. Marty put the brush in cleaning fluid and reached for furniture clamps.

"Miss Greenlaw?"

An old woman, thin white hair expertly fluffed around her wrinkled face, stood in the doorway. Dressed in yellow linen slacks and an ivory silk shirt, she looked like she might have stepped out of the pages of *Antiquing Georgetown, Virginia.* Marty looked at the clamp in her hand and then back at the woman. Usually she enjoyed working with clients, but the woman's intense scrutiny made Marty suspect she wanted more than an opinion about a family heirloom.

Still holding the clamp, Marty said, "May I help you?"

The woman bustled into the room. Something familiar, something that reminded Marty of nightmares. Why hadn't Vicki kept the newcomer in the showroom or buzzed to find out if it was a good time for a visitor? The woman was carrying Marty's spiral-bound book, *A Beginner's First Book of Antique Repair*. Maybe she wanted an autograph.

"I couldn't tell from the photo on your book, but now that I see you . . ." The old woman's voice wavered. She groped in a tapestry handbag and pulled out a tissue. "You look just like your mother."

But she didn't look anything like her mother. Polly Greenlaw was blonde and big-boned, obviously of Swedish descent. Marty was petite with curly auburn hair. The woman obviously had her confused with someone else.

"You're Martha Baker. I'm your grandmother Lois."

Baker. The name exploded in Marty's mind, howling from the part of her memory she kept deliberately locked.

"Before all our tragedy, before the Greenlaws adopted you."

Marty knew perfectly well when her name had been Baker. She also knew she didn't want to go back to that time, not even in conversation. A nightmare.

"Your daddy was my son James. Your mother was Elaine, Ellie."

Mommy! Daddy! Never coming home. Never.

"Say something, honey. Let me know you remember."

Marty chose not to remember. Just as she had chosen years ago. Something terrible.

But it seemed Lois had interpreted Marty's silence as encouragement. She moved closer, close enough that Marty caught the light scent of lavender. Granny?

"I saw you twenty-two years ago, honey, just after we buried your sweet little sister."

Ruthie. The room tipped, and Marty groped for the edge of the worktable. She didn't want to remember. It was all such a long time ago. Nothing to do with her now.

"I've upset you. I should have called, but I couldn't take the chance you would refuse to see me. Until a week ago, I didn't even know the name of the couple that adopted you."

Gene and Polly Greenlaw and their son, Ron.

"Even then, I wasn't sure we'd found the right family. But when I read your blog, I knew it had to be you. Back when you were a tiny tot you loved old things. Remember Grandpa Henry's copper box?" Lois closed the distance between them and put a gentle hand on Marty's face. "Hello, Martha."

The touch sent a shock through Marty, a shock so strong that for a moment she couldn't breathe. A long time ago, Granny Lois. Marty pushed the past away, clung to the present. "I have two grandmothers, in Chicago and San Antonio." Marty took a step back, meant to leave it there. But the words kept coming: "I don't want another grandmother."

Lois studied her with compassionate, gray-green eyes, eyes that were becoming uncomfortably familiar. "I was your very first grandmother, Martha. In Arizona, the big white house in Jerome. We had such fun together! You're sure you don't remember Granny Lois?"

Granny Lois isn't coming back. Until now.

"Your daddy used to come up my driveway with his three girls. Your mommy on one side, you on the other, and Ruth Ann on his shoulders."

Memories tumbled out of the attic of Marty's mind, landing every which way. So many memories it was impossible to sort them. Grasping the only one she was sure of, she dragged it out into the light. "I remember Granny Lois left me with a social worker."

Now it was Lois's turn to step back. "You blame me. Of course you do. That's why I've come. To explain."

But Marty didn't want an explanation. Not now. Not ever. She was doing fine without these memories. In fact, she was better off without them. Why else had she put them away?

But she didn't want to hurt this old woman, grandmother or not. "It was all a long time ago." The words came out in a rush and kept coming. "I'm a grown woman. I have friends, work I love, and a home of my own. Maybe you mean well, Mrs. Baker, but honestly, I don't need another grandmother."

"You don't remember what happened to Ruth Ann, do you?"

Ruthie! Come back, Ruthie.

"It was like that at first. You couldn't deal with your sister's death, not after everything else. It was almost as if you boxed up that terrible day and put it away somewhere."

In the attic. With the nightmare.

"But I thought—hoped, really—that after all these years, you would have healed enough to remember. I don't blame you, Martha. I tried my best to forget. But it won't work. The past is still the past, whether we choose to remember or not."

The gentle pronouncement sounded like a warning, and Marty wanted to run away from this old woman and her memories. Absurd. The past couldn't hurt her. It was over and done.

Lois pulled a checkbook in a tooled-leather cover out of her handbag. "I suppose I let my hopes run away with me. I do that. For an eighty-year-old woman who's been around the block more times than she wants to admit, you'd think I'd have learned to be realistic. Your grandpa Henry used to say, 'Lois, your optimism is your greatest virtue, but it's your greatest fault too.'" She tore a deposit slip out of the back of the checkbook. "I suppose I expected you'd be waiting for me to find you. Maybe I even expected I would be the answer to your prayers as you are to mine. But, of course, you didn't know a thing about all those prayers."

Prayers. Dear God, make this woman go away! Please!

Marty knew she should offer Lois Baker a cup of tea and listen politely to whatever had brought her halfway across the country. She even opened her mouth to speak, but nothing came out. Suddenly Marty was seven years old. Not only that, she was mute. Something terrible was hidden in the jumble of memories. Something she didn't dare remember.

So Marty watched silently as Lois dug through her bag for a pen and then took it and the deposit slip to the worktable. Turning the paper over, the old woman began to draw a tiny map. "My address is on here. If you start to remember, come home, Martha. Anytime, tomorrow, next week, next month." With warm hands, she pressed the paper in Marty's cold ones. "We'll remember together, honey. One thing at a time. It won't be so scary that way."

Scary. As Marty looked into her grandmother's earnest face, another interpretation of the text message came to her, another wolf's disguise. Who had warned her? And why?

∾

Paul Russell tossed what was left of an ancient pair of work boots onto the growing pile of trash. "Grab that hat, will you, Scott? We're finally making progress down here."

The teenager picked up the felt fedora and sailed it across the dim basement.

Scott's aim was off, perhaps not intentionally, but as Paul reached out to snag the hat, his self-control frayed. He was tired and not just physically. All morning, all week, he'd done his best to keep the tone of their work upbeat. Reclaiming the old house was supposed to give them a shared goal, bring them closer, help them heal. Instead it was driving them farther apart.

Paul put the hat on his head and sat cross-legged on the dirt floor. "Pow-wow time."

Scott frowned but came to sit across from him.

Paul patted the floor between them. "Now for a few ground rules."

Scott just looked at him.

"Ground rules. You get it?"

"I get it, Dad. I just don't think it's very funny."

Paul fought his discouragement and soldiered on. "Never mind. Here's the idea. When I'm wearing the hat, it's my turn to say what's on my mind. When I pass the hat, not for money of course, it's your turn."

Scott rolled his eyes.

At least that was some response. Paul tipped the hat back with one finger. "I'm frustrated. I thought you wanted us to work together on this house, make Mom's dream come true."

Scott started to speak, but Paul held up his hand. "I'll give you the hat in a minute. This work is drudgery. I know that. But before we can get to the creative parts of rebuilding, we have to clear out the rubbish. It may not look like it, but we're making progress. I've been doing the best I can to think of ways to make it fun or at least bearable. But it's obvious my attempts aren't working. So, help me out."

Scott shrugged.

"All right. Pick from this list. Music? Competition about who can fill up the wheelbarrow the fastest? Reciting the times tables or the periodic chart or imagining what kind of guy wore this ridiculous hat and how it wound up in our basement? Something, anything, you'll find interesting that will help us pass the time."

Scott held out his hand. Paul took off the hat and gave it to him. Instead of putting it on, the teenager dropped it in his lap. "Here's the thing, Dad. I'm not a little kid anymore. I don't need a game to get me to work. If I really thought fixing up this house was a good idea, I'd work as hard as you. But this house is a wreck. It can't be 'fixed up.' The best thing we could do is tear it down. Then if we really want to live in Jerome, we can build our own house."

"But Mom wanted . . ."

"I've still got the hat, Dad. See, that's it. You think fixing this house will somehow bring Mom back. News flash! Mom's gone. And nothing you or I do can change that."

Paul listened with growing dismay. Had he really misread his son so badly, and if Scott didn't want to work on the house, what were they going to do with their summer? More importantly, how were they going to find their way back to a relationship?

Still holding the hat, the teenager scrambled to his feet. "I've gotta go."

"Sit back down. We're not done. We have to figure this out."

Scott didn't budge. "We can't figure it out any more than we can fix up this hovel, Dad."

Most of the time Paul forgot how much Scott looked like Linda. But as he got to his feet and faced his son, he was struck with the likeness. Same blonde hair, straight and fine. Same clear blue eyes. Tall for his age, Scott would soon be Linda's height, then he would catch Paul and probably grow taller. Basketball was already his game.

"This is the first time you've leveled with me, Scott. You've got to give me time to process this new information."

"It's not the first time I've told you, Dad. This is just the first time you've heard me. Maybe these are different words, but I've told you over and over I didn't want to come here. Working on this house makes me feel worse, not better."

"I don't understand."

"It's like we're pretending Mom's coming back!" Scott handed the hat to Paul and turned away.

"Wait! You can't just tell me what you don't want. Tell me what you do want. If this project makes you feel worse, what will make you feel better?"

"Nothing, Dad! Nothing will make me feel better."

Too stunned to respond, Paul watched his son go. *Father, help me. Tell me what to do.* He was losing Scott, and he didn't know how to get him back.

A moment passed and then another. Finally, Paul sailed the hat back across the basement. Then he hefted the wheelbarrow full of trash and pushed it across the uneven floor toward the open door. He had no idea what he was going to say to his son, but he knew he couldn't let the conversation end where it had.

After the dim basement, the early afternoon light was almost blinding. Setting down the wheelbarrow, Paul shaded his eyes and checked the sky in the southwest. The cloud that had hugged Cleopatra Hill for the last week was still there, maybe a little bigger, certainly no smaller. From this angle a casual observer might take it as a welcome harbinger of an early monsoon season rather than the constant reminder of the fire that was burning out of control in the Prescott National Forest.

Sort of like the failed pow-wow. On the surface, mild teenage rebellion; underneath, a problem so large he didn't know how to begin to address it. Frowning, he raised the wheelbarrow and pushed it up the rocky incline. He left it beside the porch and went inside.

Only faintly aware of how the floor sagged or how the staircase creaked, Paul hurried up to his son's room. Not surprisingly, the door was closed. He knocked, the rat-tat-tat they used.

"Go away, Dad."

"We need to talk."

"There's nothing to say. You seriously don't get it."

"Then explain it to me. I want to understand."

Silence.

"May I come in?"

"No!"

Paul put his hand on the doorknob but didn't turn it. "We have to talk sooner or later."

The door was suddenly jerked out of his hand. Scott elbowed around him and headed for the stairs. "Later."

Paul's frustration erupted in a bellow. "Scott!"

Scott stopped at the bottom of the stairs and turned. Paul glimpsed such desolation on his son's face, it took his breath away. He wanted to cry, "Let me help you!"

But before Paul could get a word out, Scott's face settled into a mask of exaggerated patience. "What, Dad?"

Suddenly Paul couldn't cope with the emotion swirling around them. Grasping at the familiar, he demanded, "Where are you going?"

"I'm grounded? I tell you how I feel, and you ground me?"

"Of course not. But I want to know where you're going and when you'll be back."

Scott didn't answer, just turned away, walked down the hall and out the front door.

Paul hesitated. He hadn't dealt with open defiance since his son was a toddler. Then he simply picked him up and put him in the time-out chair. As Scott got older, Linda had played the part of mediator. And the last couple of years Scott had quietly complied.

Paul didn't know what to do. Chase his son, force him to talk it out? Shrug it off, pretend he hadn't seen the misery on Scott's face? He knew neither option would work. But he also knew he couldn't leave things the way they were.

Paul hurried, but by the time he stepped out onto the porch, Scott was halfway across the dirt road that ended just beyond their house. Maybe he was headed to Lois's house. A surprising friendship had sprung up between the eighty-year-old woman and the fourteen-year-old boy. Maybe Scott would talk to Lois, explain his feelings to her. Then maybe Lois could help him understand his son.

But Lois was out of town. Scott seemed to remember at the same time Paul did because he turned abruptly and began to climb Cleopatra Hill. Paul started to go after him to make sure he stayed clear of the old mine behind the Baker house. The entrance was fenced off, but the makeshift road into the hill and the collapsed shaft fascinated Scott. No matter how much parents and teachers lectured, kids never grasped the danger that radiated out from the old mines. Unseen tunnels could cave in at any moment.

Still, Scott knew the mine was off limits, and Paul understood the impulse to walk off too much emotion. Against his better judgment, he let his son go.

Chapter Two

Marty braked for the four-way stop and stared at the weathered sign: Jerome, Arizona, Largest Ghost Town in America. "I don't believe in ghosts," she announced to the empty car.

Yet less than twenty-four hours after an old woman with gray-green eyes appeared in her workshop, here she was, chasing a whole family of them. Not just any ghosts, her ghosts.

It had started with the nightmare. The little girl with the gold mist of hair ran away, looked over her shoulder, and laughed. Suddenly she screamed and disappeared. Over and over, the little girl screamed and disappeared.

A nightmare Marty had all but forgotten. A nightmare she hadn't had in twenty years. But it was the same: picture for picture, move for move, sound for sound.

She remembered it as it played in her sleeping mind. She remembered it when she sat up and turned on the Tiffany lamp that spilled red and blue across white sheets. It wouldn't let her go, not when she splashed cold water on her face, not when she stood by the dark window and sipped chamomile tea. Only when she sat at her computer and booked a morning flight to Phoenix did the nightmare finally release her.

A flurry of packing, a five-hour flight across the country, a two-hour drive across the desert, and now a narrow highway

17

up the side of Mingus Mountain. At first the road ran straight, climbed steadily. Then without warning, it began a steep zig-zag ascent. A gust of wind slammed the side of the car, shaking it so Marty had to fight to keep the car in her lane.

Midway to the top, she glanced over the flimsy guardrail. On the roadway far below, a motorcycle started up. Above her, a pickup started down. If the pickup skidded and the guardrail gave way . . . Marty brought her attention sharply back to the road. A short, straight distance right, a sharp turn left, right, and left. With a little whine, the rented Camry topped the last switchback. Across the road another sign welcomed visitors to Jerome "The Billion Dollar Copper Camp."

Copper for pennies. Copper for boxes. Old mines. Be careful, girls! Someone stepped on her grave, and Marty shivered. "I don't believe in ghosts."

She drove down Main Street, past an ice cream shop she associated with orange sherbet, past an old jail she knew was slowly sliding down the mountain, past concrete steps that climbed to the next level of the town. "A three-story town," Mommy said. "The higher you lived back then, the richer you were. Granny's house is on the second story. The Bakers were a little rich."

Nothing terrible about these memories.

At last Marty was on the old mine road Lois had drawn on the tiny map. In the shelter of the mountain, the wind was less noticeable, and Marty relaxed her grip on the steering wheel. One, two houses, an empty stretch, an old warehouse. Higher up Cleopatra Hill she glimpsed the ruined boardwalk, all that was left of the once opulent third story of the town.

A short city block of empty mountainside, on her right a tumbledown house with a blue Land Cruiser out front, on her left a white Victorian house with lavender gingerbread,

Granny's house. For a moment, the little girl from Marty's nightmare danced on the upstairs porch. Ruthie.

A shiver started at the base of Marty's spine and worked its way up.

"I do not believe in ghosts!" Gritting her teeth, Marty made the sharp turn onto the steep gravel driveway. She passed the old carriage house she knew Grandpa Henry had converted into a garage. Memories swarmed her consciousness, stinging at her like bees rushing from a disturbed hive.

A yellow Prius was parked in the driveway in front of the house, but Marty had no idea whether it belonged to Lois Baker or to someone else. The idiocy of her headlong rush to Jerome struck her full force. What had she been thinking? What if the old woman had stayed in Georgetown or gone somewhere else before coming home?

The nightmare. Marty had allowed it to catapult her into action like an overwrought child instead of a sensible adult. Right then, she considered turning around and going straight home. But if she left now, she would never return. What was it the old lady, Granny Lois, said? "Come anytime. Next month, next week, tomorrow."

Tomorrow—today.

Heart pounding, Marty turned off the engine. *Dear God, Help me! Please.* The prayer surprised her. Not that she wasn't used to praying. She prayed as much as most people, on Sundays and before family meals. But this spontaneous cry for help. Where had it come from? "No atheists in foxholes." Marty could almost hear her Grandpa Greenlaw. But she wasn't an atheist, and this wasn't a foxhole. Unless a foxhole was a place you hid from a battle you wanted to avoid.

Not allowing herself to hesitate, Marty got out of the car, crossed to the porch, and mounted the three steps. Just as she knew about the old carriage house, she also knew there was no doorbell. She grasped the heavy brass knocker that was so easy to reach now and let it fall.

No one called out. No one came. Marty waited.

Still no one came.

She grasped the knocker and let it fall again. Once, twice, three times.

And waited again.

"Beware the wolf in disguise." The text message surfaced in her mind without preamble. What did it mean? Did Lois Baker have some ulterior motive for inviting her here? The thought was an easy out, another invitation to retreat. But wolf or no wolf, she had come this far, and she had to see it through. She knocked one last time.

A square wooden planter filled with purple petunias sat at the edge of the porch, but before Marty looked for the key she shouldn't know about, she tried the shiny brass knob. It turned easily.

Marty opened the door and stuck her head in. "Mrs. Baker? Lois? It's Marty Greenlaw."

No one answered. At least no human answered. A white Siamese with seal points appeared suddenly, jogging toward her, or more accurately toward the open door. Marty had to decide quickly, in or out. In. The screen door closed behind her with hollow finality.

"Lois? Granny?" Hard enough to think, the sound of the endearment in her own voice brought her heart into her throat. "It's Marty."

Still no answer. Anxious as she was to find the old woman, Marty was glad to have a moment to get her bearings. The paneled walls of the foyer were painted a soft peach that reappeared in the muted colors of an Aubusson runner on the polished oak floor. She caught a whiff of lavender, and an impression of yellow flowered wallpaper and beige carpet flitted through her mind. Memory?

She let it go. "Lois?"

Silence. Marty went to a wide arched doorway on the right that she knew opened into a long living room. "Lois!"

No answer. But again, the light scent of lavender.

Filled with high-end antique furniture, including a rare Weber square grand piano, the living room had the look and feel of a museum display. Not like when she was a child. Then the shining wood floor had invited skating in her socks.

The Siamese yowled in another room. The sound echoed faintly, sending the shiver crawling back down her spine.

"Granny! Granny Lois, are you here?"

This time she got a sort of answer, a faint rattle somewhere in the back of the house. No longer questioning how she knew, Marty followed her memory down the hall toward a back door in the kitchen. As she passed a gilt console table, a tapestry handbag on the marble top caught her eye. The same tapestry handbag. Lois Baker had definitely come home.

"Lois? It's Marty."

Again, the only answer was the small sound, but now Marty was sure it was a door rattling. Had her grandmother locked herself out of the house? But that didn't make sense. The front door was open. Even if the back door was locked, she could just go around. Yesterday Lois had seemed perfectly alert, but maybe when she was tired, she got confused. That happened to some older people.

Another rattle. Marty hurried into the kitchen. The sound was a door all right, but not the back door, a kitchen cupboard. The Siamese, one elegant paw curled beneath a low door, pulled and then pushed at the uncooperative object. The door rattled but refused to open.

Marty laughed. "Did your mama forget to feed you, kitty?"

The cat meowed what sounded suspiciously like an affirmative. Opening the cupboard, Marty retrieved a bag of dry cat food. Lois was home but hadn't taken care of this vocal pet? Marty dropped a handful of dry morsels into a pink plastic dish painted to look like a cat's face. Maybe Lois was at a neighbor's. Or maybe the old woman, exhausted from her trip across country, was napping.

Marty filled the cat's water dish and then headed for the stairs she knew led to the bedrooms. She was hardly around the corner when she pulled up short. At the foot of the staircase on a dark blue rug lay a motionless form clad in yellow linen and ivory silk. "Granny!"

Even as she cried out, Marty knew she was too late. Lois wasn't here. This was only her body, lying in a grotesque mockery of repose. The eyes were closed, but the head rested at an impossible angle. A dark bruise covered the left side of the wrinkled face, and dried blood matted the thin white hair. The left arm was flung wide; the right was twisted awkwardly beneath the body. Kneeling beside the empty shell, Marty lifted a cold hand to her cheek. "Oh, Granny."

That was when she heard another sound. Not the faint rattle of a pantry door. The creak of footsteps overhead.

∿

Paul swung the sledge hammer at the arched doorway of what had been a formal living room. It connected with a satisfying thud. Wallboard crumbled. Like his life. He swung the heavy hammer again. Two years ago. He swung a third time. Before he could build something new, he had to clear out the junk of the past. A fourth time. Maybe once Scott saw new space emerging in the old house, he would understand. Maybe even decide to be part of it.

An hour later, Paul's t-shirt was stuck with sweat to his chest and back. The muscles in his shoulders and arms ached.

The archway was gone, in pieces on the floor. The long living room and the narrow dining room behind it now comprised a single room large enough to move around in.

Dust that most likely hadn't been stirred up for fifty years drifted in the air, settled on the scuffed wood floor, on his damp shirt, in his hair. Paul coughed and dropped into one of the molded plastic lawn chairs they were using as den furniture. He wasn't sure he would ever move again, and, at the moment, he was okay with that. More than okay. Destruction was a highly-underrated activity. Samson must have died a happy man. Or if not happy, at least satisfied. Maybe he should put a sledge hammer in Scott's hands.

Maybe they could work shoulder to shoulder and solve whatever it was between them without being forced to dissect the problem. Giving Scott permission to stay at Dan's overnight had been a good decision. After the unaccustomed confrontation, they had both needed a time out. And if Scott would listen to anyone, it would be Dan.

The boys' relationship went back to when twelve-year-old Dan had stayed with nine-year-old Scott whenever he and Linda spent an occasional evening out. They never used the word "babysitter," and Scott thought of Dan as an older brother. Dan seemed to reciprocate the feeling, Jonathan to Scott's David.

Paul hoped Scott had vented his feelings to Dan. He trusted the older boy's good sense and genuine concern. But Scott would be coming home this afternoon, and whether he had talked to Dan or not, Paul still had no idea what to do about the anguish he had glimpsed on his son's face yesterday. *Father!*

Paul didn't know how to focus a prayer. Scott had shut him out for so long, he had no idea what his son was feeling.

Or had he shut Scott out? Had he been so consumed with grief and guilt that he had left Scott to cope on his own? Paul groaned. So must Samson have felt the weight of his guilt. Maybe Scott was right. Maybe he should pull this hovel down around himself.

Forgive me, Father. Help me help Scott. Surely it wasn't too late. It was never too late for God, but it might be too late for Paul to be the human father Scott needed. *Father, please!* He knew he was wallowing. He had placed his petitions before God, and God had heard.

Paul got to his feet and started the clean-up. Maybe he would have the chance to clean up his relationship with Scott too.

It took the better part of an hour to carry the old wall-board outside and toss it on the growing pile of stuff to have hauled away. He could take the seven wheelbarrows of trash they'd brought out to dump in the back of the Land Cruiser, but that would be a full load. Not something he wanted to do today. It was almost 3:00 p.m., and the earlier the better at the dump.

Paul stood for a moment, fanning himself with his damp shirt. Maybe he could get Scott to help him load up in the morning, maybe even get him to ride along. He knew it was useless to plot and plan as if he could maneuver his son into a relationship. He had to take his cues from Scott now. But his worry was like the smoke cloud hovering over the mountain, always there.

Across the road, Lois Baker's yellow Prius was still parked in the driveway in front of the house. He had been surprised to see it there when he took his first cup of coffee of the day out on the porch. He hadn't expected her back from Virginia until later this afternoon, and he wondered if her early return meant bad news, that the search had hit another dead end. Or good news, that Marty Greenlaw was indeed Martha Baker.

Now he wondered why the car was still in the driveway rather than in the carriage house garage. And who the white Camry parked behind Lois's car belonged to.

Suddenly a young woman with long, reddish hair burst out onto Lois's front porch. "Help me! Please help me!"

The woman was wearing slim black pants with a dark blue shirt. Marty Greenlaw? But this was no time to wonder who the woman was. Something was very wrong at Lois's house. Paul ran.

She saw him then and started toward him. A split second before it happened, he saw she was going to miss the last step. And he knew he couldn't reach her in time. Her high-heeled sandals weren't meant for running. One foot went down, and the other folded beneath her as she fell, narrowly avoiding hitting her head on the railing. Then he was there, helping her sit up.

She looked at him with startled eyes, hazel eyes flecked with copper. Not the freckle-faced little girl in the photo he had expected. Not a child at all, this woman was a delicate miniature like a Dresden shepherdess in Linda's collection.

He let her go and bent over to catch his breath. "What's wrong? Where's Lois?"

To his chagrin, she started to cry. If he hadn't been afraid of breaking her, he might have grabbed her arm. He wanted to shout "Stop that! Tell me what to do!" But in his mind, he heard Linda's voice. "If I'm crying, I'm probably okay. If I'm bleeding, call 911. If not, give me a little time."

But Paul didn't think there was any time. It took effort, but he kept his voice steady. "I can't help if I don't know what's wrong."

She stopped crying as abruptly as she had begun. "Lois."

"Where?" As he moved her aside, he suddenly wanted to pull her close and promise to take care of her, a feeling he thought he'd never experience toward a woman again. Definitely not toward a total stranger.

Shaken, he hurried up the steps. Whatever his feelings, now was not the time to explore them. Lois came first.

"Don't go in there!"

This time he didn't even try to keep his frustration out of his voice. "Where is she?"

"At the bottom of the stairs, but there's nothing you can do."

Help, but don't go in? Help, but there's nothing you can do? Whoever this woman was, Marty Greenlaw or not, she was close to hysteria.

Afraid of what he would find, Paul went inside. The house was too quiet, so quiet he knew what waited for him. He ran anyway. He was almost at the end of the hall when he heard something in the kitchen. A chair scraping, a door closing, he couldn't be sure.

The next moment it didn't matter. Lois lay at the foot of the staircase. He had no doubt she was dead. Or about how she had died.

Her arms were positioned as if she had tried to catch herself from a backwards fall down the stairs. Her head was twisted at an angle that could only mean her neck was broken. Her face was bruised, and her hair was matted with dried blood.

He approached her slowly. As he touched one cold hand, Lois's Siamese appeared from nowhere and climbed onto the old woman's lap. Purring, Rahab began to knead the dead flesh.

Chapter Three

Granny Lois. The porch tilted. Marty gripped the railing and sat down on the steps. Dead. The world on both sides of the porch disappeared, leaving her looking down a narrow, dark tunnel. She put her head between her knees and concentrated on breathing. Breathe in. Granny, two, three. Breathe out. Lois, two, three. Dead, dead, dead.

It wasn't working. Marty forced the image of Granny's crumpled body away, replaced it with the image of the man from across the road. Tall. Big. Not heavy, big like a bear. Shaggy brown hair, dirty brown t-shirt, ragged jeans. A big, brown bear dressed for clearing out a cave. But that was silly. A football player out of uniform. Not a lineman, a running back.

The sound of pounding feet made her sit up. A teenaged boy, blonde and wiry, came racing around the side of the house. Marty was sure he saw her, but he didn't slow down. If anything, he ran faster. Instead of following the driveway, he cut in front of the two parked cars and went down the slope, leaping from rock to rock like a young goat.

She was about to call out when she heard the screen door open behind her. Automatic to look. The man came out. When she looked for the boy again, he was disappearing into the tumbledown house across the road.

The man stood behind her, looking across at the house. She wondered if he had seen the boy. If he had, he didn't comment.

"She's dead." His voice was pleasantly low, a resonant bass, so the words didn't sound as harsh as they might have. In a strange way, it was a comfort to have someone share the burden of the terrible knowledge. "You knew. That's why you said there wasn't anything I could do."

"Yes." Marty got to her feet and turned to face him. Even in the high-heeled sandals, she felt like she was standing in a hole beside him.

He was staring across the road. Beneath the scruffy beard, his face was as white as if he'd seen a ghost. But there was no such thing as ghosts. She didn't believe in ghosts. She didn't believe . . .

"Lois must have fallen last night."

Last night. While she slept. While the little girl with gold hair ran away.

He made a visible effort to turn his attention to her. "I'm Paul Russell. Are you Marty Greenlaw?"

The sound of her name was like a splash of cold water. Suddenly she was herself again. Still shocked by what she'd seen, but herself. "Yes. But how do you know my name?"

He ignored her question. "You look a little pale."

No paler than he did, but she didn't say it.

"Let's sit down."

She shuddered. "I don't want to go inside."

"Of course not. The porch swing."

Somehow, he had read her mind. Or maybe he was as reluctant as she was to go back inside the house. They sat side by side on a white wicker swing with lavender cushions. He pushed with his foot so the swing moved gently. No ghost, a

28

solid flesh and blood man, Paul Russell's presence was surprisingly comforting.

"I know who you are because Lois and I are, were, friends. I live across the street. She's been looking for you ever since Tommy died, a little over two years."

Uncle Tommy. She'd forgotten about him. A big boy who acted like a little one.

"Lois asked for prayers from the very beginning, but this trip to Virginia was special. She was convinced Marty Greenlaw, you, would turn out to be her granddaughter."

Grief and guilt or maybe guilt and grief gripped Marty so tightly she was glad the man was at her side and couldn't see her face. It gave her a moment to try to breathe.

But he picked up on her silence, seemed to read her mind again. He stopped the swing and turned to her. "You're not Martha Baker?"

She couldn't find her voice. She cleared her throat, tried again. "I am. But I disappointed her. At first I didn't know who she was. Maybe I didn't want to know."

"I don't understand."

Words, now that Marty had found them, tumbled out, telling more than she intended, telling more than she knew herself. "I was afraid! I don't remember much about my life before I was adopted. I've always told myself it didn't matter. When she told me who she was and who I used to be, the memories came so fast I couldn't sort them out. I let her leave without even listening to what she had come such a long way to tell me."

He searched her face so intently, it was all she could do not to push him away. But she held her ground. She deserved his scrutiny, maybe his disapproval. She had handled the whole situation badly, from letting the text message bother her to pretending she didn't remember to sending Granny Lois away.

At last he settled back against the cushions and started the swing moving again. "So why did you come?"

She didn't know what to say, how to explain what she didn't understand herself. But his interest seemed genuine, so she did her best. "Lois's visit triggered an old nightmare. I decided to come and ask my grandmother to explain it." Decided sounded like her old self, the planner. Nothing like this new self who yelled for help and fell down the steps into a stranger's arms.

He was silent, and the slow movement of the swing comforted Marty. She began to breathe more normally.

After a moment, he spoke. "Lois's death is a double loss then. The future Lois wanted and the past you need."

His comment surprised her, and she wondered who this man Paul was. He looked like a bum and lived in a house that should be condemned, but he seemed able to read her mind.

She shied away from the thought, grasped at a detail that didn't matter. "What makes you think she fell last night? Why not this morning?"

"I saw her car a little before six this morning. It's a two-hour drive from the airport. She must have come home last night."

"It's my fault then."

"What's your fault?"

"She invited me to go to dinner with her. If I had gone instead of sending her away, she wouldn't have come home in the middle of the night like that." Marty felt tears start down her face, but she couldn't stop them. "She was an old woman. She must have been exhausted and discouraged. She started upstairs to go to bed."

A siren wailed, not close, but not far. Paul reached for her hand, enveloped it in his, a warm hand with long fingers and dirt under the nails. "Lois's death was an accident. Friends have been trying for years to get her to move out of this house into something on one level."

She knew he was being intentionally kind, but she wanted to pretend it was true. Just as she wanted to pretend he was a giant Teddy bear. She could lean into him, let him wrap his arms around her, and let the tears come. The strength of her longing took her by surprise. This man was a total stranger. She must be in shock.

He squeezed her hand. "You've got to be in shock, and I'm sure the best thing for you right now would be a good cry. But, unfortunately, that siren is for us."

The wail was getting louder, coming closer. No time to give in, either to fantasy or tears.

"Our fire chief gets overenthusiastic. We don't have many fires in Jerome." His voice trailed off as he looked toward the cloud of smoke in the southwest.

Marty gulped back tears and wiped her face with her hands. Again she grasped at a detail. "The radio said the fire is on the other side of the mountain, that Jerome isn't in danger."

"Not at the moment. But if the wind shifts, we could be in serious trouble. These houses are frame, dry as kindling."

Here on the side of the hill, the air was relatively still, but she remembered the wind that had pushed her car as she drove the switchbacks. "Why is the fire truck is coming here?"

"The fire department is our first response team for any emergency. No doubt José will have Dr. Zimbelman with him. Sheriff Winston will be here shortly."

"I don't understand."

"An unexpected death. There has to be an official inquiry. It's nothing to worry about."

A compact fire truck, white with a red stripe across the side, bounced down the dirt road toward them. Shorter than average for one of its kind, but still too long to make the sharp turn into the driveway, it came to a halt in front of Paul's house. The siren stopped abruptly, as did the engine, but the lights continued to flash.

Paul got to his feet, making the swing lurch. A pudgy man clad in jeans and a red t-shirt with a fire department insignia jumped down from the driver's side of the fire truck. The enthusiastic fire chief was younger than she expected him to be, about her own age. An older man, probably the doctor, climbed more slowly out of the other side.

They were partway up the driveway when a dark blue SUV bounced into view, coming too fast for the unpaved road. The two men picked up their pace.

Spraying gravel, the SUV made the turn into the driveway as the fire chief hurried up onto the porch.

Marty had a sudden urge to laugh. Lois was dead. Speed wouldn't bring her back.

"It's okay to slow down, José." Paul was reading her mind again.

"You're sure she's dead?"

"I'm sure."

"We're all here," the doctor said. "Let's get this over with. I didn't sign up for coroner duty when I let you convince me to be on call for this sorry excuse of a rescue squad."

"Quit your belly-aching, Glenn!" the sheriff shouted, marching around the two cars. "None of us signed up for something like this."

Something like this. Marty got to her feet and tried to prepare for whatever was coming.

"Good afternoon, Larry," Paul greeted him.

"Is it?" Frowning, the sheriff turned to Marty. "You the one who found the body?"

"Yes."

"So, who in blazes are you and what were you doing in Lois's house?"

"Take it easy," Paul said. "This is Marty Greenlaw, Lois's granddaughter. Marty, this is Sheriff Larry Winston, Fire Chief José Sandoval, and Dr. Glenn Zimbelman."

The sheriff elbowed his way around the other two men. "So she found you."

Marty nodded. "Yesterday."

The three newcomers studied her, but she refused to squirm. At least she no longer felt like crying. She thought the sheriff was going to comment, but all he said was, "Let's get this over with."

The fire chief and the doctor followed him inside, oblivious to the Siamese that slid between the doctor's feet and disappeared under the porch. The screen door banged shut.

Marty looked up at Paul. "What would happen if I jumped in my car and drove away?"

"For starters, you'd get a traffic ticket and a big bill from the car rental company."

"What?"

"The sheriff is parked behind your car."

Marty groaned.

"Come on. To coin a phrase, 'Let's get this over with.' Afterwards, you can come across the road to my house and relax in a plastic lawn chair. It'll be quiet, and we can sort this out."

Afterwards. Would there be an afterwards? Probably. And bum or not, she suspected Paul would be good at sorting details. Who was he? And how had he come to live in a shack? He was standing, holding the door, so Marty got up and went inside, but she moved slowly. She told herself she hadn't really known Lois Baker. Not for a long time anyway.

The three officials were gathered at the foot of the stairs. The sheriff stood with arms crossed, watching while the doctor knelt beside the body. The fire chief leaned against the wall, fidgeting.

"How long, Glenn?" the sheriff asked.

The doctor got stiffly to his feet and ran a hand through his thin, gray hair. "Long enough for rigor mortis to have become well-established. From the state of lividity, I'd say she died sometime last night. Looks like she was on her way upstairs and fell."

The sheriff picked up a small red and white ball. "Maybe she tripped on this. What is it? A cat toy? Maybe the cat can tell us what happened."

Marty felt the blood rush to her face. A joke? "My grandmother is dead! Even if you don't care, I do."

Pushing her way around the men, she ran to the dining room, simply accepting she knew where it was. The round oak table she expected to see was gone, replaced by a Duncan Phyfe table draped with gold damask. She whisked the cloth off gleaming mahogany and hurried back to the stairs.

As she spread the shimmering fabric over the grotesque figure, José said softly, "She was a sweet old lady. She should've died in her own bed."

"Sweet, but stubborn," Dr. Zimbelman said. "My wife has been trying for a couple of years to convince Lois to move down the hill to one of those garden apartments."

"God's peace be on you, Granny," murmured Marty, "on me and . . ."

"On all who enter," Paul said.

Completing her thought again.

No one spoke for a moment. Finally Sheriff Winston spoke. "Time to call the mortuary."

"I'll do it." Taking out his cell phone, Dr. Zimbelman turned his back and stepped away from the group.

"I need to be at the station," José said. "We're on high alert."

Sheriff Winston frowned. "Itching to fight those hundred foot flames we're hearing about?"

"No, sir! My job is to be ready to evacuate this town."

"That's all we need—panicked tourists, stubborn residents, and opportunistic looters."

Marty pictured the antiques she'd glimpsed in the living room. What a shame it would be to lose them in a fire.

"Go on then," growled the sheriff. "But for Pete's sake, José, if you get the call, give me some warning before you start the sirens."

"You've got it."

Marty watched as the fire chief turned away. She wished she could go with him.

Evidently the doctor felt the same way, because he raised a hand and closed his cell phone. "Seldon's coming to pick up the body," he said. "So you don't need me anymore. I came with José."

"Go on, then." Sheriff Winston dismissed them and turned to Marty. "You the one who called in this incident?"

This incident. Situations like this. Why wouldn't these men say it? Why wouldn't they say "Lois's death?"

"I called it in," Paul said.

"Why was that? Person who finds the body usually calls it in."

The accusatory tone made Marty bristle. "I had just found Lois, my grandmother, dead. I ran out of the house." She hesitated. Should she mention the footsteps or the boy?

"She called for help," Paul said. "I heard her and came over."

Marty wondered if he had seen the teenager, his son? Was he trying to protect the boy?

"Convenient." The sheriff gave her a suspicious look.

That tone again. "I don't understand," she snapped.

35

"Your grandmother finds you one day and dies the next."

Paul took a step closer to her. "What are you trying to say, Larry?"

"Maybe an inheritance."

Marty was too surprised to reply. Surely he couldn't think she had anything to do with Lois's death.

Paul shifted impatiently. "Back off, Larry."

Before Sheriff Winston could reply, the screen door banged and a man's voice shouted, "Lois? What's going on here?"

The sheriff frowned. "Here, Lockridge! The main staircase."

Marty turned to Paul. "Who?"

"Brad Lockridge. Lois's lawyer. I wonder who called him."

The lawyer, blonde and tanned, strode down the hall. Though his khakis and blue polo shirt were casual, he carried himself as if he was entering a courtroom.

Sheriff Winston asked Paul's question. "Who called you, Lockridge?"

"No one. I stopped by to see how Lois's trip went." His gaze went to the gold draped figure on the floor. "What's going on?"

"Mrs. Baker is dead." The sheriff's tone was grudging, as if he hated giving even that much information. Marty wondered what was going on with the sheriff. He was suspicious of her, dismissive of Paul and José, and now defensive with the attorney.

"I'm sorry to hear that," Brad said. Squatting down, he lifted the edge of the tablecloth and looked briefly. "What happened? Another heart attack?"

Sheriff Winston shrugged. "It looks like she tripped on the stairs sometime last night."

Brad let go of the gold cloth and stood. "You're sure it was last night? She told me she wouldn't be back until this afternoon. I think her flight was supposed to land around noon."

The flight I took, thought Marty.

"I don't care what her plans were," snapped the sheriff. "Glenn Zimbelman says she's been dead at least twelve hours."

Brad held up his hands in a mock gesture of surrender. "Hey, Larry. We're all upset by this. No need to be defensive."

"No need for you to be here at all," the sheriff growled. "It's time for you and Dr. Russell to take your business elsewhere."

Doctor? Marty couldn't help it. She stared at Paul.

He ran a hand across the stubble on his face and looked embarrassed. "Doctor as in Ph.D. Which designation some of my students insist stands for 'Piled Higher and Deeper.' I profess history at the university in Flagstaff."

Marty felt heat start at the base of her neck and work its way up. How could she have thought he was a bum? She knew better than to judge the worth of a blanket chest by its cracks. She wanted to apologize, but she was afraid to make things worse.

He grinned. "Don't worry about it. I get taken for a derelict all the time. My son calls our house 'the hovel.' My other house, while not a fit for a Cadillac, is a respectable three-bedroom, two-bath with garage."

No doubt about it, Dr. Paul Russell was a mind reader. Marty did her best to smile.

Oblivious to the exchange, the sheriff took her arm. "I've got questions for you, Missy."

Chapter Four

Paul started to object. The sheriff was in a foul mood, and he had singled out Marty to take the brunt of it.

But Lockridge was quicker. "I'm staying, Larry. As Lois's attorney, I represent the family's interests, which are now Ms. Greenlaw's interests."

Paul felt a surge of irritation, as useless as it was irrational. Under the circumstances the attorney could probably handle the situation better than he could, but he'd never particularly liked the man. Too smooth, glib even. More than that, the gratitude on Marty's face annoyed Paul. No doubt Lockridge would charge her by the hour.

Linda's voice tugged at his memory. "You're jealous of Brad. You wish the ladies swooned for you." He'd laughed at her. Absolutely not true. Linda had been the only woman he cared about. But now, was he jealous of Brad? Ridiculous. Dresden shepherdess or not, he had just met this woman.

"I guess I can't stop you," the sheriff said. "But this sure seems like another convenient coincidence."

"Explain," Lockridge said.

"First, she shows up here just at the time her grandmother dies, most likely leaving her everything. Then a lawyer shows up to help her collect."

Paul could hardly believe what he was hearing. Was Larry Winston implying Marty had something to do with Lois's death?

For the second time, Lockridge objected first. "If you're suggesting Ms. Greenlaw is somehow implicated in this tragedy, tread lightly, Sheriff. I'm sure you don't want to be accused of slander."

"All I'm saying is I've got grounds to ask this lady some questions. Dr. Russell, like I said before, 'Go home.'"

Paul ignored the command. Marty was staring at the covered figure on the floor, and for a moment he saw the little girl in the photo Lois had carried. Marty stood silent, but he could almost hear her shout, 'She's dead! Doesn't anyone care?'

Paul answered her silence. "I'll call Pastor Ray. He'll want to come to the house. I'm sure he knows what Lois wanted. If you like, I'll stay until he gets here."

"Thank you!"

The intensity of Marty's gratitude made Paul realize how alone she must feel, how welcome the pastor would be. He should have thought of calling Ray sooner.

"Call whoever you like," Sheriff Winston said, "but I've got questions that need answers now. Miss Baker or Ms. Greenlaw or whatever your name is, you need to come with me."

Lockridge said, "You're not thinking of taking her to your office, are you, Larry?"

"If I had several hours to waste, I just might do that. But since I don't, the TV room will do just fine."

"Good call," Lockridge said. As Marty moved to follow the sheriff, he put his hand at the small of her back in a protective gesture. She looked surprised, but then she smiled at Brad.

Paul shoved away an annoying flash of jealousy. Taking out his cell phone, he went into the kitchen to make the call. He got an answer on the second ring.

"Good Shepherd. How may we help you?"

"Kathy, it's Paul Russell. Is Ray in?"

"Hold on."

Paul leaned against the doorframe and waited.

"Good to hear from you, Paul. You ready for a crew from the youth group?"

"Not yet. I'll let you know. Ray, I've got some sad news."

The pastor's shock, so at odds with the sheriff's insensitivity and the lawyer's possessiveness, was strangely comforting. Ray was a friend who knew what Lois had meant to Paul and Scott since Linda's death, and it was a relief to share the burden of the sorrow that was just becoming real.

"We're all going to miss Lois," Ray said.

"There's more. The granddaughter found her."

"So, Marty Greenlaw turned out to be little Martha? How is she holding up?"

The landline on the wall began to ring. Paul hesitated. Answer it or not? Better to find out who was calling. "Ray, can you hold on a minute?"

"No problem."

Paul put his cell phone on the table and reached for the old-fashioned receiver. "Hello."

A pause. Then, "I'm sorry. I think I must have the wrong number."

A familiar voice, a young woman's voice, but he couldn't identify it. "Are you trying to reach Lois Baker?"

"Yes. This is Carly Remick."

The young face surrounded by a mop of ginger curls came into his mind. She was little more than a teenager. He wondered what her relationship with Lois was. "Hi, Carly. This is Paul Russell. I'm here at Lois's."

"May I speak to her?"

Paul suppressed a sigh. Sooner or later, people were going to find out. Sooner if he told Carly. But there was no point in pretending. "Hold on a minute, Carly."

He went back to his cell phone and explained.

"No problem," Ray said. "I think you're right to tell her, but make sure she knows no one is to come to the house. Tell her to call me if she's got questions. I'll be up shortly."

Paul closed his cell phone and went back to Carly. "I've got some sad news," he said for the second time.

She took the news harder than Paul expected, beginning to cry when she finally understood what he was telling her."

"Dad? Are you here?" Scott's voice. At the front door.

Paul covered the phone. "Stay there, Scott! I'm coming." He did not want to talk to his son over Lois's body, covered or not. Into the phone, he said, "I'm sorry, Carly. I have to go. Do you have a friend you can call?"

"Yes. I'll call Krystal. She's a friend of mine, and she likes, liked, Lois."

Krystal Cho? But Paul didn't have time to worry about who Carly's friends were. "If you can't reach her or if you need to talk to someone else, you can call Pastor Ray."

"Thanks, Dr. Russell."

Paul replaced the receiver and took a deep breath. When had he been elected Bearer of Bad Tidings? He shook off his resentment. Not really resentment, just a delayed reaction. Poor, sweet Lois. Ray was right. They were all going to miss her.

Scott was waiting for him just inside the front door. "What's going on, Dad? I saw the fire truck and the sheriff's car."

"We need to talk, son. Let's go home."

Suddenly Scott started to tremble. Paul reached for him, but the teenager twisted away. Jerking the screen door open,

Scott flung it against the wall. Then he was gone, his feet pounding across the porch and down the steps.

Paul took a deep breath. Scott knew or suspected. *Father, give me the words.* Had he and Scott ever talked about death? About its aftermath, yes. But about death itself? So intractable.

He hesitated, torn between his need to go after Scott and his promise to Marty to stay until Ray arrived. But his son had to come first.

Paul went to the door of the TV room, intending to catch her eye to let her know he was leaving. But she was standing with her back to the door. She was focused on the sheriff, and her body was rigid with anger or the effort to keep from crying or maybe something else.

Lockridge saw him and nodded as if to say, "I've got everything under control."

The reality hit Paul again. This woman was a stranger. She was not Linda, and she didn't need him. His son did. He was turning away when he heard Marty say, "I'm telling you, sheriff, someone else was in this house, upstairs. I heard footsteps."

Paul stopped. He wasn't sure why, but he knew it was imperative to hear the rest of the exchange. He couldn't hear the sheriff's response, but Marty's voice was clear and strong, not the voice of a china doll.

"No, I didn't see anyone inside. But a few minutes later while I was sitting on the front porch, a teenager came around the side of the house. He went into the house across the road."

Paul remembered the quiet sound he'd heard as he stood over Lois's body. The back door closing? Scott slipping out?

Paul left before he could hear anymore. Whatever else he learned had to come from his son. Before the sheriff had time to follow up.

Sheriff Winston called it the TV room, but Marty knew they were in the parlor. By either name, despite the plush green sofa and matching chairs, the square room with its deep carpet was a prison cell. The sheriff had settled in a leather easy chair and propped his feet on a matching ottoman. Marty continued to stand to let him know she didn't have time for his questions.

"The kid you saw would be Scott Russell," the sheriff said. "I'll check with him, but I don't think he would have been in the house. He hikes around these hills, wants to be a geologist or something like that."

Marty didn't argue. She didn't want to cause trouble for Paul, Dr. Russell.

"Now, Missy. Let's get back to your story."

"I have a name, Sheriff Winston. It isn't 'Missy.'"

The sheriff looked annoyed, but Marty didn't care. The initial shock was wearing off, and she was getting angry. Beyond the bad luck of being the first one to discover her grandmother's body, the accident had nothing to do with her.

"I suppose you do. But it ain't Baker, is it? If you ask me, that's strange, seeing as how you claim to be Jim's daughter."

"I don't claim to be anybody's daughter! Mrs. Baker told me I was her son's child. I don't remember much about my life before the Greenlaws adopted me." What she did remember was none of his business.

The sheriff looked skeptical.

Marty decided she didn't care what this man thought or any of the rest of them, for that matter. "My grandmother abandoned me when I was seven. Under those conditions, I don't think many children would remember."

"Now, don't go tearing Lois's memory down, Miss Greenlaw."

"You asked me."

Brad touched her arm, "Let's sit down, Marty. We'll get this straightened out." He went to the sofa and gestured for her to sit beside him.

Marty didn't want to make any concession to the sheriff's right to question her, but she couldn't think of a good alternative. Her car was blocked in, so she couldn't even storm out. She went to the sofa, but she perched on the edge.

"I can shed some light," Brad said. "As you must know, Larry, Mrs. Baker has been searching for her granddaughter ever since her son Tommy's death a couple of years ago. She didn't have other living relatives, so she wanted to find Martha Baker. But she had signed an agreement not to contact the child after the adoption, so she had no information, not even the adoptive family's name."

Marty caught her breath. That was why her grandmother had never come back. What a cruel requirement, for both of them.

"Before Lois went to Virginia," Brad continued, "she consulted me about Ms. Greenlaw. She showed me a detective's report and a photo on the back of a paperback book. While the data weren't conclusive, Mrs. Baker was very excited. She was certain if she saw Ms. Greenlaw, she would know if she was Martha. I recommended she make the trip. It seemed like a long shot, but I didn't see what it could hurt. What Ms. Greenlaw is saying is correct. She didn't come to Lois; Lois went to her."

"And Lois called you after she met this woman and told you she was sure Ms. Greenlaw was her long-lost granddaughter?"

"No. That was the reason I came up to Jerome today. Lois was due back this afternoon, and I wanted to hear what she found out."

"If she found out anything," Larry said.

The sheriff was implying something, but Marty couldn't guess what it was. "Are you accusing me of something?"

"Keep your shirt on, Ms. Greenlaw. Like I said earlier, I'm of the opinion that there are too many coincidences here."

"Spell it out, Larry," Brad said.

"Happy to. First, she's the only kin, but no one's seen her in what? Over twenty years? Back then she was a little girl and now she's a grown woman. If you ask me, it's tough to tell what a little girl is going to look like in later years. Second, Ms. Greenlaw shows up on the exact day of her grandmother's death to collect what I estimate is a pretty nice inheritance. Third, a lawyer turns up just when I try to ask a few friendly questions. That's about three coincidences too many for me."

Marty stood up. "You seriously think I fooled Mrs. Baker into believing I was her granddaughter, somehow engineered her fall down a flight of stairs, and then called Mr. Lockridge to meet me here? I've never even seen this man before!"

Brad touched her hand. "Pretty far-fetched, Larry, and I'm sure you know it."

Marty gave in to the gentle pressure and sat back down.

"All right, then," the sheriff said. "Tell me why you did show up today, Ms. Greenlaw."

Why indeed? How to explain the nightmare? The urgent need to face the past? She hardly understood herself, so she couldn't expect the sheriff to understand. She decided to stick to the what and let the why go. "Lois came to my workshop yesterday. I had no idea who she was at first. But as soon as she called me 'Martha Baker,' I started to remember bits and pieces. Nothing really coherent, just that she somehow fit into my past. She wanted me to talk to her right then, but I wasn't ready." Marty had been afraid, but she didn't say it. "So Lois invited me to come here when I was ready. I decided to take her up on her invitation."

"Seems kind of quick."

It was the nightmare, but she didn't try to explain. "I was awake most of last night remembering snatches of those years. It was all pretty confusing. I needed my grandmother to explain. She said to come anytime. I found a morning flight, so I came." The flight Granny should have been on. If only . . .

"Lois wasn't due back until today," the sheriff said, "but it seems she came home last night. Maybe your meeting wasn't as friendly as you say. Maybe you had a disagreement with her. Lois was upset and wanted nothing more to do with you. She threatened to cut you out of her will. Maybe you followed her here to try to change her mind."

"It wasn't like that! She didn't even mention her will."

"Or maybe you're not Martha Baker after all. Maybe you saw the chance for an inheritance and jumped at it."

Marty got to her feet. "I've had enough."

"Excuse me." A chubby little man with salt-and-pepper hair stood in the doorway. He was dressed in a blue summer suit, white shirt, and surprising red tie. He glanced around the room and then settled his gaze on Marty.

Pastor Ray. Marty's relief was as great as her agitation had been a moment before. Surely the pastor would change the tone here. She would ask him to pray.

The sheriff grunted and got to his feet. "Come in, Seldon. You ready for the body?"

Not the pastor, the undertaker. Marty's relief crumbled.

"First I need to speak to this young lady." The undertaker came toward her, both hands extended.

It was all she could do to keep from backing away. To this man, her grandmother was "the body."

Brad took charge. "Marty, this is Seldon O'Brien, owner of the Verde Funeral Home."

"And Lois's friend," the little man said. "Don't forget that." He took Marty's hands.

Cold hands. Where was Paul? He had promised to stay until the pastor got here. She needed him to take this man away. Absurd.

"We're so sorry for your loss, Ms. Greenlaw. All of Lois's friends know how much it meant to her to find you. Now to be robbed of the precious time you and she could have had together."

The man had no way of knowing the reality behind his platitudes, but Marty couldn't respond, couldn't even muster a polite thank-you.

Seldon squeezed her hands as if he understood and then turned away. "I could use some help bringing in the gurney, Larry. I suppose there's no need for an autopsy?"

The sheriff frowned.

An autopsy? Marty thought she might scream.

"Give it a rest, Larry," Brad said.

The sheriff snorted. "All right. We'll skip the autopsy. The doctor says Lois died sometime last night, and it looks like the only one to benefit much from her death just got here a couple of hours ago. Course I plan on checking on that airplane ticket."

Marty started to object, but Brad murmured, "He's baiting you."

The sheriff studied her, but Marty refused to drop her gaze.

After a moment, he shrugged, got to his feet, and went with the undertaker. As the two men went out on the porch, Marty heard Seldon say, "What happened?"

"She fell down the stairs. Maybe the cat got between her feet. Maybe her hip broke. Who knows?"

Their voices faded, and Marty realized she was holding her breath. She let it out in a long sigh. "Was the sheriff really considering an autopsy?"

"No. He was enjoying watching you squirm."

"This is all a game to him!"

"Larry's bored and hung over. The spooks have been pretty quiet the last few months."

"Spooks?"

"Remember, Jerome is a ghost town. The locals refer to themselves as spooks. Ghosts are their chosen identity and a major source of their income."

"Surely no one believes in ghosts, even in Jerome."

"You'd be surprised."

I do not believe in ghosts, thought Marty.

Through the open door, Marty heard the clang and clatter of unloading. The hearse. No pastor, no prayer. Just the body. "Where's Paul?"

"I saw him leave with his son."

It was absurd to feel abandoned. Paul Russell wasn't her brother. He wasn't even a friend. He had a responsibility to his son. But where was the boy's mother?

None of that mattered. What mattered was getting away. "I don't want to see them load her in the hearse, but my car is blocked in."

"No problem. I'll take you up to the hotel."

"Hotel?"

"You weren't planning on staying here tonight?"

Plan? That was something that belonged to her other life. She had no plan for this trip. Certainly no plan for Lois's death. "Of course not. I'll go home. There's nothing to keep me in Jerome."

Brad looked down at her, his blue eyes compassionate. "I'm afraid you can't leave just yet. Tomorrow maybe, but certainly not tonight. You and I have to have a conversation about your inheritance."

"But Lois only found me yesterday!"

"It's an unusual will, but I made sure it's perfectly legal."

Comprehension dawned slowly. The white Victorian house on the side of Cleopatra Hill belonged to her now. How easily would it give up its secrets, her secrets?

Chapter Five

Such a shame about Lois. I'll miss her. She and I had a special friendship. Her death was a tragedy, so unnecessary. Like the sheriff said, an accident, though a chain of accidents would be more accurate. If even one of the links had held, Lois would be alive today.

Before she left for Virginia, Lois told me her schedule. She would leave Saturday, spend Sunday resting and praying. Monday, she would contact Marty Greenlaw and spend the evening with her. She would return to Phoenix Tuesday on the morning flight and arrive home around 2:30 or 3:00 p.m. A quick trip, but it gave me the opportunity I'd been waiting for so patiently.

Saturday I was eager to get to work, but I stuck to the schedule I'd made. I didn't want any accidents. So, I waited until it was full dark. Then I walked to Lois's house and let myself in the back. Getting a key to the back door was a bit tricky. I had to watch for several weeks before I got my opportunity. You see, I really was patient. It would have been child's play to go in the front door. Everyone in town knows dear, trusting Lois kept a key under the planter on the front porch. But I didn't want to take a chance of being seen, slight as it was, I planned for it. I planned for light too. I suppose it would have been safe enough to use an electric lantern, but I didn't want to take the risk of someone seeing a light in the house. I did my best to avoid any accidents! My solution to light was clever. I ordered a spelunker's helmet with a light on the front. It worked beautifully. Saturday night I worked from 9:00 p.m. until 3:00 a.m. I didn't get as much done as I'd hoped, so I was tempted to stay another hour, but, like I said, I didn't want any accidents.

Sunday night I stuck to my schedule. If only Lois had stuck to hers! I had no way of foreseeing the future. A shame really. But life is what it is. Sunday I finished downstairs and started upstairs, but at 3:00 a.m. I had a lot of house left to cover. Still, I stuck to my schedule. Keep that in mind. What happened to Lois wasn't my fault. You'll see it was her fault, but I don't mind calling it an accident.

Monday night I started upstairs at 9:00. I was in Lois's bedroom at the back of the house which explains why I didn't hear the car sooner. That was the first accident, Lois changing her schedule. I still don't know what possessed her to take the evening flight. The second accident was her decision to drive home. If she'd been sensible and stayed the night in Phoenix, nothing would have happened. It was a little after 10:00 p.m. when Lois drove up to the front door and parked. That was the third link in the chain. If she'd followed her routine and put her car in the garage, I would have had enough time to grab my pack and get out the back door. But she came in the front door about the time I realized she was home. I was trapped upstairs.

The fourth link in the fatal chain was the cat. As soon as Lois came in the house, it started squawking and carrying on as if it was about to starve to death. So she went into the kitchen to feed it. Even then I still had a chance to get away without being seen. The terminal link was Lois seeing my pack on the kitchen table. Worse, she recognized it. When she came out of the kitchen shouting my name, I knew what I had to do.

51

Waiting for Lois on the stairs was tough because I knew what was coming. Even though I knew how it was going to end, I tried to convince her to leave it alone. I had a good explanation: I told her there had been a lot of break-ins over the weekend and I was checking to make sure her house was secure. She wouldn't listen. She said I was dressed in black from head to foot. She told me she had to call the sheriff. She had no idea what she was forcing me to do.

I'm going to miss Lois. We had a special friendship.

Chapter Six

Paul found Scott at the kitchen table, head pillowed on his arms, face hidden. Too many questions crowded Paul's mind. Were you upstairs in Lois's house? When did you get back from Dan's? Why didn't you check in with me? To buy time, he went to the refrigerator and pulled out two bottles of water.

Scott raised his head. "Miss Lois is dead, isn't she?"

And now another question. Are you deliberately trying to fool me? Paul handed Scott a bottle of water and sat down across from him. "I think you already knew that."

Scott dropped his gaze, concentrated on opening his bottle. An angry red stain like a birthmark appeared on his neck, a sure sign he was embarrassed.

That, at least, was in his favor. "Talk to me, son."

Scott took a long drink of water. Still without meeting Paul's eyes, he said, "What do you want to know?"

"Whatever you have to tell me."

Scott looked up. "Okay, so I was there. Miss Lois was already dead. There was nothing I could do. I went upstairs to get something, and then that lady came in. I didn't know what to do, Dad!"

"Slow down, son. Back up and start from when you got back from Dan's. Tell me why you didn't check in."

Scott shrugged. "The Prius was there, so I knew Miss Lois was home. I wanted to see her. I was just going to say hello. Then I was going to come home. What's the big deal?"

"Nothing. Go on."

"The front door was unlocked like always, so I went in. Miss Lois never minded. She said to think of it as another home. You know, Dad!"

"I know. Go on."

"I called to her a couple of times. When she didn't answer, I got kind of worried. I started looking for her." The teenager took another long drink. When he finally met his father's eyes, Paul saw a frightened little boy. "It was awful, Dad. I never saw a dead person before, but I knew she was dead without touching her or anything. I didn't know what to do."

"Why didn't you come home and tell me?"

Scott dropped his eyes again. "I had something I had to do first."

Paul waited.

"I had to get something of mine."

Paul held his frustration in check. The only chance they had to rescue his trust in his son was for Scott to tell him the story, the whole story. If he gave into the temptation to ask questions, the answers would be grudging at best. So, he waited.

"A stamp album, okay? It belonged to her husband's father. They're American stamps, and some of them are really old. Miss Lois didn't collect stamps."

"So, you told her about your stamp collection."

The anger seemed to drain out of Scott, and the red splotch on his neck began to fade.

"Not like that, Dad. Not like I was trying to get her to give it to me. I was over at her house one day when she was going through her mail. She had a letter from some kid she gives money to in Peru, and there was a really cool stamp on it."

"So you asked her if you could have it for your stamp collection."

Scott nodded. "While she was cutting the stamp off the envelope, she said I was the only stamp collector she knew except for her father-in-law, and he's been dead for a long time. She said she never got into collecting, but she knew there was a really old stamp album somewhere. She asked me if I wanted it. I said sure."

"But she didn't give it to you then."

"She said she thought it was up in the attic. She wasn't sure, but she told me one day we would go up together and look for it." Scott hesitated. "You believe me, don't you, Dad?"

"I don't have any reason not to. But why didn't you come get me?"

"I don't know. All I could think of was Miss Lois was dead. I had to have something to remember her by. So, I went to get the stamp album."

"You'll always remember Lois, son. You don't need a stamp album to keep her alive in your heart."

Scott looked defiant. "That's what you do, Dad. You've kept everything of Mom's. Even this dumb house."

∾

Buzz. Marty's head hurt. She burrowed under the pillow and tried to shut out the sound. *Buzz.* An alarm clock, not her alarm clock. *Buzz.*

Marty pushed away the pillow and opened her eyes. She was curled on her side in a brass bed, antique but nothing special. Her hair was damp, and she was wrapped in her summer robe.

Reluctantly she rolled onto her back. The ceiling was hammered tin. In one corner a full-length oval mirror reflected a glass door that opened onto a narrow balcony. It was daylight, early evening. She remembered: Arizona, the Jerome Grand Hotel, Granny Lois was dead.

The alarm continued to buzz. She had a dinner date at 7:00 p.m. Arizona time, 10:00 p.m. her time, EDT. Marty groaned and reached for the clock radio. 6:30. She turned off the alarm and struggled up to sitting. She knew she should be grateful to Brad for insisting she go to dinner with him, but now all she wanted to do was fall back on the bed and sleep until morning. The golden-haired girl had kept her awake most of last night.

Ruthie. Nightmare or memory?

With Granny Lois dead, she might never know the answer to that question. But she had to know. Ruthie: running away, screaming, disappearing. Again and again. Marty had to live with the nightmare or find out the truth. Not a tough decision. Not a decision at all.

Marty swung her legs over the side of the bed, got up, and started the routine to get ready for dinner. First, her hair. She didn't need to look in the bathroom mirror to know it was hanging in ringlets, the consequence of lying down with a wet head. When she blew it dry immediately after washing, she could achieve soft curls that nestled on her shoulders.

But after her soak in the claw-footed tub, she'd been too tired to care. Now she had to take drastic measures or look like Little Orphan Annie. She pushed away the association to her own adoption and focused her attention on her hair. Turning on the faucet, she leaned down and poured water over her head with the hotel drinking glass. The cold jarred her fully awake, but it did nothing to erase the image of the four-year-old with golden hair running away from her or the question that came with it: Had she seen Ruthie die?

When her hair was thoroughly soaked, she wound it in a towel and squeezed out as much water as she could. Then with the hair dryer in one hand and radial brush in the other, she did her best to tame the auburn curls. Like the water, the hot air blowing on her scalp and neck did nothing to derail the track her mind was running on. One question seemed to lead into the next. When did Ruthie die, where, how? Worst of all, was Ruthie's death her fault?

Marty turned off the hair dryer and finger-combed taming cream through her curls. Maybe the nightmare was nothing more than a child's anxiety dream brought back by Lois Baker's sudden appearance. Maybe now she had come to Jerome, the reality of the present would erase the fears of the child.

But she knew different. At that moment, she experienced the same indecision she had on her arrival earlier that afternoon. Stay or go? Open the door or retreat? Step inside or stay outside? The difference was now she knew her grandmother was dead. She was on her own.

Marty gave her hair one more swipe with the brush and turned away from her reflection. She left the bathroom, but one question, the only question she really cared about went with her: Had she killed Ruthie? She slipped the black silk shell with spaghetti straps over her head, stepped into the black linen slacks and then the high-heeled sandals.

She was becoming obsessed, had become obsessed. No matter what the answer to that question turned out to be, she knew she had to find it. She had come to Jerome trusting Granny Lois to tell her what had happened. Without Granny Lois, she had no one to trust but herself. What did she have to work with? A nightmare and bits and pieces of a hundred different memories.

The house. Simply walking in the front door had triggered memories, or if not full-blown memories, at least impressions from the past: carpet, wallpaper, the location of rooms, earlier furnishings.

Marty took her makeup kit from her suitcase and carried it to the full-length mirror in the corner of the bedroom. If she had interpreted Brad's hints correctly, she owned that house now or soon would. A brush of mascara, a touch of lipstick, a dab of perfume, gold loops in her ears. It didn't make sense that Lois had had time to change her will, but nothing had made sense from the moment Marty looked up and saw Lois standing in the doorway. Why should anything make sense now?

Marty shrugged into the green silk jacket Ted said made her hazel eyes look green.

Ted. Four months without so much as a phone call. Long enough to be certain it was over, long enough to make certain she was glad it was over. A wave of loneliness washed over her, but Marty pushed it away.

She locked her room and followed sounds of laughter down the hall to the restaurant. On this summer evening, every table was taken, and it took a moment to locate Brad. He was sitting at a small table by a tall window open to the sunset. He had changed into an open-necked, russet shirt and navy slacks. Better looking than Ted, more polished than Paul.

Paul? Paul reminded her of a brother. She wasn't attracted to him. Brad wasn't much different. Marty could almost hear Vicki. "At least give him a chance, Mart. You gotta kiss a lot of frogs."

Brad saw her and waved. As she made her way between the tables, he got to his feet and pulled out a chair for her. "I thought so," he murmured. "You clean up very nicely."

His eyes were intensely blue in his tanned face. She almost said "You don't look a bit like a frog," caught herself in time, said, "You too."

"Mm."

As she sat, he brushed her cheek with his lips. "You smell good too."

The touch made her heart beat faster. Maybe it wasn't going to be so hard to give Brad a chance. "Thank you for suggesting we do our business over dinner."

Brad sat across from her. "Relax, Marty. We'll have time to talk business over coffee. Right now, I want to sit and enjoy the view."

Marty felt herself flush. He was flirting, a skill she'd somehow never mastered. A fact Ted had commented on more than once. But this wasn't Ted. "I'd hate to waste this magnificent sunset. I've never seen one quite that color of magenta."

Surprisingly, instead of lobbing the ball back, he sobered. "That's the smoke in the air."

So much for flirting. She felt stupid for having forgotten the forest fire. "Has the wind shifted?"

"No. The fire is far enough away that we'll have plenty of warning if it does."

"What will happen if it does?"

"I'll whisk you away. So, forget about the fire and enjoy the Asylum." He handed her a leather-bound menu.

"An odd name for a restaurant."

"It's a play on words. This building was a hospital for the miners. The third floor was the psychiatric ward, hence the name."

Asylum for poor souls driven by nightmares, an appropriate place to begin her stay in Jerome. But Marty didn't say it.

The choices surprised her. She could order anything from spinach pasta to duck. After a brief consultation, she settled on salmon and he on filet mignon.

When the waiter had taken their orders and their menus, Brad leaned back in his chair. "Now, tell me about Marty Greenlaw."

"What would you like to know?"

"Anything. Everything. I have the feeling we don't have a lot of time to establish a relationship I hope will be long and fruitful."

If he was flirting Marty didn't get it. "I don't think I understand."

"Premise: I was Lois's attorney. Premise: I'm the administrator for her will. Conclusion: You and I will be working together for at least a year, maybe longer, depending on what you decide to do with your inheritance."

"Okay. But why don't we have much time to get to know each other?"

"From what you said this afternoon, I assumed you plan to go home tomorrow. I thought after dinner tonight we would be working together long-distance."

He was right, but suddenly Marty was confused. To cover her confusion, she looked out the window. The sunset had changed, just as something in her head had changed. Outside magenta had deepened to an angry purple. Inside?

She looked back at the man across the table, smiled, heard herself say, "I've decided to stay at least until after the funeral. I'm the last of the Bakers." But she was a Greenlaw.

Brad looked as surprised as she was. "I didn't know you felt that way."

She almost said "I didn't know I did either," but that was not exactly accurate. She'd been a Baker her whole life. She'd just kept that fact locked in the attic with the memories of her early life. Now she wasn't sure who she was. But she wasn't ready to admit that to this man she had just met.

"I did some thinking this afternoon," she said. Thinking? While she was asleep? But the words kept coming one after the other, composed, inevitable. "If my grandmother left me her house, she obviously still thought of me as family. I want to at least do her the courtesy of attending her funeral."

Brad nodded. "Good. That gives us a couple of days. But I still want us to begin getting acquainted this evening. The sum total of my knowledge about you is that Lois went to Virginia because she was convinced you were her long-lost granddaughter. You agree with her. So, tell me how you lost touch so thoroughly she had to hire a private detective to find you."

Marty took a roll from the bread basket. Warm in her hand. "I don't know much more than that. Until yesterday my early years were a total blank. I told myself whatever happened before I was seven didn't matter. I was Marty Greenlaw, and that was all I needed to be."

"But then Lois walked into your workshop."

"Yes." Marty split the roll and took a bite. Pumpernickel.

Brad took a small piece of bread with a crust that looked like sourdough and buttered it. "What have you remembered?"

"Just bits and pieces. I must have been in Jerome a good bit because as I drove into town, I remembered odd details and fragments of conversation. The same with the house. Going inside triggered, not memories exactly, more impressions of the past."

Brad studied her. "What else?"

Marty reached for her water glass and put her hands around it. Cold. The present. Not the past.

"Obviously, something upsetting."

"Why obviously?"

"You arrived practically on Lois's heels."

But not soon enough.

"And now you don't want to tell me."

"We're not in a courtroom, Mr. Lawyer."

Brad sat back. "Of course not. I'd like to help you, Ms. Greenlaw, but if you'd rather I keep out of it, I will."

Marty put down the water glass. She wasn't making any sense, even to herself. First, she hoped he would help her, then

61

she snapped his head off when he tried. "I'm sorry, Brad. I had a younger sister, Ruthie. She died, but I'm not clear on those details."

The waiter appeared with their salads and a choice of dressings, saving her having to decide whether to tell Brad the rest of it or not. So much easier to decide on blue cheese. Brad chose thousand island, and then the waiter was gone.

Brad picked up his fork. "What happened to your parents?"

"I'm sure they died before Ruthie did, but so far I haven't remembered how."

"Have you remembered the circumstances of your adoption?"

The question was too close to her nightmare. Marty shook her head and stabbed a forkful of baby greens. "I don't. I really had no idea of anything before the Greenlaws until Granny Lois walked into my workshop yesterday."

"Didn't you ever ask your parents?"

"Once in a while. Mother always said, 'It's better not to dig up the past, sweetie. Enjoy the present and look forward.'" Was that true now? What would her parents say when they found out where she was?

"Most adoptive parents are quite open about the past," Brad said, "especially with children who are a little older when they were adopted."

Marty considered. "I think all they knew was my parents were both dead." Or maybe they had wanted to protect her.

Not knowing had been fun in a way. She had imagined story after story about her parents: explorers lost on an expedition to the Bermuda Triangle; king and queen of a tiny country spirited away because of a revolution; missionaries lost in a jungle on the other side of the world.

"That may be," Brad said. "Attitudes toward adoption vary from place to place and family to family. They may never have been told. They may not have asked."

Marty was tired of questions. "Your turn. How did you meet Lois?"

"She was one of the first people I met when I moved here from L.A. She was a greeter the first Sunday I went to Good Shepherd. When she realized I was new in town and alone, she sat beside me during the service and insisted on taking me to lunch. You knew Lois. She never met a stranger."

But she hadn't known Lois. A wave of grief, the first one really, washed over Marty. For a moment, she lost track of the conversation. Granny, Why? But that question didn't have an answer. Marty pushed it away. The past was the past.

". . . one of my first clients," Brad was saying. "I'd come from a large law firm in a big city. I was tired of divorces and bankruptcies. I hoped practicing law in a small town would offer more variety."

Now was now. The man across the table was Brad Lockridge. "Has it?'

"Yes."

"Are people in a small town so much different?"

"Maybe not in most small towns. But here? You bet. Residents of Jerome call themselves spooks. A large portion of them are hippies grown up to be yuppies. You'll see if you stay around a while. But most of my clients are in Sedona. It's definitely in a class of its own."

"I don't understand."

"Sedona is a very expensive place to live. Real estate in the red rocks is limited, the views are spectacular, and the climate is moderate. Add all that together, and you have a population that is wealthy and retired. I wanted to specialize in wills and trusts. Sedona seemed like the logical place. I was right, but it took longer to get established than I had expected. Lois recommended me to her friends."

"She must have liked your work."

"She knew she could trust me."

The waiter appeared with a large tray and stand. As he traded their salad plates for their entrées, Marty realized how hungry she was. The salmon was just crisp around the edges. With the first bite, a delicate flavor of apricot tickled her tongue.

Across the table, Brad cut into his filet, releasing a flow of red juice. Marty stared at it for a moment, unable to swallow. Feeling the gorge rise in her throat, she covered her mouth with her napkin and got to her feet. Noticing her distress, a waitress pointed. Oblivious to everything except the need to keep from throwing up in the elegant dining room, Marty rushed out.

She didn't actually throw up, just retched miserably over the toilet a couple of times. As she put a wet paper towel on the back of her neck, she tried to push the picture of her grandmother's bloody head out of her mind. Dried blood, brown, not red. Brown. *Dear God!*

She splashed water on her face, just barely kept herself from pouring water over her head as she had earlier.

Dear God! Her prayer had no voice, no words. But as she cried out, the horrific images faded into a picture of a younger Lois, smiling and holding out her arms for a hug. It was a long-forgotten memory, one that comforted. She had known her grandmother, not in the way Brad knew her. In a different way. Maybe a better way.

As Marty patted her face dry with a paper towel, another prayer formed, not exactly a prayer. *God, is that you?*

She didn't get an answer with words any more than she had prayed with words. But in that moment, she was not alone. Feeling more herself than she had since Lois Baker walked into her workshop, Marty finger-combed her hair away from her face, straightened her jacket, and left the restroom.

Brad was in the hall waiting for her. "Before you say anything, let me apologize. I should have realized." With a touch so light she almost couldn't feel it, he brushed a damp curl off her face. "I know you must want to go home, but I do have some business I need to talk over with you. Give me a few more minutes this evening."

Did she want to go home? It would make more sense. She could talk to her parents, maybe even track down the social worker who had handled her case. Then she could come back and investigate the past in an orderly manner, the way Marty Greenlaw did everything. Somehow, she knew that wasn't going to happen, but Brad had already left that question behind.

"What we need to do won't take long, Marty. I promise." Putting his hand under her elbow, he steered her toward the dining room. "I sent our entrées back, but we both need to eat."

Just the mention of food made her want to retch again. She shook her head.

"Butternut squash soup. A specialty of the house. I promise you won't be sorry."

The soup was already at their places. Pale gold swirled with white. While it didn't exactly make her hungry, it did look soothing. She took the chair the waiter pulled out for her and waited until Brad was seated.

The first spoonful went down easily. Pureed squash mixed with cream and a hint of spice, cinnamon perhaps.

Brad studied her. "Glad I talked you into it?"

"Mm."

"Good. I'll get straight to the point. Lois made her will several years ago, long before she ever considered looking for you. It was a simple document with the house and its contents to be sold. If she predeceased Tommy, the proceeds were to go into a trust fund for his care until his death. If Tommy died first or if they died together, the proceeds were to go to a foundation that offers scholarships to adopted children who can't afford to go to college."

It took a moment for the implications of the bequest to sink in. For adopted children. To provide for the granddaughter she hoped would have the opportunity to go to college. That meant Lois had continued to care about her. Then why had Granny sent her away?

That was the past. She had to stay in the present. Brad seemed to be waiting for a response. She said, "That's a good cause. I was lucky. My parents were able to send me to the University of Virginia."

"That was the original will. Two years ago, after Tommy died and Lois began to search for you, she added a codicil. If you were found, everything was to go to you."

"You mean the house."

"I mean everything. It comes to quite a lot. Your grandmother was a wealthy woman."

Marty remembered the antique furniture she'd glimpsed in the living room. A small fortune there, but what else?

"She came into the money about ten years ago. It was one of those stories you hear every now and then. An eccentric second cousin she hadn't heard from in years died, leaving Lois a fortune she didn't know he had."

Marty put down her spoon. Here was something else that didn't make sense. How could Lois Baker have left a fortune to a grandchild she'd put up for adoption?

But Brad wasn't finished. "Larry was trying to scare you, but he was essentially correct."

"What do you mean?"

"You are Lois's sole beneficiary and her sudden death just when you came on the scene can be construed as surprisingly convenient."

Chapter Seven

Paul scooped half of the instant mashed potatoes onto each of the plates and then ladled canned beef stew over the potatoes. As he carried the plates to the card table, their only table, he called a third time, "Scott!"

"I'm here, Dad."

The resentment in his son's voice grated. Paul knew he had blundered in their discussion about the stamp album, but he had no idea how. Fourteen was turning out to be a confusing age for both of them. For a moment, Paul wished his son were twelve again or twenty. "Good." He retrieved the two bowls of fruit cocktail he'd sliced a banana into. "Get the milk, please."

Scott obeyed in silence, pouring each of them a glass.

When they were seated, Paul bowed his head and held out his hands. At first, he wasn't sure Scott was going to take them, but after a moment he felt his son's hands, warm and seemingly larger every time he held them.

It was Scott's turn to say the blessing, but when the teenager didn't speak, Paul said, "All glory and honor are yours, Father. For the food we are about to receive, we give you thanks. Bless it to the nourishment of our bodies and us to thy service."

As he lifted his head, Paul prayed silently, *Father, keep me calm. Give me the words I need.* He picked up his spoon and took a bite of the potato-stew mixture. He chewed and swallowed, but he didn't taste it. He ate mechanically, waiting for Scott to break the silence. When his plate was half-empty, he said, "Talk to me."

"You don't get it, do you, Dad?"

Paul wanted to snap 'I don't even know what it is!' But answering rudeness with rudeness wouldn't get them anywhere. "I get that our conversation about the stamp album was about something else, but no, I don't get what that was. Please explain it to me."

Scott's jaw relaxed suddenly, and once again Paul caught a glimpse of the frightened little boy. "Why did Miss Lois die, Dad?"

"She fell down the stairs sometime last night."

"But why? Why did she fall?"

"Sheriff Winston thinks she tripped on one of the cat toys."

"Rahab doesn't play with toys. Remember when we bought her that catnip mouse? She just ignored it. Why Miss did Lois die?"

"It was an accident, son. Accidents happen."

"Mrs. Potter told us in Sunday School everything happens for a reason. What was the reason for Miss Lois to die, Dad? Why did God decide she had to die now?"

Paul picked up his glass and drank the cold milk. He wanted to argue with the assumption, wanted to guide his son through the theological struggles he'd gone through when Linda died, wanted to say, 'Accidents are accidents, free will is free will, evil is evil, and God is God. Always there. Always with us, no matter what happens.' But now was not the time. His son was expressing grief, not asking a theological question. It was the grief he had to answer.

"Miss Lois is still your friend," he said. "You'll see her again."

"In heaven? Like I'll see Mom again someday?" Shoving his chair back so hard it fell over, Scott shouted, "I don't believe in fairy tales, Dad!"

~~~

Marty stared at Brad. "You agree with the sheriff? You think I had something to do with my grandmother's death?"

"I'm simply attempting to see the situation from all possible angles." He looked noncommittal, the way he must look in court.

"You think maybe I sneaked into town last night and pushed Lois down the stairs for an inheritance I knew nothing about? Or maybe you agree I'm not really Martha Baker." The words tumbled out, tripping over each other. She knew her anger was out of proportion to his offense, but she had thought he was on her side. She needed someone on her side.

"Take it easy, Marty."

She wanted to shout, 'Don't patronize me!' But she had to rein in her emotion or lose control completely. She drew in a deep breath, then let it out slowly. A second breath. A third.

She was gripping the cold, water glass again. He covered her hands with his warm ones.

"I want to help you. I don't think you were directly involved in Lois's death, but I agree with the sheriff on one point, it's hard to accept the timing of her death is a coincidence."

She let go of the glass and pulled loose from his hands. "What then?"

"Cause and effect, indirectly. Maybe Lois tripped on her way upstairs because she was overexcited by finding you."

Or disappointed.

"She could just have easily been in an accident with the car. She was distracted, not paying attention."

Marty knew he was right. It was exactly what she'd told Paul. If she hadn't sent Lois away, if she'd invited the old woman to dinner, to stay the night---would've, could've, should've.

Brad shrugged. "You may have been the underlying cause of Lois's death, but it wasn't your fault. You heard the doctor. His wife tried to convince Lois to get out of that house. And Jan wasn't the only one to warn Lois. I told her repeatedly those stairs were an accident waiting to happen."

He held out his hands. "Come on, Marty. I'm just analyzing Larry's thinking so we can deflect his accusations."

We.

"You're on my side?"

"Of course, I'm on your side. Come on, give me your hands."

Clean hands, well-manicured, very different from Paul's. She thrust the comparison away and put her hands in his.

He squeezed them. "The blueberry cheesecake here is superb. I'll order a piece, and we can eat it on your balcony." He let go of her hands and signaled to the waiter.

She started to refuse. Her emotions were in turmoil, and she wanted to be alone.

But maybe that was wrong. Ted had accused her of always running away from her feelings. She remembered his words as if he were sitting across from her, "I won't marry you unless we live together for at least a year. I have to find out if you're even capable of the emotional give and take of a real relationship."

She'd gotten up and walked out on him then. His final words had followed her. "That's exactly what I mean, Marty. You always run away."

Brad didn't know it, but he was offering her another chance. What did she have to lose?

So she waited while he went to the cash register to pay. The waiter brought a covered basket and a thermos of coffee to their table. Curious, Marty lifted a corner of the red-checked napkin and looked. It was a real New York style cheesecake. And fresh blueberries. The soup had been delicious, but not filling, and it had been a long time since the yogurt at the Phoenix airport.

Brad put a generous tip on the table and picked up the basket. "I knew you wouldn't be able to resist. You might be able to say no to me, but not to the cheesecake. Or is it the blueberries you have to have?"

"Definitely the blueberries."

She got to her feet and slipped a hand into the crook of his arm. If she was going to deal with her emotions, she might as well deal with them all. He gave her a smile that made her pulse quicken. She said hurriedly, "Just for a little while."

"Of course."

"And you'll leave with no fuss."

He laughed. "No fuss. Not tonight anyway."

She flushed and looked away.

Her room was on the same floor as the restaurant at the far end of the hall. They were even with the elevator when Brad said, "Remember I told you this was the psychiatric ward? Though I've never seen her myself, a ghost is supposed to haunt this hallway."

"I don't believe in ghosts."

He gave her a quizzical look. "Don't be so quick with your judgments. When I first started coming up to Jerome, I didn't believe in ghosts either."

"Now you do?"

"After seven years, I don't exactly believe in ghosts, but I don't exactly not believe in them either. The case is open."

"So what does this ghost look like?"

"A woman, a nurse. She's dressed in white and carries a clipboard."

Not terribly imaginative for a building that used to be a hospital. Marty was glad they were at the end of the hall and she didn't have to comment. Drawing the room key out of her pocket, she inserted it in the lock.

Brad reached around her, turned the key, and pushed open the door.

He followed her inside, so close she could feel the warmth of his body. As she was about to step away, he caught her arm and studied her with an expression she chose not to understand. But she didn't look away. Finally, he turned her toward the glass door, gave her a gentle push, and said, "It's a great view."

Marty laughed, part relief, part regret.

As she stepped out onto the balcony, cool mountain air embraced her. It stroked her face, sighed against her neck, and whispered through her hair. The hint of a breeze, a broken promise of rain. While Brad unpacked the picnic basket onto the tiny café table, she went to the wrought iron railing and looked over.

Beneath the balcony, there were three cars on a ribbon of blacktop with nothing but a flimsy guard rail between them and a sharp drop. One of the cars was Brad's Lexus, gleaming silver under a lone lamppost. Below the parking lot, squatted a great, unlit building with the look of a warehouse or a school, empty and abandoned to ghosts. On the other side of a deep ravine, she could see the ruins of the copper mine, the heart of Jerome that no longer beat. Farther out, the lights of Cottonwood scattered across the dark valley floor, unfamiliar constellations in an inverted night sky. Headlights moved at random, meteorites shooting across empty space.

"Coffee?"

Brad's voice brought her back to the balcony, back to cheesecake and blueberries, back to whatever she had let herself in for. "If it's decaf."

"Of course."

Marty settled herself in one of the two wrought iron chairs and accepted the steaming mug he offered. The coffee tasted so much like the real thing, she wondered if the kitchen had made a mistake. No matter. Despite the nap, exhaustion was starting to catch up with her. Nothing would keep her awake once she collapsed into bed.

Except a golden-haired girl. Marty pushed her away. Now was now.

Brad angled his chair so he could stretch out his legs. The soft light from the open door illuminated the side of his face. Straight nose, full mouth, strong chin. A good candidate for an old-fashioned, black paper silhouette.

He turned suddenly. "A penny for your thoughts or, adjusting for inflation, a quarter."

"Just admiring the view." As she heard her own words, she wanted to call them back. What was she doing parroting his earlier double entendre, inviting the very flirtation she had declared off limits? One thing was for sure, she was dangerously tired.

Brad either missed it or was gentleman enough to ignore it. "I told you. The valley looks different in the daylight, of course, but the view is just as spectacular." He cut a bite of cheesecake and held it out to her. "How about a bit of local history to lighten the mood?"

If he meant for her to eat off his fork, he was going to be disappointed. She had slipped, but now she was on her guard. She took the fork from him. "Short snippets. And only a few." She put the cheesecake in her mouth. Like the soup, it was superb.

"You can trust me to keep my side of our bargain."

He hadn't missed it then. She felt herself flush. Grateful she was sitting in shadow, she murmured, "Good."

"You know, of course, Jerome was a mining town. From the 1880s to the early 1950s, the United Verde Mine pulled a billion dollars' worth of ore out of Cleopatra Hill. Mainly copper, with gold and silver mixed in. In 1929 Jerome had a population of fifteen thousand."

Brad took the second fork from the picnic basket and cut another bite of cheesecake. "After the mine closed, everyone moved out. In 1955 there were fewer than a hundred people here." He held the bite out to her, but instead of taking the fork, she leaned around him and cut a bite for herself. He chuckled and ate the bite he had meant for her.

"When did the town become an artist community?"

"Not all that long ago. Jerome was a true ghost town for about ten years. In the sixties, a few hippies discovered the empty houses and moved in. That's when the ghost stories began."

He took her fork, cut a bite with it, and held it out. She should take his fork and cut her own bite, but she was enjoying the sound of his voice, a rich tenor, and she didn't want to interrupt. She took the bite off the fork with her teeth.

"Jerome, like all mining towns, had its sordid underbelly. Knife fights in the saloons, in the brothels, in the hotels where the rooms rented for eight hours at a time. People tell stories of a miner that haunts the old cemetery." He offered her another bite of cheesecake.

Before she took it, she said, "If you're trying to scare me, it won't work. I told you before. I don't believe in ghosts."

"Keep an open mind. Too many people have too many stories from too many places in this town to dismiss them all as kooks. If you don't believe me, talk to Krystal Cho. She's our resident expert on Jerome's ghosts. She swears the Baker house, your house, is haunted. She told me she's heard footsteps in the house when she was alone."

Footsteps . . . Marty wondered if she had accused the teenager unjustly. But she didn't believe in ghosts!

"Krystal owns Mystic Glass, a little shop you might find very interesting."

The ghost stories were getting too close to home, and Marty was tired of flirting. She needed Brad to leave. "I'll keep that in mind, but right now I want to go to bed." As soon as the words were out, she wondered if she'd blundered, again.

He let it pass. He offered her the last bite of cheesecake. When she shook her head, he ate it. "One last story, about the ghost of a woman crazy with grief over the loss of a child."

Ruthie. Absurd. Brad was talking about events that had taken place a hundred years ago.

"Guests have seen her pace this balcony. It was the only place patients could get outside for a breath of air. The iron railing went all the way to the roof back then."

"I'll be sure to lock my door."

"You're being flippant." Brad got to his feet and moved behind her chair. Putting his hands on her shoulders, he began to work the tight muscles at the base of her neck. "We'll see how you feel tomorrow. Ghost hunters come to the Jerome Grand from all over the country, hoping to catch a glimpse of the wailing woman."

Brad's hands moved along her shoulders and down her arms.

Beware the wolf in disguise.

That ridiculous text message. It had to be from someone at home. Yesterday no one in Jerome could have known she would be here tonight. Lois hadn't even identified her as Martha Baker when the text came in.

Brad ran his fingers through her hair.

Warning bells clanged, but she ignored them. She was being illogical again. Two minutes ago, she had wanted him to go home. Now . . .

"Do you have someone, Marty?"

"I thought I did."

"What happened?"

Edgy was giving way to groggy. "He didn't want to get married. He wanted us to live together instead."

"A lot of people think that's okay."

"I don't. I thought he agreed with me, but I was wrong. What about you?"

"I was married, but small town living wasn't for her. She left me for another man."

"I'm sorry." The response was automatic, but even as Marty said the words, she knew they weren't completely true.

Brad leaned over and whispered in her ear, "I'm not. Not now."

His breath was warm on her neck, and she almost turned her face for a kiss. The warning bells went off again. This time she heeded them. Getting to her feet, she turned to face him. He was so close, too close, and she was aware of the warmth of his body and the hint of spice.

Ted always smelled of pine. Paul probably smelled of sweat. There was Paul again, a complete stranger, a married stranger with a teenage son. Suddenly she was wide awake. "Thanks for a lovely evening, Brad. I had a nice time."

He stepped back as if she had slapped him. "Had a nice time, as in time's up?"

She smiled and turned him toward the door. "Don't push your luck, Mr. Attorney. I had a nice time. Nice dinner. Nice dessert. Nice neck rub. Now be nice and go home."

He laughed and, before she knew what he was doing, kissed her lightly on the lips.

Chapter Eight

Paul leaned back and stared at the computer screen. Thomas Jefferson, 1818. What could he say about the man that hadn't already been said? Nevertheless, that was his task for the summer, to write ideas no one had written before. And not just an article or two, an entire book. So far, his work consisted of an outline and two sample chapters, the proposal that got him the book contract six months ago. Since then, not one new word. And without the book, he didn't have a hope for promotion.

The cursor blinked at the top of the outline like the steady beat of a drum calling for action. But the topics and subtopics marched down the page in stiff formation like a regiment of British Redcoats unprepared for real-life guerilla warfare. The spark that had fueled the revolution of his book proposal had been extinguished.

That kind of fanciful thinking was nothing more than a new avoidance technique. Paul got up from his desk chair, an ergonomic design intended to allow him to sit for hours in relative comfort. For all the good it was doing, he could have left it at the house in Cottonwood or in pieces in the shipping box, for that matter.

He circled the room restlessly, moving from the hollow core door supported by two sawhorses that was his desk to the crude bookshelves made from planks held up by cinder blocks and back again. Not since college days had he tried to work in such crude conditions. Maybe he needed a decent desk.

That useless thought propelled him out of the study and across the hall to his bedroom. Linda's picture waited on the metal filing cabinet he used as a dresser. She smiled at him from beneath the brim of a straw hat she was holding on her head. The wind whipped her yellow flowered sundress and stirred the Pacific behind her into whitecaps.

Had it only been three summers ago? Scott was away at camp. Driven by some force they couldn't name, premonition maybe, they ignored the budget and went to Hawaii.

He remembered Linda beside him as they snorkeled in water so clear it seemed they could touch the sea turtle far below. Linda in front of him as the boat raced to catch lava glowing red against the night sky, hissing as it flowed into the sea. Linda behind him as they explored the Japanese garden across from their hotel.

Paul picked up the wicker frame and studied his wife's photograph as though he had never memorized her face. The blue pigment didn't capture the sparkle of her eyes. Nor the flesh tone the glow of her skin. Even the smile was inadequate. The photo held nothing of the warmth, nothing of the joy.

Sometimes the twenty-six months since the crash seemed like so many breaths, as though Linda had just walked out of the room. "Honey, what can I tell that boy of ours? He's so angry."

Tonight she didn't answer. Tonight, the months seemed like years, as though he had been on his own his entire life.

Breaths or years. It didn't matter. Linda was gone. This nostalgia was simply another ruse to keep himself from working. In this moment, his personal life was unimportant. In this moment, all that mattered was the book.

Paul put down the photograph, left the room, and pulled the door closed, a symbolic act. Silly. Or not.

Back in his chair Paul forced his mind to focus. Thomas Jefferson at his desk in Monticello. Thomas Jefferson cutting out sections of Matthew's gospel for his own book, *Life and Morals of Jesus of Nazareth.* The white-haired statesman pasting the verses that related Jesus' teachings onto a manuscript page with Latin, Greek, Hebrew, and English versions lined up. The old man crumpling every passage that reported a miracle and tossing it onto the floor.

A man ahead of his time. Postmodern long before the modern era began, choosing the parts of the gospel that resonated with his experiences of life, rejecting the parts he couldn't get his head around.

In his darkest moments, Paul understood. Linda, her blue eyes closed, her blonde hair dark with blood. *"Please, Father. Please, please, please!"*

Paul had learned what it meant to pray without ceasing. Riding in the ambulance, holding Linda's hands slippery with her own blood, pacing the hospital halls, even drinking the bitter coffee, all prayers. The forms he was required to fill out, the phone calls he dreaded making, the long hours of waiting, even the dreams that came as he dozed, all prayers. Each breath a plea.

He wasn't the only one who prayed. Their families, their friends, friends of friends, their churches, present and past. And Scott. A twelve-year-old kid. Twenty-four hours. Forty-eight hours. Fifty-two hours. Then God answered, "No miracle."

Who had Thomas Jefferson lost? Paul decided to find out. Perhaps this was a line of inquiry no one had yet written.

"Dad?" Scott, eyes swollen and red, stood in the doorway of the study.

Paul glanced at the time displayed at the bottom of the screen. Well after midnight. How long had Scott been crying? He went to draw his son into his arms.

"I'm sorry, Dad." The teenager started to cry again, not the wails of a child but the choking sobs of a man.

Paul started to pat his son's back the way Linda had taught him when Scott was a tiny baby, an automatic reflex dredged up from his subconscious. The soothing tone came from the same place. "It's okay, son. Whatever it is, we'll work it out. It's okay."

Meaningless words. But Paul meant them, with all his strength he meant them. These tears were the first Scott had shed in his presence since the funeral. As he held his son, Paul accepted responsibility for Scott's loss of faith, his anger.

For the first time, he glimpsed the months following Linda's death through Scott's eyes. He had abandoned his son. Drowning in his own grief and guilt, he hadn't had the strength to reach out to Scott. He had lived by habit. Every morning he got out of bed because that was what he had always done. He fixed meals for the two of them because they had always eaten. He took Scott to school because Scott had always gone to school.

Every night he went to bed, but not to sleep. Whenever he closed his eyes, he struggled to see the road to Flagstaff through the fluke spring snowstorm, not lazy flakes falling on the road, needles of ice shooting straight at the windshield of the Forester. He saw the red glow of the motorcycle's taillight leading them from a safe distance, the red glow that was suddenly golden, not the taillight but the headlight coming toward them, gyrating wildly behind the screen of snow as the big bike skidded on black ice. He felt the steering wheel twist in his hands like a living thing with a deadly purpose of its own. He heard Linda suck in her breath, felt her grip his arm.

Night after night it was the same: his intense concentration, his determination to steer into the space between the motorcycle and the guardrail, the impact of his airbag as it exploded, blinding and paralyzing him. That was when he reached for the bedside lamp and sat up, drenched in sweat, but shivering so violently his teeth chattered.

It never worked. Despite the light, despite the feel of the carpet between his bare toes, he remembered Linda's mangled face. Her airbag, they told him, failed to deploy. That was when he staggered into the bathroom to turn on the shower and stand beneath cold water until it ran so hot he had to turn it off.

Then his struggle really began. Like Jacob, he grappled till dawn. With himself? With the angel of death? With the great I AM? Night after night after night. Then one night he was too exhausted to fight anymore. Linda was dead. God was still there. God refused to explain. Paul limped away, without Jacob's blessing or Job's restitution. But he limped with the hope of seeing Linda again. He limped with the truth of the Apostle Paul's assertion that we don't grieve like people who don't have that hope.

But we do grieve, he thought. And he had been so caught up in his identity of a grieving husband, he had utterly failed in his identity of father to a grieving son. No wonder Scott resented this house. *Father, forgive me. Help me reach my son.*

Gradually the intensity of the teenager's weeping lessened. As Paul was about to release him, Scott hiccupped, ending his crying fit exactly as he had as a little boy. The sound startled them both. They stepped apart, and after a moment they laughed.

Scott hiccupped again.

Paul put his arm around his son's shoulders. "You need some water to stop those hiccups."

"Dad . . ."

"Let's get the water. Then we can talk." Paul led the way, turning on lights until the downstairs was ablaze. Another prayer. *Father, shed your light on our confusion.*

They took their water bottles into the living room. Scott went to the lawn chair, leaving the couch for Paul. The body language was clear: Scott had retreated. After a moment, Paul said, "I'm sorry, Scott. You deserved better from me. I was so caught up in my own grief, I failed as a father."

Scott's silence was more damning than anything he could have shouted. Paul took a deep breath. "You now have my full attention. I want to hear what you've been trying to tell me about this house, about how I can help you, about anything else."

Scott got up and began to pace. "We have to get on with our lives, Dad. I know Mom loved this house. She and I used to talk about it. She had a whole story about how this house was before and another one about how it was going to be when we moved up here to Jerome." Scott crossed the room to stand in front of Paul. "That was Mom's story. I don't want to live here without her!"

Out of the mouths of babes. Linda's story had ended. It was time to get on with their own stories. "Okay. What's your idea? What do you think we should do?"

Scott's answer was a long time coming. Finally he said, "Maybe we could move. Go someplace that wouldn't remind us so much of Mom." Scott paused. "Maybe if we moved, maybe you would meet somebody."

Paul blinked. Was his son telling him to start dating?

Marty. The thought of the young woman he'd met that afternoon took him by surprise. What was she doing in his head? Red-gold curls he wanted to run his fingers through, hazel eyes with flecks of copper.

Marty opened her eyes in darkness. She was in bed, but not her own bed. Granny Lois dead. The hotel at the top of the mountain. Brad Lockridge. Jerome, Arizona. As she sorted through bits of memory and put them in chronological order, something moved in the corner of the room.

Not exactly a movement, the reflection of a movement in the antique pedestal mirror. Hardly daring to breathe, Marty turned her head to see who was there. No one. She looked back at the mirror. The hint of a shape whispered on the glass, a woman in a long, white dress. A haunted hotel, a ghost.

A shiver crawled across Marty's scalp and down her back. Pushing herself up on one elbow, she said firmly, "I do not believe in ghosts."

Instead of disappearing, the reflection sharpened. A woman with wild, white hair hanging over her face stepped out of the mirror and came toward her. *Dear God!*

"In the name of Jesus Christ, I rebuke you! Go back to wherever you belong." Even as she said them, the words surprised her. Immediately the mirror was only a mirror reflecting the glass door that opened onto the balcony.

Marty fumbled for the bedside lamp. She knocked it over, righted it, fumbled again, and turned it on. The light was a weak, dirty yellow, but it was enough. With a sigh of relief, she lay back against the pillow and tried to breathe. Deep breath in. Slow breath out. Deep breath in. Slow breath out.

It was no use. Her breath came short and fast, her heart hammered in her chest, and her pulse pounded at her temples. Sitting up, she swung her legs over the side of the bed and put her head between her knees.

Where had the notion of rebuking the ghost come from? Had God answered a prayer she hadn't put into words? *Thank you! Lord, Thank you.* Gradually the fear faded.

No longer afraid but wide awake, Marty went out onto the balcony and looked over the railing. The cars, the schoolhouse, the mine, even the lights of Cottonwood, everything was as it should be. High, white clouds covered the sky, leaving only a rainbow luminescence where the moon floated. A nightmare. Not the same one, but still a nightmare.

She stood until the cool mountain air raised goose bumps. Rubbing her arms with her hands, Marty turned back to the room. As she settled to sleep again, she reached for the bedside lamp to turn it off. It was an automatic gesture, but after a moment she pulled her hand back and left it on. Closing her eyes, she tried to compose herself for sleep. Deep breath in: one, two, three, four. Slow breath out: one, two, three, four, five.

Once.

Twice.

A dozen times.

Marty sat up and considered her options. It was 1:00 a.m., and the night stretched ahead with nothing to do but wonder about nightmares, regret what she hadn't done, and ask questions without answers.

Or she could spend those same hours starting the search for answers. Thanks to her grandmother's will, the Baker house was now hers. Even assuming the sheriff had locked the house when the men left with the hearse, she knew where a key was. Brad had driven her to the hotel, so she would have to walk, but it wasn't far, no more than a mile.

It took less than a half hour to repack and dress in gray joggers, t-shirt and sneakers. She let herself out of the room and moved as quietly as she could down the hall. Remembering the clank of the doors and the grinding of gears of the antique elevator, she took the stairs.

The tiny lobby was empty. A lamp with a red glass shade burned at the counter, but the clerk was nowhere in sight. Not wanting to wake anyone, Marty put down her bag long enough to scribble an explanatory note. Leaving the key on top of the note, she pulled out the handle on her weekender and went out into the night.

Into fog. In the last few minutes the high, white clouds had settled on the mountain. She considered returning to her room and waiting for morning. But she knew she wouldn't sleep. Not ideal weather for a nighttime stroll, but the air was calm and the route was straightforward.

Marty zipped her hoodie and set off. As long as she had light from the lamppost, she could walk at a fairly normal pace. She passed the cars she had seen from the balcony earlier and a few more parked at the side of the hotel. But as she left the pavement behind, the fog thickened. Maybe the rain that wasn't due for another month was on its way. Maybe the fog was a good thing.

But not for her. Forced to pick her way down the rocky drive and carry her weekender, Marty began to think it would take the rest of the night to get to her grandmother's house. She needed light, a flashlight, a lantern, a torch, even a candle. Or the penlight on her keychain.

She had to put down the weekender to grope in her bag for her keys, but the little light rewarded her the first time she pushed the switch. Not much more than a pencil of illumination, but if she kept it trained on the ground directly in front of her feet, she could see well enough to keep from falling. She picked up the weekender and started walking.

A large building loomed on her left, surely the derelict apartment house with the windows broken out she had noticed right before the hotel came in view. A dog yelped. She stepped around a large stone. She stepped over a pothole.

The slope evened out, and she walked faster until she almost collided with a car enveloped in a canvas cover. Marty stood for a moment, afraid she'd stumbled off the path, maybe even walked in a circle back to the hotel. Then she caught the heady scent of night-blooming tobacco.

She remembered flowers, yellow pansies, pink petunias, red geraniums. Through the mist, she saw the white stucco bed and breakfast she and Brad passed when they first left the highway for the narrow road that climbed to the hotel.

Another few yards. A breeze stirred the fog, giving her a glimpse of the highway. A pair of red taillights headed up the mountain toward Prescott, toward the fire. Otherwise the road was empty. She crossed and kept walking.

Not long after, the light from her tiny flashlight wavered and went out. But by then she was on Lois's street. Almost there. Taking care where she placed each foot, she crept along the old road. A light breeze stirred the fog, and for a moment moonlight illuminated the landscape.

The Camry sat where she'd left it. The key was still in her purse where she dropped it after Brad retrieved her luggage. She had come to start her search, but she could be in Phoenix in two hours, and, with a little luck, home in time for a late breakfast. She could put all this behind her. Except she would take her questions with her. Like it or not, she was on a quest, and she couldn't rest until it was done.

Taking advantage of the uncertain moonlight, Marty walked more quickly. The key was under the planter, as Lois had told her it would be. As before, the cat greeted her at the door. Quest or no quest, the sense of déjà vu almost stopped her. What would she find at the foot of the stairs this time?

"I do not believe in ghosts," she said as she turned on the hall light. Not at the hotel, not here. Lois was with the Lord. And so was Ruthie. She had come for memories, memories that would be on the second floor in the room she shared with her sister, attached to their books and toys. Marty marched down the hall, past the place she'd found Lois, and up the stairs.

Though she had come to find memories, it was still a shock to know exactly who all the bedrooms had belonged to when she was a child. Granny Lois's room and tiny half-bath were at one end of the hallway, overlooking the back of the house to the mountain and the old mine. The little girls' room, the one she and Ruthie shared, was at the other end of the hallway, overlooking the front of the house. Her parents' room and the full bath everyone shared were on the right side of the hall. Uncle Tommy's room was the on the left side.

The warm cat rubbing against her leg brought her back to the present. As Marty reached down to stroke it, black spots swam before her eyes. She was dizzy with fatigue, emotional and physical. It was time for bed. But which bed? Like Goldilocks, she considered them all: Granny's, Mommy and Daddy's, Uncle Tommy's, her and Ruthie's? She decided on Tommy's as the least likely to trigger dreams or nightmares, the nightmare.

She barely remembered her uncle, a big boy who fought with Ruthie sometimes. Still, when she flipped on the light in Tommy's room, she found herself abruptly back in the past. Bunk beds made up with red and blue bandana quilts. A dresser with horseshoes for drawer pulls. A ten-gallon cowboy hat on the wall.

It would have to do. If the least familiar room in the house brought back memories with such force, what would happen in the other rooms? The memories were good news of a sort, but now, she needed the escape of sleep.

Chapter Nine

Paul studied Scott. The set of his jaw and the clenched hands told him his son's weeping hadn't been the catharsis he'd hoped it was. Something other than a desire to move was going on here. Something had already happened or was happening now. But what? What could be going on that would catapult Scott into leaving his friends?

His impulse was to ask straight out, but Scott looked on the verge of another outburst. He decided to try an end-around play. "Let me be sure I understand what you're saying. You don't want to work on this house because it reminds you too much of your mother. You want to move away from here. Do you mean just Jerome or Cottonwood too?"

"Both! We could start completely over, Dad. Find a house where Mom never lived. Find a church where no one knew her."

"You'd have to change schools."

"It doesn't matter. I start high school this fall. It's a perfect time to move."

That fast. "Have you thought about where we could go? It's not easy to find another job teaching history at the university level."

"You could keep your job. We could move up to Flagstaff. I know it's more expensive than Cottonwood, but if we live there, you won't have a commute."

"That's true . . ."

Scott rushed on. "If we can't find a house we can afford in Flag, we can move to Williams. You'd have a commute, but it wouldn't be any farther than what you drive now."

The level of detail. "You've thought about this a lot."

"It's important, Dad! Can we do it?"

"I don't know. I have a lot to think about."

"That means no! Whenever you say you've got to think about something, all you do is think of the best way to tell me no."

Paul felt himself getting angry. But now was not the time to lose his temper. He had to find out what was driving Scott's desperate plea. Paul got to his feet. "I want to show you something."

"What?"

"One of the things I have to think about." Paul crossed to the dining room and flipped on the light. With the archway gone, the space was wide open, waiting to be reimagined, repurposed.

Scott didn't comment.

"I did this while you were at Dan's."

"You want me to say I should have been here to help you. You don't get it, Dad!"

"You're the one who doesn't get it, son! I listened to you. Now it's your turn. Are you willing to listen to my side?" Just barely Paul managed not to say "Or are you a three-year-old who has to have his own way no matter what?"

"Okay, you've got the hat."

It was a grudging consent, but Paul accepted it. "Tearing down that archway felt really good. Look at this room! We can make it anything we want to: a den with a big screen TV or a game room with a pool table or a study with a computer station for each of us. We could put in a display cabinet for your mineral collection or a library or both."

"But that would mean staying here!"

"Not necessarily. We could fix it up so someone else could see the potential. Then we could decide to sell it or keep it."

Scott didn't reply.

"I agree we need to start living our own lives again. But I'm not ready for the level of change you're talking about. I'm not saying I won't ever be ready. I am saying I need some time."

Still Scott didn't speak.

Paul tried again. "Tell me you understand what I'm saying, son. I think we agree on the goal. If we disagree about the method of reaching that goal, we need to talk, find a compromise. But we can't compromise until we understand each other's point of view."

"I get it, Dad. I understand. You need to finish what you started with Mom before you move on. But I don't, Dad! I'm ready to move on now. How can we compromise between now and later?"

Paul did his best to smile. "How about a little later?"

Scott shook his head. "I'm sorry, Dad! I'm sorry!"

"What are you sorry for?"

But Scott was gone before Paul got the question out. Scott's feet pounded on the stairs. Paul started after him. Scott's bedroom door slammed, but Paul kept going. He stopped in front of the closed door and stood for a moment, listening. If Scott was on his cell phone to the kid with the motorcycle, he would be forced to ground him until they worked this out.

Silence. He knocked.

No response. Paul opened the door and looked in.

The room was dark, but the light from the hall showed Scott lying on the inflatable bed. His eyes were closed, and he was wearing his headphones. Paul wondered what rock group he was listening to. How long since Scott had shared a song he liked?

Too long. He had a lot of catching up to do, and now was always the best time to start. He considered turning on the overhead light but decided against it. He didn't want Scott to feel as if the inquisition had arrived. He retrieved the bean bag chair from the corner and put it at the end of the bed in Scott's field of vision.

As he folded himself into the chair, his movements caught the teenager's attention. Scott pulled off the headphones but didn't sit up. "My door was closed, Dad."

"I knocked. You didn't hear me."

"Because I don't want to be disturbed. We agreed to honor closed doors."

"We did. But you ran out on our discussion. You didn't answer my last question. Answer it, and I'll leave you alone."

Scott frowned and raised up on one elbow. "What?"

"What are you sorry for, son? You've apologized a couple of times, but you haven't told me why."

Scott didn't answer immediately. Finally, he lay back and stared at the ceiling. "I guess I'm sorry for everything."

"You need to be more specific. You're sorry about not coming home right away after you found Lois, about your outbursts, about not cooperating lately, about the things you've said about the house? What?"

"All of it, Dad. You've listed everything just fine."

Paul shook his head. "That's not good enough. You've been trying to tell me something, something important. But I can't read your mind, son. You have to come right out and say it. Whatever it is, we'll work it out." There were those words again.

"Just forget it." Scott put his headphones back on and closed his eyes.

Conversation over. But whatever else he might do with tonight's talk, Paul was certain he wouldn't forget it.

～

Marty expected to fall asleep easily. As tired as she was, she should have collapsed and slept like the dead. Under the circumstances, not a good metaphor. Going to sleep should have been like rolling off a log. But that cliché was no good either. The bottom bunk was almost as narrow as a log, and if she rolled over, she would find herself wide awake on the floor.

So, what was the problem? For one thing, June or not, she was freezing. It was almost as cold in the house as it was outside. Her walk in the fog had chilled her to the bone, and her shortie pajamas weren't heavy enough to warm her up. To top it off, the sheets were cold and the bandana quilt thin.

Shivering, Marty got out of bed. She found a much-too-large flannel robe, probably Tommy's, in the closet and wrapped herself in it. Socks came out of her weekender and a blanket from the bottom drawer of Lois's bureau. Meant for a queen bed, it was big enough to fold double and use like a sleep sack. Marty had to squirm to get robe, blanket, sheets, and bedspread settled, but she managed.

As she warmed up, she expected to fall asleep. Instead her mind began to chatter about the mysterious text message, the horror of Lois's death, the task of inventorying the old house, the work that was sure to pile up at home, and the people she'd met, especially Brad and Paul. Having reached the end of current topics, her mind started to do another lap: the mysterious text message, the horror of ... Absurd!

She needed to talk it through with Vicki. Not only her current problems, but she should also explain her sudden departure. Because Vicki was her best friend, Marty knew she sometimes presumed on Vicki as her employer. Not showing up for work with nothing more than a text message for notification took a lot of nerve.

Suddenly Marty's need to talk to Vicki became urgent. Maybe it was late enough now for the three-hour time difference to work in her favor. She sat up so fast she banged her head on the top bunk. Massaging her scalp with one hand, she retrieved her cell phone from her purse with the other. 2:15 in Arizona meant 5:15 in Virginia. Vicki might already be up. Her Chihuahua was an early riser. Husband Owen, on the other hand, liked to sleep in, "at least until 7:00 a.m." he often joked.

Back in bed, swathed in every layer she could pull around herself, Marty decided on a text.

Are you awake?

The answer bounced back.

Where are you? Call me!

Vicki's phone rang once. "Where are you, girlfriend?"

"Didn't you get my message?"

"I got it. But how am I supposed to interpret 'Gone for a couple of days. Urgent family business?' What happened? Did someone die?"

"Sort of."

"How does someone sort of die?"

"In a minute. Did you text me yesterday morning?"

"No, I don't think so. What makes you think I did? You know my number."

"Would Ted be texting me? Is he still bent out of shape I won't go out with him?"

"No and no. Ted's ego took a hit. But he's got a new girlfriend, maybe two. What are you talking about, Mart?"

"I got a creepy text with the sender blocked. I thought it might be Ted's idea of payback."

"Are you kidding? Ted wouldn't let you know he cared that much. What did it say?"

Suddenly the text message seemed silly, unimportant. "It doesn't matter. I'm sure it was a random prank."

"Forget random pranks. Where are you? What happened to make you drop everything and take off like that?"

"Arizona. Do you remember the old lady you sent back to the workshop Monday afternoon?"

"Sure. She wanted to surprise you. She was well-dressed and in her right mind. I didn't see what it would hurt."

But it had hurt. Not in the way Vicki meant. "You know I'm adopted?"

"Of course. I think you told me that when you pledged Chi O."

"That well-dressed old lady was my grandmother on my birth father's side."

"You're kidding! I thought you didn't know anything about your birth family."

Didn't know. Didn't remember. Didn't want to talk about it. "Monday was the first time I'd heard from her since I was six."

"Hang on. Chiquita's digging up my snap dragons."

In the sudden silence, Marty heard a board creak overhead. Then another.

Vicki said, "Okay. The critter's back on leash. I take it your grandmother lives in Arizona. Are you at her house?"

Another board creaked. Footsteps. Marty remembered Brad telling her Jerome's resident ghost expert had heard footsteps in this house.

"I don't believe in ghosts," she said. "But if I did, I'd think there was one in the attic."

"Your grandmother's attic? What on earth makes you say something like that?"

"The house is empty, but I swear I hear someone walking up there."

"You're there by yourself? Where's your grandmother?"

Another creak. And another. "I've got to go, Vicki. I've got to find out what's making the sounds I'm hearing."

"Take it easy, Marty. Old houses settle. It could be the wind. Or squirrels."

Or the cat. There were a dozen reasonable explanations for the sound of footsteps. Then Marty heard a sound like a door opening.

"I'll call you back, Vick. I've got to go."

"Where are you, Marty? Do you want me to call 911?"

"No! I'll be fine. Later." Marty cut the connection and fought her way free of the blankets. Dropping the phone on the bed, she felt her way across the dark room. When she reached the door, she flipped the switch for the overhead fixture, a concoction of deer antlers and light bulbs covered with miniature bandana lampshades. Red light spilled across the polished wood floor. Like blood. "I do not believe in ghosts!" she shouted at the floor over her head.

Silence.

Whatever it was, she had scared it. Pulling the belt of the robe tighter, she left the room, switched on the hall light, and marched to the door that led to the attic stairs. Though she was sure it had been closed, it now stood slightly ajar.

The cat. The memory of the Siamese rattling the pantry door surfaced in her mind, clear and reassuring. Surely she could simply close the door and go back to bed. But she knew she would lie awake, listening. She had to catch the cat and put it outside.

To make sure whatever was in the attic knew she was coming, Marty flung the door open. Light from the hallway illuminated the first few steps of the steep staircase. Above that, nothing. As she peered into the darkness above, Marty suddenly remembered the attic: low ceiling, unfinished floor, a jumble of broken furniture, odd-shaped boxes stacked on trunks, an old green filing cabinet.

She also remembered begging to play in the attic. But never after dark. Had they told ghost stories about the attic? It didn't matter. She wasn't about to let a ghost send her scurrying back to bed like a frightened six-year-old.

Marty ran her hand along the wall, searching for the light switch she knew had to be there. She found it and pushed, but nothing happened. She went up one step. Another. Two more steps, after that she would be climbing blind.

Granny Lois, her head twisted at that awful angle. Cat or no cat, Marty had no desire to risk a fall down a flight of stairs. She needed light, a flashlight. Hers was no good. She was sure her grandmother had one. But where? In the pantry? A bedside drawer? The hall table? It was no use. The memories that had begun to surface were flashes, nothing she could search through for details.

A candle, then. This was a recent memory, a scented candle in a glass jar on the bureau where she found the blanket. She hoped Lois kept matches handy.

Lois did. A small box of wooden matches sat beside the glass jar. As Marty lit the candle, the scent of lavender tickled her nose, fresh and comforting. Perhaps lavender chased away ghosts like wolf bane chased away werewolves. Cheered by the silly thought, Marty dropped the box of matches into the pocket of Tommy's robe and hurried back to the attic stairs.

Cupping her free hand to protect the flame, she started the climb. The fat candle with the short wick provided more fragrance than light, but she found that by holding it in front of her she could see one step at a time. As she inched her way up, she wished for an old-fashioned candlestick. Like the heroine of a gothic novel, she could have held it above her head illuminating several steps at a time.

Marty was almost at the top of the staircase, eye-level with a large steamer trunk, when the candle went out. Dank darkness smelling of rotting fabric, dry paper, and dust closed in around her. She stood very still, trying to determine what direction the draft had come from. A broken window or a chink in the siding. But the air was so still she felt as if it were sucking the breath from her lungs.

As she stood, she listened for the sounds that had brought her up here. Silence. Had the cat caught its prey? Or squirrels scurried out into the night? Or bats? She shuddered at the new possibility. The silence lengthened, somehow worse than any sound.

At that moment, Marty almost turned and ran back down the stairs. But the thought of her grandmother's broken body at the foot of the other staircase stopped her. Had Lois heard footsteps and fallen as she hurried to escape?

"I do not believe in ghosts," she whispered.

The trunk would serve as a table. She could set the candle down. The goal gave her the courage to move. Without a rail to hang onto, all she could do was grope her way along the wall. It wasn't far. Holding the candle in her left hand, she stretched out her right hand and moved carefully toward where she hoped the trunk was.

Something whispered against her face. A cobweb? With a little yelp, she dropped the candle and tried to brush it away. Nothing.

Then it was there again, clinging to her face, tangling in her hair. She fought with it, but the more she batted at whatever it was, the more entangled she became. Suddenly a shape darker even than the darkness in the attic loomed in front of her. A human form without a face.

Too terrified to scream, Marty took a step back. She connected with a piece of furniture that wobbled and then slid out from under her. Suddenly she was disoriented. Flinging her arms wide, she grasped at nothingness. She fell backwards. Her head struck a glancing blow on something that tossed her sideways. For a moment, she spun in darkness. Around, around, around. Then nothing.

Chapter Ten

Marty's head pounded and every muscle ached. She should open her eyes, discover where she was. But she didn't want to know. Maybe she was afraid of the answer. Still, she needed to move, and before she moved, she needed to know where she was.

She compromised and continued her inventory with the rest of her senses.

The air smelled of dust, musty fabric, old beeswax.

Silence. She half-expected to hear footsteps. Nothing.

She had on shortie pajamas and a flannel robe that was much too big. She was on her back, legs draped over something wooden that cut into the back of her knees.

Marty opened her eyes. Weak moonlight fractured into a thousand shards by a broken shutter scattered across a junkyard of family cast-offs. The attic.

She remembered the creaking overhead, the dark staircase, the faceless human form. With a groan, Marty untangled her legs from a child's rocking horse, Ruthie's, and struggled to sit up. A few feet away a broken-down sofa dusted with moonlight waited for her.

She managed to get up on it. She lay back carefully, stretched out cramped muscles, touched her head with experimental fingers. Dried blood on her forehead, a scrape along her cheekbone, a lump on the back of her head. She should go downstairs, wash, and doctor her wounds. But her head pounded, and she was too tired to get up. Marty reached for a crocheted throw spilling out of a box, pulled it around her shoulders, and slept.

When she opened her eyes again, sunlight struggled through the broken shutter. Faint sounds of early morning birdsong drifted in. She still ached from head to foot, but the pounding in her head had eased. It was time to go downstairs.

Marty sat up. The room spun, throwing out dark spots like drops of water. Too fast. She doubled over, put her head between her knees, and concentrated on breathing. When the vertigo passed, she sat up, slowly this time. Settling carefully against the back of the sofa, she let her eyes wander around the attic. The rocking horse, a length of rotted lace, the trunk. She remembered Granny Lois, the younger version she'd re-membered in the ladies' room, opening the trunk, pulling out dress-up clothes, old high-heeled shoes, a Raggedy Ann doll with one button eye missing, and a copper box.

Marty's gaze went back to the rocking horse and the yel-lowed lace, fine as a cobweb. But how had she gotten tangled in it? And that ghostly shape.

"I don't believe in ghosts," she told the rocking horse. "Not at the hotel and not here."

So how had she walked into the lace? Where had it been? Marty looked up at the ceiling. It was low with exposed beams. No hooks or nails for the lace to be snagged on. Nothing.

She looked for a dressmaker's form, a chifforobe, something tall she could have interpreted as a human shape. Nothing.

It didn't matter. The ghost was a tattered wedding veil. The footsteps were the creaking of the old house. The whole experience was a trick of her imagination, pieced together from

Brad's ghost stories, her nightmare at the hotel and a jumble of memories of the attic.

Marty stood up slowly. No black dots whirled before her eyes. That was good. Just to make sure, she waited a moment. When she was ready, she moved slowly toward the stairs. Without a handrail, she had to lean forward and brace herself on the floor as she took the first few steps down. Then she stretched out her arms and touched both walls of the narrow staircase.

One careful step at a time, she made her way to the bottom. She breathed a prayer of gratitude and reached for the doorknob.

It didn't move. She twisted it the other way. Still no movement. She shook the door and tried again. The knob didn't budge. She was locked in.

❧

Paul backed out the rickety screen door onto the sagging front porch. In one hand, he held his Bible, in the other a travel mug of coffee. Usually he relished these early moments when he could read and pray without interruption. Especially here. On Mingus Mountain, the only sounds this early were bird calls and wind rustling the junipers.

This morning Paul hardly noticed his surroundings. *Father, Scott needs, I need . . .* No matter how hard he tried, Paul couldn't get the last few conversations with Scott out of his mind. His son had held up a mirror, and Paul didn't like his own reflection. He had been self-absorbed and careless. He owed Scott time and attention. And Scott's unfinished apology haunted him. What was that about? What did his son need to tell him?

Paul put his coffee on a plastic crate and sat in an ancient wooden Adirondack chair he had hauled up from the basement.

Father, Scott. Paul was about to open his Bible when a flash of red caught his eye across the road. Red? Down in Cottonwood it might have been a male cardinal, but not up here on Mingus Mountain.

Paul got to his feet and moved to get a better look. A crude rope made of red and blue fabrics twisted together fluttered from the upper porch of the Baker house. An auburn-haired child in shortie pajamas leaned over the railing.

Not a child, a Dresden shepherdess. But how? After supper, the house had been dark. The white Camry had remained parked in the driveway, so he had assumed Pastor Ray, the sheriff, or Lockridge had driven her to a hotel. But that figure on the upper porch couldn't be anyone else.

As he watched, she moved to the corner of the porch. After a slight hesitation, she boosted herself up onto the railing. The idiot was going to try to climb down the ridiculous rope.

He shouted as he ran. "Stop! Marty!"

She heard because she got off the railing. "Paul!"

He stopped on the front sidewalk and looked up at her. "What do you think you're doing?" Even to his own ears his tone sounded harsh. He had no right to talk to her that way. But she had scared him. If she had fallen . . .

"I'm locked in the attic. I'm escaping."

"You're going to break a leg that way or kill yourself."

"Then do something. Get me out of here!"

"Hang on."

The front door was locked, and the key Lois kept under the planter was gone. But the back door opened easily. As Paul went inside, the cat shot out between his legs. He let it go and hurried through the kitchen, across the hall, and up the stairs to the second floor to the attic door.

As Marty had said, it was locked. He didn't really expect to find a key, but just in case, Paul ran his fingers along the top of the doorframe. Dust.

"Hurry!" Her voice came to him through the door, strained, almost desperate. "I've been in here for hours, and my head hurts."

Paul had a sudden urge to break down the door with his bare hands. Ridiculous. "Are you hurt? Do you need a doctor?"

"No. Just get me out of here!"

"Hang on. I've got to get my tools."

He took the stairs two at a time. Then he ran down the hall, out the back door, around the side of the house, across the rocky slope, and around his own house. Flinging open the basement door, he grabbed his toolbox and raced back.

By the time he got back to the attic door, he was pretty well out of breath. Between gasps, he said, "How are you doing, Marty?"

"Just hurry."

Still gulping air, Paul reached for a hammer and screwdriver. He started with the middle hinge. The metal was rusty, but after a few minutes he could work the bolt out. The bottom hinge gave way more easily. The top hinge was the hardest, but finally he jerked the door out of the way.

Marty was right there. For one crazy second, he thought she might throw her arms around him. Then she squeezed past muttering, "Got to make a pit stop."

Paul wanted to laugh, not at Marty, at himself for fantasizing like a teenager. He leaned the door against the wall and turned his attention to the dark stairwell. Surprised that Marty hadn't turned on the light, he flipped the switch.

Nothing happened. He tried it again. Still nothing. A burned-out bulb, then. Curious, he went upstairs. He knew the attic well enough to go right to the simple overhead fixture. He reached up to get the old bulb, but the socket was empty.

A little thing, but it wasn't like Lois to leave a light fixture not working, especially in a dark stairwell. Somewhere he would find a new bulb.

He found it on top of a tall chest of drawers. But it wasn't a new bulb.

Paul told himself it didn't mean anything. But the analytical part of his mind began trying to fit pieces into a puzzle for which he had no template. A steamer trunk, a scented candle on the floor, an open box of blankets, a piece of lace draped across an overturned rocking horse, a green filing cabinet, a sofa, an iron bedstead, mismatched chairs. Nothing unusual, nothing that didn't belong.

"Paul?" Marty's voice floated up the stairwell. "Are you up there?"

"Yes. Do me a favor. Turn the light switch off."

"Done."

Reaching up, he twisted the bulb back in place. "Now turn it on."

Light. Paul's mind returned to the puzzle. Who? When? Why?

"What was wrong with it?"

"It was missing a bulb."

He turned. She was right there, pajama top dirty, auburn curls a tangled mass, a scrape along the left side of her face. "You're hurt."

Without thinking, he turned her head toward him and tipped up her chin. He bent to examine the scratch. And almost kissed her.

They pulled apart at the same instant. He could have kicked himself. Talk about a teenager! "Marty . . ." He thought he was going to apologize, but instead he heard himself say, "I know my way around Lois's kitchen. What if I make us some breakfast while you get dressed?"

She looked surprised. "Okay. Thanks."

Then she was gone, and he was left wondering what, if anything, had just happened between them.

∿

Marty meant to take a quick shower, but as warm water flowed over her head and down her back, she hoped the house had an extra-large hot water tank. She ached from head to toe, and she could see the beginnings of a large purple bruise on her right hip. Getting thrown from a horse, even a rocking horse, was no joke. Besides, she needed a few minutes to sort through the chaos of her feelings.

She squeezed shampoo into her hand. Very gingerly she began to work the dried blood from her hair. The footsteps must have been the house settling. A draft had blown out the candle. The ghost was a castoff wedding veil. Her fall the result of panic. What about the door? How had it gotten locked?

Marty bent her head to rinse the suds from her hair. She remembered flinging the door wide open before starting up the stairs. It might have been locked when it closed, except that it was ajar before she ever opened it. And what closed it? A draft? The cat?

The water began to cool. As she stepped out of the shower, she decided to quit worrying about the door. It was nothing more than an idiosyncrasy of the old house. Everything else had a perfectly logical explanation.

She dressed quickly in jeans and a green t-shirt. After a short debate with herself, she decided to put on sneakers instead of the high-heeled sandals that gave her four more inches. She couldn't imagine needing extra confidence today. Then she turned her attention to the scrape on the side of her face.

It wasn't deep, but it was long, beginning at her eyebrow and ending at her chin. As she dried it gingerly, she remembered Paul's touch, light and gentle.

A deep longing washed over Marty. Ted, but Ted had wanted something she couldn't give. And Paul. Paul?

Why did he keep showing up in her head? He was ten years older, and he had a teenaged son. He acted like he was single, but his wife might just be gone for the summer. He wasn't even her type. What about Brad? He might be her type.

University professor not, Paul, though clean enough this morning, seemed to favor the scruffy look. A friend. Paul would make a nice friend. He lived close by. He had known her grandmother. He was thoughtful and kind. Had he been about to kiss her? Absurd. Still, when he leaned in to look at the scratch on her face, he was so close she'd caught the scent of wintergreen soap.

Marty shook her head and told herself to get a grip. Now was not the time to consider romance, especially not with the complicated Dr. Paul Russell. Even though it meant her hair would dry in ringlets, Marty didn't take time to blow it dry. She didn't care how she looked. Her goal for the day was the same as it had been last night, to find out if being in the house would help her remember what happened to Ruthie. She swiped at her dry lips with vanilla balm and headed downstairs.

The smells of coffee mingled with bacon frying made Marty's mouth water. The soup and cheesecake had been a long time ago.

As she entered the kitchen, Paul looked up from the stove. "Perfect timing. How do you like your eggs?"

"Scrambled with fresh basil pesto and sprinkled with grated Parmesan."

"Sounds great! We've got the eggs."

"But no pesto or Parmesan."

"Probably not. But you can always look." Paul lifted a strip of bacon out of the cast iron skillet and set it on a paper towel.

The refrigerator was surprisingly empty, but Marty found a package of shredded cheddar in the hydrator drawer and a partial loaf of rye bread. While Paul beat four eggs with a fork, she put two slices of bread in the toaster.

As she took mugs from the cupboard and poured coffee, she said, "I hope you take it black. I didn't see any milk."

"I drink coffee any way it's offered."

"Me too. Lois didn't keep much food around, did she? That feels different to me. I associate this kitchen with corn muffins, ham, and apple cobbler."

Paul tipped the eggs into the hot skillet and sprinkled them with cheese. "You're forgetting she was traveling. We're lucky to find this much. Lois wouldn't have wanted to come home to a carton of spoiled milk. She was always careful about details."

And this man, was he careful about details? She wouldn't think so from his unkempt appearance. His brown hair curled over his ears, and he would soon have a full beard. But there had to be more to him than shaggy bear man. Surely he didn't teach in his current state. Maybe his wife was away.

Before Marty had time to chide herself for her thoughts, she heard herself say, "Where's your son this morning? Is he with your wife?"

"I'm sure Scott's still sleeping. Seven a.m. is the middle of the night to a teenager. My wife died a couple of years ago."

She could have kicked herself. "I'm sorry. It's none of my business. I don't know why I asked either of those questions."

"It's natural to be curious about people we've just met. My wife died in a car accident. It was a real blessing Scott wasn't with us."

Marty didn't know what to say. "Sorry to hear," "lucky for Scott," "sad about your wife?"

Paul gave her a smile that made her forget his shaggy hair and scruffy beard. All she saw was his deep brown eyes.

As he spooned eggs onto their plates, he said, "Your turn. I'm as curious about you as you are about me. Are you married? Do you have children?"

"No." She started to leave it at that, but he had offered details. "I thought I was engaged, but it turned out to be something different."

"Just as well to find out ahead of time."

He carried their plates to the round oak table. As he pulled her chair out for her, she was struck again by how very tall he was, maybe because she was wearing sneakers. He was at least a foot taller than her five feet and two inches.

Paul sat across from her and held out his hands. "Shall I say grace or do you want to?"

Ted had never offered to pray. Feeling awkward, Marty put her hands in his and bowed her head. "You say it, please."

"Father, we come to you this morning sad about Lois's death. We know she's home with you, but we're going to miss her, Lord."

His tone surprised her, not formal at all: friend to friend, child to parent. *Father God, help me remember.*

"Thank you for this food Lois provided for us," Paul said.

Granny gone. Even as loss washed over her again, Paul's deep voice comforted.

"Be with us today, Father, and help us make choices that please you. For we pray in Jesus' name, Amen."

Paul held her hands a moment longer than was necessary.

A friend. A friend with brown eyes so dark they were almost black.

Chapter Eleven

Paul sipped coffee and studied Marty. The scratch on her cheek must sting, and she had to be sore from a fall that had knocked her unconscious. But she ate with relish. She had downed two thirds of the scrambled eggs, four strips of bacon, and a piece of toast. So far, he didn't see any sign she was ready to quit. She was a good bit smaller than Linda and shorter than Scott, but obviously not the china doll he'd thought she was.

"Shall I scramble more eggs?"

Marty flushed. "I know. I'm eating like a pig. I'm making up for yesterday. I was too upset to eat breakfast, lunch was a plastic cup of yogurt at the airport, and dinner was a disaster. I promise I don't usually eat this much."

"I wasn't passing judgment, just asking if you're still hungry."

She reached for the last piece of toast and the strawberry preserves. "This will be fine. Thanks though."

She smiled. Relaxed, fully recovered from the scare she'd had. He hated to alarm her, but she needed to know. If his conclusion was correct, he had to warn her.

But not this minute. "Another question, in the spirit of getting to know each other, are you always impetuous?"

"I'm not impetuous at all. I'm a planner."

"Really? What did you plan to do after you broke both your legs?" Just in time he kept himself from saying "both your beautiful legs."

"I wouldn't have broken anything. I planned to climb down, get the key from under the planter, and go in the front door."

"Your rope, while colorful enough to attract attention, was nonfunctional. The instant you put any real weight on it, it would have ripped. The fabric in those curtains was rotten, and the bathrobe wasn't much better."

She bristled. "The curtains were old, but they would have held me long enough to get me down."

"I humbly ask pardon, milady, but you're wrong. They ripped when I detached them from the railing. If you want to examine the evidence for yourself, you'll find them on the ground out front waiting to be taken to the dump."

"I didn't know what else to do. I didn't have my cell phone, and I didn't think I could yell loud enough to wake you up inside your house."

"You could have waited. I was bound to come outside sooner or later."

She flushed. "I had to use the bathroom. The closest one was through a locked door."

He grinned. "And you call yourself an antiques expert. Ever heard of a chamber pot? No doubt there are several in that attic."

She shrugged. "I repair antique furniture, not chamber pots. I suppose as a historian, you must encounter chamber pots all the time."

They laughed together. How long had it been since he'd laughed like that?

"Hello. Anybody home?" A woman's voice, vaguely familiar, but before Paul could decide who the voice belonged

110

to, a young woman barely out of her teens rushed into the kitchen. Right away he recognized the willowy blonde clad in white shorts and a hot pink halter top. He was surprised. What was Carly Remick doing here?

"Morning, Dr. Russell."

"Good morning, Carly."

Whirling on Marty, she said, "You are Martha! I knew you were going to be the right one." She slid out of a lime green backpack, deposited it on an empty chair, and dug through it. "I absolutely love your book. You have to autograph it for me." With a dramatic flourish, she produced a copy of A Beginner's First Book of Antique Repair and held it out to Marty. "Write 'To my new friend Carly' because we're going to be friends."

Marty made no move to take the book. "Who are you?"

Carly looked bewildered. Paul decided to intervene, although what he could do with oil and water, he had no idea. He started with the basics. "Sit down, Carly. Take a deep breath and start over."

The girl moved her backpack to the floor and dropped into the chair. "What did I do wrong?"

"For starters," Marty said, "you walked in without even knocking."

"I always walk in here like that! Lois told me her house was my second home. You don't knock when you walk into your own home."

"You know she died?"

"Of course I know. Everyone in town knows."

"Then you don't care."

"Of course I care!" Carly looked at Paul as if she expected him to rescue her.

Doing his best to keep exasperation out of his voice, he said, "Start over, Carly. Introduce yourself. Offer your condolences. Give Marty a chance to breathe."

111

"You mean like name, rank and serial number?"

"And your relationship to Lois. And how sorry you were to hear of her passing."

Carly burst into tears. This time Marty gave Paul the rescue-me look.

Now what? Water. He felt like pouring a glass of it over Carly's head. Instead he went to the sink and filled an empty mug. As he handed it to the weeping girl, he looked helplessly at Marty. "Would you like some water?"

She smiled, part amusement, part sympathy, part pure sunshine.

Sunshine? What was he thinking? Sunshine that broke through the confusion, the welter of emotions, the helplessness. It was all Paul could do to keep from throwing his arms around Marty and waltzing down the hall. If Carly hadn't been there, he might just have done it.

Oblivious to the fate she had only narrowly escaped, Marty said calmly, "How about some more coffee?"

As he refilled their mugs, Carly reached in her pack and pulled out a tissue. "I'm sorry. I was trying to be cheerful because I know that's the way Lois would want me to be. But her death is an absolute tragedy for me. You have to understand. We had a special relationship. She was like my grandmother. Whenever I needed anything, anything at all, I went to her. She always helped! Every single time."

"I understand," Marty said. "Now tell me who you are."

"Carly Remick. My brother is Bill. He's four years older. Our parents got divorced when I was eight and Bill was twelve. We stayed with our mom, but she's a drinker. That's why Dad left. Bill is part brother, part father to me."

"Whoa," Paul said, sitting back down. "Too much information. Focus on Lois. How did you meet her?"

Carly swallowed a mouthful of water, set the mug on the table, and began to turn it in her hands. "When my grandmother died last year, she left everything to Bill and me. Nothing really valuable except for a few nice pieces of really old furniture. A bedroom set, a dining room table and chairs, a few other odds and ends. Bill is in grad school at NAU in the history department. You know him, Dr. Russell."

"He's a good student." Distracted much of the time, but now Paul saw why. Trying to deal with Carly had to be a full-time job.

"Bill got the brains in the family. I got the energy."

An understatement. From the twitch at the corner of her mouth and the way Marty avoided his eyes, Paul thought she must agree. What was it with this woman? They seemed to be on the same wave-length. He wondered what she would do if he reached across the table and brushed those quivering lips with his fingertips.

"Back to how you met Lois," Marty said.

"She and my grandmother were friends. When Grammy died, Lois was so sweet to me. I started coming to see her whenever I missed Grammy."

"And Lois told you about me."

Carly shook her head. "I already knew about your book. After Grammy died, Bill and I decided to turn Grammy's house into an antique shop. Clarkdale, where I live, is known for antiques, little things mainly, but some furniture. Her house is right downtown, so we got permission."

Paul wanted to stem the flow of Carly's talk. Hadn't anyone ever taught the girl conversations were supposed to be two-way? But he wasn't the girl's father.

"Bill and I are doing okay, but we need to keep finding new things to sell. Lois understood. She promised me when she decided to downsize, I could get some of her antiques appraised and sell them for her. Now she's gone, I'll do it for you."

Marty made a capital T with her hands. "Slow down, Carly. I haven't had time to even look at what's here, much less think about selling any of it."

"No worries. First I do the inventory."

Marty frowned, and Paul wondered if he should intervene again, but a knock at the back door caught everyone's attention.

Scott stuck his head in. "Dad?"

Carly waved. "Scott! I was just thinking about you. How about a part-time job?"

"Slow down," began Paul.

Scott ignored him. "What job?"

"Helping me do an inventory of this house."

"Hang on," Marty said.

"Does it pay?" asked Scott.

Carly looked at Marty. "That depends. What---"

"Whoa!" Paul said. "Everyone stop talking." Not surprisingly, Carly looked resentful and Marty grateful. Scott, however, looked almost apprehensive. What was that about?

"Okay," Paul said. "Let's back up. Good morning, son. Would you like some breakfast?"

Scott shook his head. "I had some cereal."

"Okay. What can I do for you?"

"Nothing."

"I think you were going to ask me something."

"I just wanted to find out if you were over here." Scott looked away, a sure sign he wasn't being entirely truthful. But Paul didn't want to confront him in front of the others.

Carly raised her hand and waved it. "May I say something, Dr. Professor?"

"It's Marty's house. I suggest you ask her."

Marty said, "Go ahead, Carly."

"The inventory is a job for Lois's estate, so maybe Scott and I could get paid for doing the work."

"I haven't even decided if there's going to be an inventory, much less whether I want you to be involved."

Carly looked puzzled. "I just assumed you would want to settle things before you go back to Virginia today."

"I'm not leaving until after the funeral. I hadn't thought of an inventory. I admit it's a good idea, but I'm perfectly capable of doing it myself."

Paul could almost see Carly rearranging her ideas about Marty. Whatever else the girl was, she was quick to grasp the situation.

"Okay," Carly said. "I'll help you with the inventory. I already know most of what's here. We can do it in a fraction of the time, especially if Scott helps. I can talk to Mr. Lockridge about us getting paid. We can start in the living room."

Marty leaned forward and put a hand on the girl's arm. "Carly, stop. This is my house. I make the decisions."

Carly's face fell. "I've made you mad, haven't I? Krystal keeps telling me there's a line between assertive and pushy. She says I'll never get anywhere with my business until I learn where that line is."

No kidding. Paul purposely avoided looking at Marty.

"Who is Krystal?" Marty said. "You'll never get anywhere with your business if you keep talking in circles with prospective clients."

"Krystal Cho. She's my mentor."

"She runs Mystic Glass, a shop in town," Paul said.

Marty nodded. "The resident expert on ghosts."

"She's really nice," Carly said. "She's helping me learn how to be a business woman. She's going to be disappointed when I tell her how I handled my meeting with you. Am I fired?"

You bet you are, thought Paul. At least the girl had solved the problem for them.

But the corner of Marty's mouth twitched. After a moment, she laughed. "I rarely fire volunteers, even pushy ones."

Paul was glad Marty could see humor in the situation. But then she didn't know Scott, couldn't know how to interpret the closed expression on the teenager's face. What opportunity with his son had Carly snatched away?

∿

Marty didn't make a conscious decision to start with the bedroom she and Ruthie shared, but once she decided to let Carly and Scott start in the living room, her feet took her upstairs and down the hall. Though Lois had left Tommy's room untouched, she'd completely redone this room. Where Marty expected two white beds with pink spreads she found a walnut escritoire and matching file cabinet. Where two white dressers should have been stood floor-to-ceiling bookcases. Even the bentwood rocker was gone, replaced by a blue plush recliner.

All of this as she stood in the doorway. What memories waited for her inside the room? Would she remember pushing her little sister off the balcony? In the nightmare, Ruthie ran away and then disappeared. She might have run out onto the balcony and disappeared over the railing.

Suppressing a shudder, Marty edged into the room. Nothing. Just a study. She crossed to the French doors, opened them, and stepped out onto the balcony. Nothing. Just a view of mine tailings.

Below the balcony, Paul folded himself into the little red car that must be Carly's. He backed it down and parked it in the street. As he walked up the driveway, he saw her and waved. She waved back.

He pointed at her rental car and called, "Keys?"

"In the ignition!"

He came even with her and looked up. "Okay if I move your car to the street? I want to put Lois's car in the garage."

"Good idea."

"Making any progress?"

"Not much. I keep getting sidetracked with memories."

"That's why you came, isn't it? Not to do an inventory."

He was mind-reading again. Suddenly Marty wanted to tell him about Ruthie, about her fears, even about the nightmare. Paul might know what happened to Ruthie. Just because Brad didn't know didn't mean none of Lois's friends knew.

But the top porch was no place to have that conversation. "May I talk to you later?"

"Any time. Once I get the cars moved, I'm going to count things in the garage."

"Carly's orders?"

"I don't mind. I've always been curious about that old carriage house. It might be a good place to talk without being interrupted."

A good place to avoid Carly. Not that she blamed Paul. She had done the same thing by coming upstairs.

Hopeful her quest might be easily resolved, Marty went back into the room. She might as well get something accomplished while Paul moved the cars. The filing cabinet promised to be a long, slow process, possibly something better left for Brad. The books would be slow, too, because she knew she would stop to read bits and pieces.

She decided to start with the closet. Winter clothes or items to give away could be sorted quickly. It might even be empty.

At first, she thought the white toy chest with "Martha" and "Ruth" stenciled in pink on the top was another memory, except it had stood beside the French doors. She lifted the lid with a trembling hand. Raggedy Ann lay face up on the jumble, looking at her out of a single black button eye. As Marty reached for the doll, a needle of pain stabbed her chest, so intense it took her breath. She doubled over and fought for air.

The room rushed away from her, and just in time, she sat down on the floor. *Dear Lord.* She wrapped her arms around herself and began to rock back and forth. No longer twenty-eight, she was six. Mommy and Daddy gone. Ruthie too. My fault.

"What did I do?" She hadn't meant to speak the words aloud, but there they were. A question without an answer. Nothing came into her mind, nothing at all.

She was grateful when the tears finally came. How many years had she held these tears back? Twenty-two.

Marty didn't know how long she cried, but gradually her weeping lessened. Finally, it stopped. The room stabilized. She returned to the present. The pain in her chest eased. Her breath came normally. She slid into sleep.

Ruthie was on the balcony outside their room. In her hands was a little, shiny box. The copper box. "Granny Lois will be mad."

Ruthie laughed, her heart-shaped face surrounded by a halo of golden curls, her blue eyes bright with excitement. Then the box tipped. Jewels spilled out: red, blue, green, yellow, purple.

Marty tried to scream, but what came out was only a half-sound, a gurgle that worked its way out of her throat. Heart pounding, she opened her eyes.

Memory? Nightmare?

Both.

"The best way to get rid of a nightmare is to face it down, sweetie." The voice that whispered in her memory wasn't her mother's voice. It went farther back, to the time before the Greenlaws. Mommy's voice.

Face the nightmare. Face the reality. Was there a difference? The past was past. Now was now. Marty sat up and took a deep breath, then let it out slowly.

Kneeling beside the little white chest, she began to take toys out one at a time. Raggedy Ann was hers; Raggedy Andy was Ruthie's. A gray stuffed cat with blue marble eyes was Ruthie's. A pink stuffed dog with floppy ears was hers. The tea set belonged to both of them. Two plastic telephones so they could call each other. A set of Russian nesting dolls was hers, but she let Ruthie play with it. They shared Candyland. Sometimes she let Ruthie win.

At the end of an hour, the toy chest was empty. But something was missing. Something important. Marty closed her eyes and tried to remember. A clear plastic ball with blue and yellow butterflies that danced when it rolled. The ball was missing, but it wasn't important.

The copper box. Not just a product of her afternoon's dream. Surely Lois Baker had mentioned it. "Remember Grandpa Henry's copper box?" And when she was driving into town, copper for pennies and boxes. And now in this new dream.

Granny Lois had let them play with the copper box. Or with the treasures inside: sea shells no bigger than a penny, coins that rolled across the floor, black buttons set with shiny rhinestones and something else, something she couldn't remember.

The copper box wasn't a toy. It was an heirloom. She hadn't known the word twenty-two years ago, but she had understood the concept. A box that was Great-Grandpa's before it was Grandpa's, a box that would be hers after it was Daddy's.

Marty lay back on the floor and studied the ceiling. It was white tin, embossed with a vine pattern. She chose one tendril and followed it with her eyes as it branched into leaves and curled around a clump of grapes and then crawled on to join another vine and then another.

The copper box was like the vine. It crawled from one memory to the next. If she could find the copper box, she could connect the memories. She was sure of it.

Marty closed her eyes and let herself drift back in time. She held the copper box in her lap and counted the seashells: one for Ruthie, one for herself; two for Ruthie, two for herself. The coins: one for Ruthie, one for herself. The buttons: one . . . Suddenly Martha was tired of sharing. Ruthie didn't care. She wasn't even watching. Martha grabbed the treasure from both piles and put it all back in the box. She closed the lid. She would hide the box where Ruthie would never find it.

That was all. Where? Where had she hidden the box? Marty opened her eyes and sat up, got to her feet and paced. No matter what she did, that "where" persistently eluded her. But suddenly she knew when---the day Ruthie died.

Marty's cell chimed, jarring her out of the past into the present.

A text message from Vicki. She'd promised to call Vicki back hours ago. Their conversation had ended with ghosts, and the story of her experience in the attic wasn't much better. Marty imagined Vicki rolling her eyes.

Except the number wasn't Vicki's. Or any number she recognized.

Only one word of the text was different, a word that made Marty look over her shoulder.

Beware the ghost in disguise.

Chapter Twelve

"Paul . . ."

Marty sounded hesitant, making Paul wonder what she wanted to talk to him about. "Half-a-second." Twenty-five, thirty, thirty-five. He stacked the last of the horseshoes in the corner of the garage. "Thirty-eight."

He dusted his hands and turned to Marty. Except she wasn't alone. Lockridge was there with an angry Scott in tow.

"Let me go," Scott said, jerking his arm loose from the attorney's grip.

"As long as you don't try to leave until we settle this."

"I'm not going anywhere. My dad knows the album is mine."

"We'll see," Lockridge said. The attorney's voice was under better control than Scott's, but he looked as angry as the teenager did.

"What's going on, son?"

"It's mine, Dad! I told you about it."

Lockridge took a slim, oversized book from Marty and handed it to Paul. "I caught your son leaving the premises with this. He would have succeeded if I hadn't arrived at the exact moment I did."

Paul ran his fingers over the leather cover, cracked with age. Using extreme care, he opened the album: "October 10,

121

1939. To my son, Henry, on his 10th birthday. May the habit of collecting stamps bring you as much pleasure as it has me. Your loving father, William."

Paul caught Marty's eye. "Henry Baker was Lois's husband, your grandfather, right?"

Marty nodded.

"William was your great-grandfather. That's a long way back."

"You bet it is," Lockridge said. "I don't know much about stamps, but some of those are from before 1900. I'm certain that collection contains some valuable items."

Paul turned the page. The first stamp in the album was a head of Benjamin Franklin cancelled in red. He couldn't guess its worth, but he knew it must be exponentially more than the five cents it sold for in 1859.

"I told you yesterday, Dad. Miss Lois gave it to me!"

Lockridge snorted. "You want those stamps so you can sell them for drug money."

Scott flushed. "That's not true!"

Paul felt his temper flare, but getting angry would only make the situation worse. "You're an attorney. You ought to know better than to make slanderous accusations."

"The truth isn't slander."

Marty stepped between them. Paul was struck again by how small she was. But her voice was firm. "Our discussion is about the stamp album. It's not about Scott."

"You're right." Paul handed her the album and moved to stand beside Scott.

"Tell them, Dad. The album is mine!"

Lockridge looked directly at Scott. "Verbal promises are irrelevant. The moment Lois Baker died, the terms of her will defined ownership. Specific written bequests will be honored. Everything else belongs to the estate. As such, it can't leave the premises until after the will is probated. Even then, Ms. Greenlaw will have final say on what stays with her and what is sold. Your attempt to remove this album from the premises constitutes attempted theft."

Paul put a restraining hand on his son's shoulder. "That's a serious accusation, Brad."

"It's meant to be. I caught your son sneaking out of the house with a valuable asset."

"I wasn't sneaking out! I was taking it home."

"You've been searching for the album," Marty said suddenly. "That's what you were doing upstairs yesterday afternoon. And you were up there again last night."

"No! I didn't go anywhere last night. Did I, Dad?"

Paul studied his son. Under the bravado, he could tell Scott was scared, and that worried him. He didn't think Scott had left the house, but he couldn't be sure. It wasn't as though he'd sat up all night listening.

His hesitation was disastrous. Scott twisted away and headed down the driveway. "Thanks a lot, Dad! Thanks for nothing."

"Come back, Scott. We're not done here!"

For answer, Scott began to run.

Angry at himself for bungling the situation and ashamed of his son's behavior, Paul didn't know what to say. He wasn't ready to believe Scott had locked Marty in the attic, but he wasn't able to flatly deny it either.

After a moment, she said, "It's okay."

At least he knew how to answer that. "No. It's not okay. When I get to the bottom of whatever is going on here, I'll let you know."

"That's fine," Lockridge said. "But nothing's going to change. As I said, legally this album is part of the estate. It's not going anywhere except into the safe in my office."

Paul wanted to shout, "This isn't a courtroom!" but Scott had been childish enough for both of them. The best thing he could do now was talk to Scott. "I apologize for my son," he said stiffly.

The walk home took less than two minutes, but it felt like two hours. His emotions were in total disarray. Protectiveness struggled with embarrassment, anger with sorrow, determination with confusion. And beneath it all a dreary acknowledgment that the best he could hope for with Marty Greenlaw was friendship.

The quiet house somehow reverberated with feet pounding on the stairs and doors slamming. *Father.* Paul took a deep breath and let it out slowly. Then he went upstairs. As he'd expected, Scott's door was closed. *Father.* Paul knocked, not their rat-tat-tat signal, a formal, adult knock.

"What?"

"May I come in?"

"No! You don't believe me any more than the rest of them do."

"That's not true, Scott. I believe Lois promised you the stamp album. I'm confused about some of the things Mr. Lockridge said." And the conclusions Marty drew. But he didn't say that. He needed to take one thing at a time. "We have to talk. May I come in?"

"No!"

That was when Paul heard the motorcycle. It was still a long way off, but it was getting closer by the minute. Forcing himself to keep his voice even, he said, "Scott, you're not to leave this house until we get this straightened out."

The door opened then, and his son stood in front of him, angry and rebellious. "There's nothing to straighten out, Dad. I told the truth, but you don't believe me. That's about as straight as it gets."

Outside the motorcycle roared ever closer. "I mean it, Scott. You're not to go with that boy on his bike."

"Are you going to lock me in my room and starve me until I change my story?"

The sarcasm stung. It was a weapon Paul was careful never to use, a weapon Scott had learned from someone else. "Of course not," he said, taking a deliberate step back. "I'm asking you to stay home until we talk this out."

"Sorry to be such a disappointment to you, Dad." Pushing around him, Scott started down the stairs.

"I mean it, Scott. You're not to get on that bike with that boy!"

Scott stopped at the bottom of the steps and looked up at Paul. "'That boy' has a name."

Paul forced his voice down. "I'm sure he does, but since you've never introduced him to me, I have no idea what it is."

"B.T."

"Okay. What do the initials stand for?"

"It's a nickname."

"What's his real name?"

"Why are you cross-examining me about him, Dad?"

Paul started down the stairs. "I'm not cross-examining you." He couldn't do anything about Scott's belligerence, but he could at least change the body language between them, put them on the same physical plane if not the same emotional plane. "I like to know your friends."

Scott backed away. "You think he's a bad influence on me, don't you? Why can't I be a good influence on him?"

"I'm sure you can. Does he need a good influence?"

"I didn't mean it like that. He needs a friend. Okay? I'm his friend."

"That's good, Scott. But why doesn't he have any friends?"

"He's new around here."

Normally Paul would have given up the question and answer session and come back to it later when Scott was more receptive. But the motorcycle was definitely on their street now, and it would be much better if Scott would cooperate of his own free will. If he could just get Scott to hear himself. "Just being new doesn't keep someone from making friends. Is there a reason the other kids don't want to be friends with B.T.?"

"B.T. is different. So what? He still needs friends."

Paul was sure Scott was getting close to giving in. "Of course he does, son, but you need your other friends too. I haven't seen Jason around for a while."

In the front yard the motorcycle revved its engine. Scott jumped and looked defiant. "Jason doesn't have anything to do with it. You don't even know B.T. You don't like him because he has a couple of tattoos."

"It's not the tattoos; it's the lifestyle that generally goes with tattoos I object to."

"Why don't you say it?" shouted Scott. "You think Mr. Lockridge is right about me! You think B.T. is a druggie, and you think because I'm friends with him I am too."

Scott turned and ran out, slamming the screen door against the wall of the house. Anger and frustration rose like gorge in Paul. As he followed his son out onto the porch, he shouted, "If you get on that bike, you're grounded the second you get home!" He recognized his blunder as soon as the words were out, but it was too late. *Father!*

Scott climbed up behind the biker, an older teenager with shaggy black hair and dark tattoos. Fighting for self-control, Paul deliberately lowered his voice. "We agreed you wouldn't ride on a motorcycle, Scott."

"You made a pronouncement, Dad. I didn't agree. I don't agree! There's nothing wrong with bikes. They're fun."

"Fun? You think it was fun when that motorcycle came out of nowhere in front of your mother and me?"

Pumping the brakes as the Forester skidded, sliding in a long, slow arc across the road, Linda clutching his arm, tipping, rolling, the roar of the bike. Linda! When he came to, the paramedics were working on her. The biker stood looking on, banged up but not seriously injured.

"It wasn't the motorcycle, Dad," Scott said quietly. "You lost control of the car. It's your fault Mom is dead."

~~~

Marty closed the door behind Carly and went upstairs to collapse. It was only 4:00 in the afternoon, but she was wrung out, physically and emotionally. Even at home it was only 7:00, but she'd had very little sleep the last two nights.

She pulled her cell out of her pocket and stared at it. She should call Vicki, tell her about the second text message, ask her to help make sense of utter nonsense. But the thought of trying to string two words together to make a sentence was overwhelming. No way did she have the energy to explain anything to Vicki.

She went into Tommy's room and crawled into the bottom bunk. For just a minute.

"Yankee Doodle went to town. Yankee Doodle . . ." Just the tune, but the words sang along in her head. Her cell phone. Marty opened her eyes. A dark room. An unfamiliar bed.

". . . dandy. Yankee . . ."

Her cell phone wasn't in her hand. Or on the narrow bed. "Doodle dandy." She sat up and banged her head on the top bunk. The phone blinked at her from the floor. "Yankee . . ." She grabbed the phone and punched it on. "Hello."

"You were going to call me," Vicki said.

"What time is it?"

"I'm not sure what time it is in Arizona. In Virginia, it's time for bed. Owen and Chiquita have both deserted me."

"Hang on a minute. I've got to turn on the light."

"So, it's bedtime in Arizona too. Why didn't you call?"

Marty staggered to the door and flipped the switch. The red bandana shades lit up among the deer antlers. "It's a long story. The short version is I fell asleep."

"Sorry to wake you, sweetie. Start talking."

Marty looked around the room for some place to sit besides the bottom bunk. Not a single chair. "Vicki, I've got to call you back."

"No way."

"Not in the morning. After I splash some water on my face and find a place to sit."

"I'll call you back. Five minutes."

The phone went dead in Marty's hand. She considered turning it off. But only briefly. There was a limit to how much she could presume on Vicki's friendship.

While she was in the bathroom she decided the recliner in the little upstairs study was a good compromise. She could turn on all the lights and still put her feet up.

She had barely gotten settled when her phone rang. "Yankee . . ."

"All right," Vicki said. "Start talking."

"I don't know where to begin."

"How about with where you are. I got Arizona. But that's a big state."

"I'm in Jerome."

"Never heard of it."

"That's because you're not a ghost hunter."

"A what?"

"Someone who follows ghost sightings."

"Okay. I'll bite. What ghosts have been sighted in Jerome, Arizona?"

"None," Marty said. "Since ghosts don't exist."

"Cute. Tell me something that does exist."

"Okay. Jerome was a copper mining town that became a ghost town when the mine closed. Reports of ghosts are a major source of income to the current residents."

"Your grandmother is one of those residents?"

Marty hesitated.

"Is that a hard question?"

"My grandmother was a resident, Vicki." Until yesterday. "She died."

"When? You told me the old woman I sent back to the workshop was your grandmother. You have two grandmothers in Jerome?"

"No. When I got here, I found her." What to say? I found her body, I found her dead or something else? "She fell down the stairs during the night. I was the one who found her."

"Oh, Mart! You went all that way, and she died the day before you got there? You must be devastated."

Was she devastated? Disoriented might be closer to the truth. Two days ago, she hadn't known about Granny Lois. Or about Ruthie. That wasn't right. She'd known. She just hadn't remembered, had chosen not to remember.

"Marty? Are you still there?"

"Sorry. I suppose I'm having a hard time processing it."

"I can imagine. When are you coming home?"

Not until I find out if I killed my little sister. But she couldn't say that without trying to explain a nightmare she didn't understand herself. "I need to stay for the funeral."

"Why? It's not like you were close to her. Are there other relatives?"

"No. I'm all that's left of the family." The refrain that started when she drove into town picked up again: Mommy and Daddy are gone. Ruthie too.

"Then come home, Marty."

"I can't, Vicki. Granny Lois left everything to me. I can't just turn around and come home as if nothing happened."

"I suppose not. What did you inherit?"

"An old Victorian house filled with antique furniture. Not family hand-me-down antiques, a high-end collection. A Weber square grand piano, a gilt mirror that's got to be three hundred years old, and a lot of things I haven't had a chance to take a good look at."

Vicki didn't reply immediately. Marty could almost hear her thinking it through, how to ask tactfully if she could handle the sale of the pieces. After a moment, Vicki said, "Do you need some help? Do you want me to come out there?"

More than anything. But not yet. Not until she found the copper box. Not until she remembered how Ruthie died. "Maybe in a few days. After the inventory. You can help me decide the best way to handle the pieces I want to sell."

"Don't you need help with the inventory?"

"No. There's a young woman here who knew my grandmother."

"Okay. If you change your mind, let me know. Do you want me to contact the clients you've got projects going for? I can tell them there's been a death in the family."

More than one death. "Would you? The list of current projects is on the bulletin board over my desk. I'll call every one of them as soon as I get back. If anyone seems upset, promise a discount on the work. Mr. Clarkson, for example."

"All right. Now, girlfriend, tell me what you heard up in the attic. That was quite a cliff you left me hanging on."

"It wasn't a ghost."

"I didn't think it was. It was just the creaking of an old house, right?"

"I wish. I'm pretty sure it was the teenaged boy who lives across the road. I'm not sure how to handle it."

"That should be easy enough. Tell his parents."

The overhead light went out. Not just that light, the desk lamp and the hall light. Every light in the house. Downstairs something crashed.

Chapter Thirteen

Another crash in the room directly below the little study, the living room.

"Marty?"

"Sorry, Vicki. Gotta go." Marty cut the connection and pushed herself out of the recliner.

A heavy thud in the front hall. The cat in the dark? But cats could see in the dark. An intruder.

She punched the phone on. The light was only intended to illuminate the tiny screen, but it was like a candle in the heavy darkness. In the moment of sight it gave her, Marty looked for something to use to as a defensive weapon. The desk lamp. She jerked the cord out of the wall and wrapped it around her hand.

The chink of china in the dining room. Not just once, a series of crashes as if someone were throwing dishes at the wall.

Suddenly Marty didn't know whether to be frightened or angry. She did not believe in ghosts. A living, breathing person was methodically demolishing Lois's house. But who? And why?

A door opened and slammed shut. Then another door. Coming this way. Marty didn't intend to be trapped or forced out onto the upper porch. Gripping the lamp, she blundered across the room.

Silence. For a single breathless moment.

She was in the doorway when a new sound sliced the silence. A sound that stopped her heart, the wail of an infant. Dear Lord! Not a baby, a cat. It must be the Siamese.

Whatever it was, Marty knew she had to get out of the house before she changed her mind about ghosts. She shifted the lamp to her right hand and put her left hand on the wall. Her eyes were beginning to adjust to the dark, so she could pick up her pace. But not too much. The stairs were ahead, but how far?

Without warning the lights came back on. Not just the hall light and the other upstairs lights she had turned on, but also light from downstairs filled the stairwell, lights she was sure she had turned off. She was surrounded by light, blinded by it. The next instant the lights went out, plunging her into darkness. Then into light. Dark, light, dark until it took every scrap of Marty's will power to stifle a scream.

Scott! It had to be the teenager, angry she had agreed to Brad taking the stamp album to his office.

The lights came on again. She shouted, "Stop it! Stop it, Scott!"

She was at the top of the stairs when the lights went out again. Somewhere a door slammed. Once, twice, three times.

Marty started down the staircase. An angry screech and then something warm and heavy struck her chest. Something with claws. The cat. The cat!

Cat, lamp, cord. Marty fought to untangle herself. The lamp struck the banister. As it went over, the plug on the end of the cord hit her cheek, narrowly missing her eye. The cat scrambled loose and shot up the stairs.

Marty almost lost her balance, coming so close to falling that she sat down abruptly. She flashed back to the sight of Granny Lois, a crumpled yellow form at the bottom of these stairs. Fear swallowed her anger. But she couldn't let it paralyze her. She couldn't stay where she was.

Why didn't she hear a siren? Surely Vicki had called 911. The fire truck should be here by now. Fire truck or not, she had to get out of this house. Had to get out! Marty fought the urge to fling herself down the staircase. She would not give into the fear. So far nothing had actually happened. Noises, lights, the cat. Maybe the destruction was imaginary, like ghosts. Marty pushed away the thought of ghosts and concentrated on her feet.

One step at a time. Down. One foot at a time. Right foot. Left foot. She would ignore the crashes. She would reach the bottom of the stairs, walk down the hall to the front door, open it, and go out onto the porch. Then she could hurry down the driveway and go across the road to Paul's house. She would demand Paul discipline his son.

More crashes. More thuds. The tinkle of breaking glass at the bottom of the stairs.

Marty froze. Her cell phone. Where was it? Not in her hand, not in her pocket. She must have dropped it. In the hall? In the study? Should she go back for it? Or keep going downstairs?

She had to decide. Up to the cell phone. Down to whatever, whoever, was tearing the house apart.

Up was the sensible choice. But if she went back, she would be trapped. Marty kept going down. One step at a time. Down. One foot at a time. Down.

Thuds at the front of the house. A rush of water in the kitchen.

It couldn't be. The teenager couldn't be in two places at one time. *Dear Lord!*

"Mar … tee …" Pounding at the front of the house. Water running in the kitchen.

"Marty!" Her name? Her name! Not Scott.

"Marty!" Paul?

Light.

Silence.

"Marty!"

Paul. At the front door.

He was shouting. "What the devil is going on in there?"

Not the devil. Not a ghost. A disturbed teenager. Marty stumbled toward the front of the house, as blind in the light as she had been in the dark. Broken glass crunched under her feet, proof the destruction wasn't imaginary.

"Marty! Are you in there?"

She tripped on something that might have been a book and staggered before slamming into the wall and catching herself.

"Marty!"

She tried to answer, but no sound came.

Finally. The front door. She groped for the dead bolt. Found it, pulled it, opened the door.

Paul was there, and she was glad. So glad. But she pushed around her rescuer. "Stop him!" Her voice was hoarse, a croak more than a voice, but he understood.

He turned, gripped her shoulders, and looked over her head. "Who?"

The light spilling out the door behind them was kind to her beleaguered eyes. She could see without having to look into light or being surrounded by it. In the driveway, the Camry; on the slope below, rocks; on the road, nothing. Not a car, not a running figure. No one.

Paul's presence was somehow natural. His arms went around her, encircling her waist, and she relaxed against his warmth.

"What was going on in there, Marty? I saw lights flashing on and off all over the house. Who was here?"

She didn't have the strength or the desire to argue with him about his son. Besides, she didn't actually know it was Scott. "I wish I knew." She shivered, not from cold, not even from fear. It was from delayed reaction. Whatever it was, it was over.

"You're cold. Let's go inside."

"No!" She heard the edge in her voice, willed herself to control it, and said more quietly, "Not yet."

He turned her around and looked down. He was framed in the bright doorway, a faceless outline backlit. She shivered again. Not Paul. Scott. Or someone else.

"What happened in there, Marty?"

She didn't know the answer or maybe she simply didn't have words for it, so she shrugged.

He studied her, cocking his head so his outline shifted. She tried to find words to give him. "I don't know why the lights went off and on. I heard sounds of dishes breaking, but I don't know who was there. I was trapped upstairs. All I know is I had to get away."

He pulled her close and held her. "You go to my house. I'll take a look around here, turn out the lights, check for clues to the intruder's identity. When I'm sure no one's here, I'll come home. We'll have a cup of cocoa, and you can tell me what happened."

Scott. She stepped back, shaking her head.

"Scott's not home. We can talk."

Grateful he had read her mind again, she pushed her hair out of her face, took a deep breath, and tried to think. Her cell phone. "Would you look for my cell phone? I dropped it somewhere upstairs. In the hall or the little study."

"Consider it done. Are you sure you're okay, Marty?"

His concern was more than she could bear, and suddenly tears were sliding down her face. She didn't want to cry.

She wasn't hurt. She swallowed her tears, coughed, and kept crying.

He pulled her close again, murmured, "It'll pass more quickly if you don't fight it."

She gave in and sobbed. Her tears stopped as suddenly as they had started. She stepped back, wiping her face with her hands.

Paul said, "In the old movies, this is where the hero pulls out a clean, white hankie and hands it to the girl. I, however, am fresh out of hankies, clean or dirty, white, red, blue, or plaid. In fact, I don't think I've ever owned a handkerchief. My granddad carried them."

Marty dabbed her face with the hem of her shirt. "That's okay. My mother told me when she was a little girl one of her chores was to press her father's clean handkerchiefs. Since I didn't bring an iron, we'd be in a mess if you had one to give me."

He chuckled. "I'm glad your sense of humor is intact. You're going to need it when you see the hovel. Scott thinks it should be razed. You'll probably agree."

"I'm not in the mood to pass any judgments. As long as I don't have to go back in this house until you give the all clear, I'll be happy."

"If you don't mind camping out, you're welcome to stay the night."

She expected to refuse, but she heard herself say, "I don't want to be any trouble."

"No trouble. We have two air mattresses." He paused, then added, "I don't expect Scott home tonight."

Something about the way he said his son's name made her wonder if Paul had his own suspicions of the teenager.

∾

The moon slid into view, momentarily eluding the clouds. Paul stood on the porch and watched Marty make her way down Lois's driveway. When he was reasonably certain she wasn't going to fall, he turned and went into the house. Shading his eyes against the blaze of light, he surveyed the hallway.

Shards of glass shone among a welter of books from the den, silverware from the dining room, mugs from the kitchen, and family pictures that had hung in the stairwell. The aftermath of an earthquake, except an earthquake wouldn't fling items from one room into another. He could imagine the noise. No wonder Marty was in shock.

Paul righted the gilt hall table and picked his way across the debris. A short walk down the hall and around the corner to the stairway, but it was slow going. He did his best not to step on anything that wasn't already broken, but glass crunched almost every time he put his foot down.

He was almost to the kitchen when he heard the water. Whoever had done all of this had turned on the faucet, full blast from the sound of it. That was when Paul's own shock gave way to anger. Clearly the point of all this destruction had been to frighten Marty into thinking a poltergeist was on the loose in the Baker house. But he didn't believe in ghosts, and the water was pure spite.

Paul went into the kitchen and shut off the faucet. As he turned to leave, he kicked the cat's dish. Where was poor Rahab? He wondered if they would ever see her again. No doubt she was already on the prowl for a new home.

The stairs were largely uncluttered, and nothing was out of place on the second floor. The poltergeist had evidently been careful not to get too close to where Marty was. He found the cell phone on the floor in the doorway of Lois's study. He pocketed it and turned off the desk and floor lamps. The only other light burning on the second floor was the overhead fixture in Tommy's room.

He was surprised to see Marty had taken that room as her own. He wondered why. He couldn't imagine she was comfortable in the bunk bed. He could understand why she might not want to sleep in Lois's room just yet, but the guest room was ready. Perhaps there was more to Marty's story than a simple lapse of memory. Back downstairs he decided to take a few minutes and start the clean-up. He didn't think Marty would mind the time to herself in a neutral environment.

An hour later the kitchen was marginally functional, and it was possible to walk down the hall without stepping on anything. While he hadn't actually put everything back where it belonged, he had returned most of the unbroken items to their rooms of origin. Articles he judged repairable waited on the dining room table. Broken pieces filled two large garbage bags.

Armed with broom and dustpan, Paul made his way to the front of the house. Steeling himself for the sight of more destruction, he ventured into the living room. A pair of table lamps with ornate silk shades glowed pale pink. He was so unprepared for what the soft light revealed, he stopped in the doorway. It was as if an unseen hand had brushed lamb's blood on the lintel. The angel of death had passed over. Nothing in this room had been touched.

Vaguely troubled, he turned off the lamps and went to put the broom away. The pristine condition of the living room worried him. The value of all the broken articles together didn't add up to as much as the price of the antique mirror hanging on the wall in the living room. The vandal had been remarkably selective in his or her demolition. What at first glance was simply an attempt to frighten Marty now looked like a calculated plan. But the goal eluded him. What he couldn't understand worried him. Turning out the rest of the lights, he picked up the bags of trash to add to the load he planned to take to the dump and headed home.

Marty was asleep on the shabby brown couch he'd bought in the resale shop. If he had found Linda there, he would have gone quietly to her and kissed her forehead. But he knew very well this wasn't Linda.

Marty must have heard the door close behind him because she stirred, stretched, and opened her eyes.

He said, "Hi."

She frowned slightly.

"Jerome, Arizona. Paul Russell. The hovel."

"Sorry. I was really out. I was dreaming. I hope what I think happened at Granny Lois's house was a nightmare."

He took her cell phone out of his pocket and handed it to her. "Sorry. I'm afraid it happened."

She swung her legs around and sat up. "Is it as bad as I imagine?"

"It depends on how you look at it. The damage was largely superficial."

"What do you mean?"

"Lots of things were broken, but nothing of real value was damaged."

"That's good, isn't it?"

"Yes."

"But?"

He moved one of the lawn chairs to sit directly across from her. Not quite knee to knee. "I'm afraid the culprit has a motive other than simple vandalism."

"I don't understand."

"I think you're supposed to draw the conclusion that a poltergeist was on the loose in your house."

"A poltergeist? A mischievous ghost?"

Paul nodded.

"But that's ridiculous. I don't believe in ghosts."

"Neither do I. I think someone is trying to scare you into leaving here."

"But why?"

"No idea. But I think the incident tonight is the second attempt."

"The first one being locking me in the attic."

So, she had thought of it too. Good. Maybe she would be easier to warn than he'd thought. "Yes. I don't know someone was up there. My conclusion is conjecture, but it's conjecture based on concrete facts."

"What facts?"

"First, the light bulb. It wasn't burned out. Someone removed it from the fixture. I found it sitting on a bureau."

"Second," she said, "the door didn't slam shut. It was locked, right?"

"Yes."

"At least that explains the wedding veil."

"The wedding veil?"

"I kept running into something in the dark. In the morning, I realized it was a piece of lace, but I couldn't figure out what it was hanging from. Someone was waving it in my face, the same someone who just trashed Granny's house."

"Probably."

"Beware the ghost in disguise."

"What?"

"Another piece of the puzzle that doesn't make any sense, a text message I got yesterday afternoon. It wasn't the first one either."

"Sorry. I'm not following you."

"Someone is sending me weird warnings. Yesterday I got one that said, 'Beware the ghost in disguise.' When you said the trashing of Lois's house was intended to look like the work of a poltergeist, the meaning of that message clicked."

"Okay. I see that 'ghost' could mean the poltergeist. I don't understand the reference to a disguise. What is a 'ghost in disguise?'"

"No idea. That was the second warning. The first one came right before Granny Lois showed up in my workshop."

"You got a warning about a ghost?"

"No. That one said, 'Beware the wolf in disguise.' At first I thought it was some sort of joke. Later when I remembered the wolf disguised as the grandmother in *Little Red Riding Hood*, I thought someone here in Jerome must have sent it."

"Warning you about Lois. Why would you need to be warned about your grandmother?"

"I don't know. None of it makes sense."

"No clue to the sender?"

"The sender was blocked in the first text. There was a number for the ghost-in-disguise text, but I don't know how to find out whose it is. I tried it. Of course, no one answered. No voice mail."

"Do you still have the messages?"

"I erased the first one, but I kept the one from yesterday."

Paul held out his hand. "If you'll let me see it, I can at least tell if it's a local number."

She got the phone out of her pocket, scrolled, and then handed it to him.

928-982-2892. Paul felt sick, but he couldn't let Marty see his reaction. He retreated into objective-teacher, nothing-shocks-me mode. In a steady voice, he said, "It's a local number. That's all I can tell you."

Not a lie. It wasn't all he knew, but it was certainly all he could tell her. The number was more familiar than his own. It was Scott's.

142

Chapter Fourteen

Marty is becoming quite a problem. Don't misunderstand, I don't have anything against her. In fact, I like her. If we had met under different circumstances, I imagine we could have become special friends. Now, however, she's in my way. From the very start her presence was a complication. At first, I hoped she would go straight home after she found poor Lois.

When she announced her intention to stay until after the funeral, I was disappointed, to say the least. A fine family sentiment, but I'm surprised she didn't realize no one cares. It's not as if people know her. And as if that isn't enough, now it seems she's on some sort of a quest. She wants to find out what happened to her little sister, though I can't see the point of worrying about something that happened over twenty years ago. Unfortunately, it seems quite important to her. On top of that, I've learned she's searching the house for something. I have no idea what it is, but her search is almost certain to cross mine, and when that happens, I'm afraid I'll be forced to take direct action.

She's turning out to be quite stubborn. Almost as stubborn as Lois. It's an unfortunate family trait, unfortunate for them. I was quite annoyed when she showed up in the house the first night she was in Jerome. I put on a pretty good show for her, given the fact I had to improvise. I had her pretty scared, and I hoped she would at least move out of the house!

Marty keeps fighting the idea of ghosts, though I don't know why in that house. Everyone knows the Baker house is haunted, even though Lois denied it until the day she died. I hadn't realized until now, but her insistence that she didn't believe in ghosts was another factor in her death. If she'd been willing to at least play along, I could have put on a show for her and scared her out of the house long enough to give me a chance to get away. Never mind, that's all water under the bridge.

Back to Marty. Since my haunting of the attic didn't scare her sufficiently, I had to up the ante with the poltergeist. In one way, I hated to break those lovely dishes, but in another way it was fitting. If Marty refuses to believe in ghosts, I hope she at least gets the message I'm getting angry. If the poltergeist doesn't scare her away, I suppose I'll wait until after the funeral tomorrow to see if she'll keep her word and go home. If she doesn't, I'm not sure what I'll do next. What I do know is the situation is becoming serious. Serious problems require serious solutions.

Chapter Fifteen

Marty walked toward town, following the narrow sidewalk that bordered the highway. Early afternoon and the road connecting Jerome and Prescott was almost deserted. If not for the forest fire, it would have been busy on a summer afternoon. But because no one could predict where the wind would carry the fire from one hour to the next, it was safer to drive the extra miles along the interstate and loop into Prescott from the other side.

Marty's morning had been like the road was now, empty and slow. When she opened her eyes and studied the patch of blue framed by the lopsided window, she knew almost immediately where she was. On the air bed in Paul's spartan bedroom. Maybe it was the faint scent of wintergreen soap or the biography of Thomas Jefferson or the filing cabinet with the carefully rolled socks on the top that told her. Whatever the clue, she knew exactly where she was, and, in spite of the poltergeist of the night before, she was content. An hour later, breakfast had been peanut butter toast and coffee accompanied by casual conversation that meandered anywhere but along the path that led from Lois Baker's crumpled body to the chaos stirred up by a ghost in disguise.

Marty walked past the fire station and crossed the narrow road that led up to the Gold King Mine. That was when the view caught her. She leaned against the railing and tried to take it in. Impossible to do anything but process successive mental snapshots of the panorama that began at the edge of the sidewalk, dropped down the kudzu-smothered hillside, spun across the wide valley, touched the scattered town of Cottonwood, skipped along the silver line of the Verde River, slid up the ridge of blue mountains that defined the horizon, and stretched into infinity in azure sky far from the fire.

The last four days felt like the view. Impossible to comprehend except as a series of unrelated events: an encounter with a forgotten grandmother, the discovery of Lois Baker's body, a neo-gothic night in the attic, the task of creating an inventory of the Baker house, the destruction wreaked by the poltergeist. Not to mention the people: Paul, Scott, Brad, Carly.

How did it all fit together? Because it must. Beneath the chaos lay a pattern she couldn't identify, someone with a hidden agenda.

The two men were easy to read. Both friends of Lois saddened by her death. Both wanted to make things as easy as possible for the granddaughter who had come too late. Beyond that, Paul was a father worried about a teenager, appropriately worried from what Marty could see. Brad was an attorney determined to carry out his client's wishes according to her last will.

Scott and Carly weren't so transparent. Marty wasn't positive Scott was behind the mayhem, but so much seemed to point to him. Locking her in the attic might be nothing more than a prank gone wrong, though she couldn't imagine why the teenager would want to play a trick on her. But the damage to Lois's belongings could hardly be called a prank.

And Carly. The girl had showed up this morning at 9:30, ready to work on the inventory, seemingly shocked at the state of the first floor. But was she really? For starters, why had she arrived so late? The day before she'd showed up before 8:00. Was she late because she expected Marty to send her away? Besides her early arrival, Carly almost immediately suggested calling a friend of hers with a pickup to move the most valuable antiques down to her store, not to sell, of course, but to move out of harm's way.

"Martha Baker?"

Marty started. A petite woman with skin the color of manzanita bark stood at her elbow. She was wearing a white peasant blouse and a long patchwork skirt of yellow and red batiks. Black hair threaded with silver was swept up and secured with tortoiseshell combs.

"I'm Sofia Lopez. I think you're Martha Baker. Lois and I were good friends. She told me so much about you, I feel as if I already know you."

A friend. Marty knew she needed a friend here in Jerome. She smiled. "I'm glad to meet you, Sofia."

"I should have come to the house as soon as I heard about Lois." Sofia looked out at the blue distance. "I'm not sure why I didn't. Maybe I didn't want to believe Lois was gone." She brushed away a tear and smiled at Marty. "We never know when we'll be called Home, do we?"

Called home. A different way of thinking about death.

Sofia took Marty's arm. "You can't imagine the plans Lois made for the time when she found you. Now it's up to us to pick up where she left off. Come across to my shop."

With nothing across the road except a rough amphitheater cut into the hillside, Marty wondered what Sofia meant. They waited for two cars to pass and then hurried across. Sofia led her to a kiosk bright with silk scarves, lengths of hand-dyed cotton, and colorful string bags. "Welcome to my shop."

Marty reached for a silk scarf that shimmered magenta and gold. "Do you dye these yourself?"

"I do. You like bright colors?"

"Yes. Very much." Letting the scarf slide from her hand, Marty reached for a second one, a swirl of green and copper large enough to wear as a shawl.

"That's a good one for you. It brings out the green in your eyes."

"I'd like to buy it."

"Take it as a gift, a gift to my dear friend's beloved granddaughter."

As Marty was about to refuse, Sofia reached up and touched Marty's mouth with her index finger. "If I may, I'll come to the house tomorrow and haggle over the price of a gift.

Marty smiled. "I'd like that very much. I have so many questions."

"Questions you hoped Lois would answer for you."

"Yes. She told me she wanted to explain."

Sofia sat in a canvas director's chair and pointed to another one for Marty. "Do you know what she meant?"

"Not exactly. I hoped she would explain why she gave me up for adoption."

"You know she had Tommy to take care of."

"I don't remember Uncle Tommy very well. He was a special needs child, wasn't he?"

"He had Down syndrome. He was a surprise baby, born to Lois and Henry late in life. They loved him very much, and Lois was determined to keep him at home as long as she could. When he died a couple of years ago, her first priority was to find you."

Marty took a deep breath. Now was the time to ask The Question. "Did my grandmother tell you how my little sister died?"

Sofia didn't answer for so long Marty was sure she was looking for a way to say, "My dear, surely you remember. Surely you didn't forget how you pushed her."

Finally, Sofia said softly, "I thought there was another grandchild. Lois would never talk about those years. She said they were very painful. I assumed the other child died in the car accident that killed your parents. I assumed you were the only one who escaped. That's not true?"

"My sister's name was Ruth. She and I were here in Jerome when our parents were killed." The words came automatically from a place in her memory Marty had thought inaccessible.

"Perhaps her diary holds the answers you need."

"My grandmother kept a diary?"

"Sí. Every night she wrote in it. She told me it was a conversation she had with God before she went to sleep. You haven't found it?"

"No, but I wasn't looking . . ."

"Sofia, amigá!" A stocky middle-aged woman speaking rapid Spanish approached the kiosk.

"Un momento, Dolores." Sofia folded the green and copper scarf into tissue paper and put it in Marty's hands. "Mañana."

Marty slipped the scarf into her bag.

Dolores touched Marty's arm. "We are all sorry for your loss. The memorial service for our sister Lois is tomorrow, is it not?"

Marty forced a smile. "At 4:00 p.m."

It was unsettling to realize these women she'd never seen knew who she was. She wondered what they imagined her loss to be. The deep sorrow of a grandchild for a beloved grandmother? Marty wished she could feel sorrow, but shock was as far as she'd gotten. Shock and frustration Lois Baker had died before she could explain the past Marty so desperately needed to retrieve. Perhaps if memory returned, sorrow for Granny Lois would come with it.

Marty settled her bag more firmly on her shoulder and headed down the street as if she knew where she planned to go next. Almost immediately she came to a flight of concrete steps cut into the side of the mountain. She looked up.

The angle was too steep for her to see what was at the top, but she knew anyway. A park with a swing. Nothing more than a flash. Not enough to be classified as a memory.

If she climbed up and sat on the swing, could she conjure up the full memory? It was worth a try. The steps were steep. A child would have to be helped. Who had helped her? Nothing came. The tiny park was there: a handkerchief of grass, a single picnic table, a swing set with two swings.

She sat in one and closed her eyes. Who stood behind to give her a push? Mommy? Daddy? Granny Lois? Nothing. Where was Ruthie? Nothing. No matter how hard Marty tried, she couldn't bring back the memory.

She was halfway down the steps when the next flash came. Orange sherbet. As before, it was hardly a memory. Just a sense that after a picnic it was time for ice cream. She remembered passing the ice cream shop when she first came into town. At the end of this street.

She walked past the sheriff's office. To her relief, it looked closed. She had no desire to renew her acquaintance with Sheriff Winston. Brad had tried to reassure her by saying the sheriff was bored. Even so, she wanted to stay out of his way.

The sidewalk was crowded with all sorts of people: gray-headed bikers in red bandanas and leather pants, teen-aged girls in halter tops that showed off tattoos of butterflies and rainbows, families with young children who tugged ahead or lagged behind. She studied the children, especially the little girls, grasping for something that might connect her to her childhood. Orange sherbet.

The ice cream shop was almost at the end of the block. She pushed open the door, setting a small bell jangling, a bell that belonged only to the present. She looked hopefully around the long narrow room, but nothing was familiar. The little round tables looked like they might have been there for twenty years, but she couldn't pick one out as a place she might have sat when she was six. Orange sherbet.

Marty took her place in line behind a bearded grandfather holding a little girl with curly brown hair high enough to see the tubs of ice cream.

"I want strawberry!" shouted the little girl.

"In a cup," the grandfather said.

The server, a teenaged girl with long, blonde hair slicked back in a ponytail, dipped without comment.

Orange sherbet in a waffle cone. What else? What did Ruthie want? But Ruthie didn't seem to be in the memory. Or if she was, she was being very quiet. Ruthie, asleep in the car. Mommy in the car with her. Daddy . . .

"What'll you have, ma'am?"

"Are you going to order or just stand there?"

Marty turned to see who had poked her. A tired-looking girl with a baby on her right hip and a toddler hanging on her skirt said, "It's your turn."

"Sorry. I was thinking about something else."

"What'll you have, ma'am?" repeated the server.

"Orange sherbet in a waffle cone." Daddy. Behind her the baby started to wail. Three years old when Ruthie was born. But that memory was too far back. She traded three dollars for the extra-large cone and made her way back outside. She stood for a moment in the shadow of the building and licked the sherbet, savoring its cold sweetness on her tongue. Daddy handing her orange sherbet in a waffle cone. But nothing more came.

She looked farther down the street to where the sidewalk divided, half of it dropping steeply as it followed the road down the side of the mountain, the other half meandering around the side of the mountain as it followed a side street off to the right. Still nothing.

Suddenly the sherbet was too cold and too sweet. Marty dropped what was left of the cone into a trashcan and turned back the way she had come. On this side of the street, the buildings were narrow and tall, three or even four stories, and so close there was barely room to walk between them. On the other side of the street, buildings had collapsed and tumbled down the mountain so she could see a lower level of the town.

Mommy had called Granny's street the second story of the town, making this level of shops and offices the first story. Did that make the lower level the basement of the town? She could see a row of tiny shops, almost like a row of apartments. As she was trying to decide whether to go down or turn around, one of the signs caught her eye.

Leaded letters set in colorful stained glass spelled out the words "Mystic Glass." What was it Brad had said? "If you want to talk ghosts, Krystal at Mystic Glass is the best source in town." Elusive memories weren't exactly ghosts, but on a sudden impulse, Marty headed for the shop.

∾

Paul stared at the computer screen. It was no use. He couldn't keep his mind focused on Thomas Jefferson. Was it possible? Could Lockridge be right? Was Scott mixed up with drugs?

Paul wasn't naïve enough to assume his son was immune to the temptations every teenager faced these days, but Scott had always been a dependable kid. Scott was the child who noticed when another child was hurt or being left behind. He was the kid who stood up to the bullies, who remembered adults had feelings.

But that was the little boy Paul remembered. What of the teenager who blamed his father for his mother's death? What might that kid get into if his father was too caught up in personal grief to pay attention to the son? Might that teenager turn to drugs?

Paul knew the warning signs: withdrawal, defiance of authority, an unexplained drop in grades, friendships with troubled kids. With a sinking feeling, he admitted they all applied to his son. As hard as he tried, he couldn't remember the last time Scott had initiated a serious conversation with him, at least before the morning's fiasco over the stamp album. He could remember plenty of instances when Scott withdrew into his room and closed the door.

Going off on the motorcycle had certainly been defiant, but if Paul was honest with himself, he knew rebellion had been building. Scott had always been a straight-A student, maintaining his grades with dogged determination even during the weeks immediately following his mother's death. But he had finished the eighth grade with a C in English and another one in history. Paul had debated with himself about how to respond, but in the end, he had kept quiet. Though not up to Scott's usual standard, Cs were acceptable grades. Or so he had reasoned. Now, however, those two Cs seemed nothing short of ominous. And there was no escaping Scott's new friendship with B.T. If ever a boy looked like a troubled kid, that one did.

Paul closed his laptop and pushed back his chair. There was no point in arguing with himself any further. He knew what he had to do. The only question was why he hadn't seen it sooner.

The door to Scott's room was closed, as it always seemed to be lately, but Paul opened it without hesitation and went in.

No matter that he felt awkward about invading his son's space. He had always respected Scott's privacy, but he had never had cause to suspect Scott was involved in anything that might require his intervention. If there were even the slightest chance his son was doing drugs, Paul needed to know.

Like the rest of the house, the room contained only the bare necessities of living: an air mattress and sleeping bag, a battered four-drawer chest they'd found at a thrift store, and a makeshift set of shelves. Pushing aside his uneasiness, Paul went to the chest and opened the top drawer. Not surprisingly, it was a jumble of underwear and socks. The other three drawers were just as disorganized, but it didn't take long to see Scott hadn't hidden anything in the chest.

He checked under the air mattress and inside the sleeping bag. Like so many houses in Jerome, this one had been built before closets were common, so he turned to the shelves. The bottom shelf was empty. The top shelf held three large cardboard boxes, all the things Scott had brought along for the summer in Jerome.

The first box contained sports equipment. A baseball and a catcher's mitt, two Frisbees, a ping pong ball, and two paddles. As Paul went through the box, he realized with a pang he hadn't once suggested they stop work to play. Vowing to do better, he closed that box and went to the next. It was filled with books.

Scott's own stamp album lay on top. Paul picked it up and paged through it. It contained penny stamps, nickel stamps, and commemorative stamps. Paul understood Scott's desire for Lois's stamp album, and he believed his son's story. No matter what Lockridge might think, he knew his son wouldn't steal a stamp album to sell. He closed the album and set it aside. The rest of the books were books on the subjects that interested Scott: stamps, astronomy, and geology.

The third box held geology equipment: rock picks, a magnifying glass, a field notebook, a guide to rock identification, safety goggles, empty sample bags, and the daypack Scott kept for rock hunting. Paul almost skipped the pack, so light he thought it was empty. But he decided he might as well be thorough. Inside were two more sample bags, but unlike the others, these weren't empty. One held a stack of small white papers ready for rolling. The other one was filled with crushed gray-green leaves.

Chapter Sixteen

Marty watched the wind push the sign one way, pull it the other: push, pull, push until the dark letters seemed to dance across the stained glass. That was how she felt, pushed to go inside, pulled to pass by. What did it matter? She didn't believe in ghosts. Mystic Glass was just a tiny shop with a seductive sign. A gust of wind pushed against her back. Marty gave in and opened the door.

As she entered the shadowy interior, a shimmer of blue came toward her, more substantial than colored light, but not an identifiable shape. The farther she advanced, the closer it came. With an involuntary shiver, she stopped. The shimmer stopped. It didn't retreat, holding steady. She took another step, and the blue came closer. With a sudden suspicion, she stepped to the right. Whatever it was moved with her.

Behind her, a woman laughed.

Marty turned to see a tall, slender woman about her own age studying her with heavily accented almond eyes. A black satin dress with a mandarin collar and cap sleeves hugged her figure. Her long black hair was twisted into a tight chignon, and slender crystals dangled from her ears.

"Welcome. I'm Krystal Cho, owner of Mystic Glass. My mirror is intended to pique your interest in the enchantment of glass. I think perhaps it has worked for you."

Marty smiled. "It has. Why doesn't it reflect my face and hands? It seems to only pick up my shirt."

"If I told you that, my mirror wouldn't intrigue you, would it? Just as my mirror interests you because you don't know anything about it, you interest me because I don't know you."

"I'm Marty Greenlaw." She hesitated and then heard herself add, "Martha Baker. Lois Baker was my grandmother."

"Ah. I'm glad to meet you, Martha. I won't pretend sorrow that Lois has passed over, but I will miss her. She and I were friends after a fashion. I once saw a mirror in her attic---"

A telephone pealed, and Krystal waved a hand that glittered with rings toward the shelves and cases that lined the walls. "My mirror is only the beginning of the enchantments of glass. For now, explore."

Shaking off a vague sense of uneasiness, Marty turned her attention to the contents of the shop. Mirrors of all shapes and sizes hung in unexpected places around the room. Blown-glass figurines stood on a corner shelf. Vases filled with silk flowers sat on counters and small tables. Paperweights, some in a variety of colored glass, others in odd shapes, and still others containing fanciful figures, filled shelves on one entire wall. A sparkling glass mobile hung from the ceiling, twisting gently in an air current.

But the kaleidoscopes drew her across the room. The first one she picked up was silver and no bigger than a pen, but when she looked through it, miniscule flowers danced across her vision. The case of another one was polished wood, and when she looked inside, mirrors reflected the room around her in a series of hexagons.

"You've found my kaleidoscopes," Krystal said, so close Marty jumped. "They were my inspiration for the shop. Or one particular kaleidoscope was."

Something in the other woman's tone made Marty reluctant to hear about Krystal's inspiration. Putting the wooden tube back on its stand, she said, "I've never seen so many kinds of glass in one shop. You have an eye for the unusual."

Krystal gave Marty a cryptic smile. "It's more than an eye. I don't think you will believe me when I say some of these pieces came to me of their own volition."

"I don't believe in inanimate objects with volition any more than I believe in ghosts."

Krystal made a delicate clucking sound. "I'm surprised you're willing to speak so boldly after your experience last night."

It was clear this woman knew all about her poltergeist. Jerome was a small town, but who had called this woman? She knew as soon as the question crossed her mind. "Carly called you."

Krystal shrugged. "I hoped you would think I was clairvoyant. Sometimes I am. But in this case, you're right. Carly called me about an hour ago. She knew how interested I am in any sort of manifestations that take place in the Baker house."

"Manifestations?"

"Carly told me about your poltergeist."

"I don't believe in ghosts."

"What kind of ghost don't you believe in?"

Marty picked up a tiny unicorn fashioned from spun glass and turned it in her hand. "What do you mean?"

"Is it just poltergeists you don't believe in? Or ghosts that appear in mirrors?"

Marty put down the unicorn with a shaking hand. This woman couldn't possibly know about her experience at the hotel.

"Or shadows of memory that linger in old houses? Or restless spirits that appear as orbs of light?"

Marty reached for a fluted glass vase filled with blue, silk irises that looked so real she had to touch them to make sure they were artificial.

"The Baker house has all of those. I'm surprised you haven't encountered the other ghosts."

Suddenly Marty was angry. "If you're trying to frighten me," she said sharply, "it won't work."

"Why would I try to frighten you? I'm explaining why you should sell me your house."

"I don't know what you mean."

"Brad didn't tell you? I thought that was why you came in."

He'd told her Krystal was an expert on ghosts, but Marty didn't think that was what the other woman meant. "I came in because your sign caught my attention."

"Shame on Brad. He should have told you! I want to buy your house. Ever since Tommy died, I've been trying to convince Lois to sell it to me."

Marty shook her head firmly. "I'm sorry, Ms. Cho. This is the first I've heard anything about selling the house. I have no idea what my long-term plans for it will be." Plans were something that belonged to her life in Virginia. Would she ever make plans here?

"Never mind. We can talk about it another time. Come, let me show you a very special kaleidoscope. It's in the garden."

Marty started to refuse, but she was curious. A kaleidoscope in the garden?

They went down a wide staircase into a room that looked more like a library than a shop. Afternoon light streamed through floor-to-ceiling windows, catching prisms that spilled color across the white carpet. Tall shelves filled with books of various shapes and colors lined two walls. The smell of coffee and a variety of overstuffed chairs invited a visitor to stay and browse. At the back of the room a large, round, oak table with eight ladder-back chairs suggested a meeting place.

Krystal beckoned to her from a small door. "Come outside."

A narrow garden clung to the hillside. Wildflowers in all the colors of the rainbow danced around their legs: yellow poppies, blue lupine, white yarrow, red paintbrush. Names Marty didn't know she knew whispered in her mind, echoes of long ago.

At first glance the garden looked haphazard, as if Krystal had taken a handful of mixed seed and broadcast it across the side of the mountain. But as Marty looked more closely, she realized the riotous garden followed a subtle design. The colors might be random, intermixed like a child's bucket of crayons, but not so the planting. The flowers grew, not in rows, but in concentric circles that followed a path of white stones laid out like a labyrinth.

A large telescope stood in the center. Rather than being tilted to the sky, however, it pointed across the ravine below. A narrow road snaked down from the highway into a parking lot off to the right. Marty tried to get her bearings. She thought she was below the Jerome Grand Hotel looking across the ravine from a lower point on the mountain.

Krystal moved to the center of the garden and looked through the eyepiece of the telescope. "Do you know what the word kaleidoscope means?"

"Not exactly. A telescope is an instrument for viewing things far away, and a microscope is for viewing tiny things. I guess a kaleidoscope is an instrument for viewing things that are splintered in some way."

"Close. It comes from three Greek words that mean instrument for viewing beautiful objects. Some kaleidoscopes, like this one, show the viewer more than beauty. Come look."

More curious than she wanted to be, Marty looked into the eyepiece. The white building loomed before her just as if she were looking through a powerful telescope, but what she saw was more than an enlargement; it was a jumble of angles and colors where they didn't belong. The blue of the sky was in the center of a hexagon. Around the edges green and white alternated, bushes and walls. Light flashed in odd places, windows reflecting light perhaps.

"That's the Douglas Mansion," Krystal said. "James Douglas, owner of the Little Daisy mine, built it. 'Rawhide Jimmy' lived there with his wife for over twenty years, from 1916 to 1938. You're looking at it through the lens of one of the most powerful kaleidoscopes in the world."

"It's an interesting perspective."

"We're just beginning."

Marty watched the scene in front of her change. Now the green was in the middle, the white formed a hexagon around it, and the blue sky was on the outside. Then the whole image changed again."

"What do you see?" Krystal said.

"The colors are different. Rose, brown, and purple."

"That's 1918," murmured Krystal.

As Marty watched, a shadow flitted through the angles, first one way and then another.

"You're seeing a miner heading up to the mansion with the news of a fire deep in the earth, a fire that burned for twenty years. Some people say it's still burning."

Another shadow moved across the scene. "It's changed again."

"What colors do you see?"

"Yellow and shades of green."

"That's 1929. The population of Jerome is up to 15,000."

The images began changing more quickly, and Krystal's commentary picked up speed. It was as if she knew ahead of time what Marty was seeing. It was a trick, a slide show. It had to be. But as still another shadow moved across her vision, Marty began to feel dizzy, dizzy and irritated. Stepping back from the kaleidoscope, she said, "That's an odd game you play with a very expensive toy."

Krystal shook her head. "No game. This is an enchanted kaleidoscope. It shows the viewer slivers of the past, especially in the moonlight. Some might call the shadows you see 'ghosts.'"

A haunted kaleidoscope? The idea was ludicrous. Marty wanted to laugh, but as she met Krystal's gaze, the humor of it died. The woman actually believed what she was saying.

"Come back tonight. I'll show you more."

I don't believe in ghosts. Marty wanted to say the words out loud, say them more firmly than she had ever said them before. But this time the words wouldn't come.

∽

Paul's first call was to the hospital: "No, no motorcycle accidents. No, no teenaged boys admitted in the last twenty-four hours."

His second call was to Dan's cell phone. When the older boy answered, Paul said, "I want to thank you for letting Scott spend the night Monday. He and I needed a timeout. We had a pretty intense discussion that afternoon." Intense discussion, who was he kidding?

"No problem, Dr. Russell. I like Scott. He's pretty grown up for his age."

"He's not with you now, is he?"

"No. Haven't seen him since the other night."

"You wouldn't happen to know where he is?"

"Sorry. What's up?"

"All I know is he's angry at me, justifiably so, I might add. I'm afraid I left him on his own emotionally when Linda died. I don't suppose he told you anything that might help me understand?"

"No. We ate pizza and played some chess. He seemed okay."

He seemed okay. Paul had to admit the phrase just about summed up his parenting for the last year and a half. "Thanks, Dan. If you ever change your mind about accepting payment for the time you spend with Scott, just let me know."

"Won't happen. Scott's my man. If I hear from him, I'll tell him to call you."

Paul started calling Scott's friends. Jason's house. "No, Scott isn't here. Jason's at a softball game. I'm sure Scott isn't with him. We haven't seen much of Scott lately."

"Do you know the name of a kid who goes by B.T.?"

"The one with dark shaggy hair and tattoos on both arms?"

"That's the one."

"No, sorry. Jason won't have anything to do with him."

Curt's house. "Not here."

"B.T.'s name?"

"Sorry."

It was the same at Bobby's and at Tim's.

Finally, because he couldn't leave any possible source of information untapped, he dialed the number for Madison's house. Madison was the closest thing to a girlfriend Scott had ever had, and Paul liked her a lot. As he listened to the phone ring down the mountain in Cottonwood, he realized why he was reluctant to ask Madison about B.T. It was almost as if by linking Scott's name with the other boy's, he would reveal a shameful secret. But there had been nothing secret about the motorcycle.

"Hello."

"Hi, Janet. It's Paul Russell." He knew good manners dictated some sort of small talk like thanking Madison's mother for the work she and Madison's dad were doing with the youth group or asking about their vacation plans, but he was too tense, too focused on the task at hand. He let himself off the manners hook and blurted, "Is Scott there?"

"No." Janet paused. "You don't know where he is?"

Paul wasn't sure if the hint of criticism was in her voice or only in his imagination, but he struggled to keep from sounding defensive. "Scott and I had a misunderstanding, and I'm not sure where he went." Yesterday. Or where he spent the night.

"I imagine you've tried calling him."

He wanted to snap at the woman. Did she think he was a simpleton? Patience, he told himself. Patience, she's only trying to help. "No answer. Sometimes he forgets to recharge his phone." He was making excuses for Scott, but he wasn't ready to take Janet Logan up on her implied offer of help. He wasn't ready to tell her his fears.

"Maybe Madison's heard from him. Would you like to talk to her?"

"Please."

The moments of dead air increased his tension. He got to his feet and began to pace, making the boards of the dilapidated front porch creak.

Then Madison's young voice said, "Sorry, Dr. Russell. I don't know where Scott is. I think he's mad at me."

"That makes two of us."

"I'm sort of worried about him."

Paul felt his tension ease. Here was a kindred spirit, never mind she wasn't much more than a child. He was tempted to ask if she knew about the marijuana, but if she didn't know, he didn't want to be the one to let her in on a guilty secret. He said, "Scott left with a kid who goes by B.T. Do you know him?"

"Yeah. He's the reason Scott's mad at me."

Paul waited for her to tell him more.

"I told Scott I didn't think he should be friends with B.T."

He waited again.

"He's a druggie, Dr. Russell."

Not exactly a surprise, but Paul was suddenly short of breath. "Do you know his name?"

"Sorry."

"Where he lives or anything that would help me find him?"

"I know he's in the tenth grade. He bragged he was going to quit school, but he can't. He flunked again."

The high school. "Do you know who any of his teachers were?"

"No. You should call Mr. Ramos. He's the assistant principal, and B.T.'s always in trouble."

"That's a good idea. Thanks, Madison."

"Dr. Russell? When you find him, tell him . . ."

Her voice trailed off, and Paul knew she faced the same problem he did, what to say to Scott. "I'll ask him to call you."

Paul tried Scott one more time. This time he didn't leave a message. What was there to say besides begging him to come home?

Paul closed his cell phone and wondered what to do next. He was reluctant to call the assistant principal. He would need to give a reason for asking for B.T.'s name, and any explanation would include the fact his son was with the kid. He didn't want to brand Scott as a troublemaker before he even got to the high school.

Paul put his head in his hands and whispered the question he had asked so many times in the last year and a half. "What am I going to do, Linda?"

Sometimes he'd felt she was still with him, but now there was nothing. As his grandfather used to say, Linda was dead and gone. A desperate loneliness filled Paul, and he looked across the road. Lois. But Lois was as far out of reach as Linda was.

Maybe Marty was home. He could talk to her. About what? About how he'd messed up things with his son? About how much he missed his wife? That was when Paul knew what he had to do, at least what he had to do first.

The day pack was where he had dropped it on Scott's air mattress. He picked it up and took it to the bathroom. The sample bag was still there, still filled with marijuana. Paul emptied it into the toilet and flushed. As the gray-green leaves swirled in the water and finally disappeared, it seemed as if he was watching his life.

Chapter Seventeen

Marty stood on tiptoe, put her hands in the air, and stretched. She leaned down and put her palms on the floor. The book inventory was taking more time than it should. She kept getting sidetracked, scanning a table of contents in one book, skimming a chapter in another, reading still another. She wasn't getting as many hash marks on the inventory sheet as she could have, but she was accomplishing something much more important than counting books. She was getting to know Lois Baker.

Roughly two-thirds of the collection was nonfiction: cookbooks, gardening books, Bible study guides, books on antiques. *The Beginner's First Book of Antique Repair* was missing. With a pang, Marty realized it must still be in Lois's car, not the first thing she would have brought in the house with her.

According to the sheriff, Lois had arrived in Phoenix at 8:30 p.m. which would have put her back in Jerome between 10:00 and 10:30. With the three-hour time difference, she would have been up since 4:00 a.m. Arizona time. An eighteen-hour day, even without the emotions of finding a long-lost granddaughter, would have worn anyone out. But at eighty-two, Lois must have been utterly exhausted, running on adrenaline. Marty had found her grandmother's purse on the hall table. Evidently, she'd left everything else in the car.

Marty's memory of Granny Lois was clear. An old woman carefully dressed in yellow linen slacks and ivory silk shirt, with thin, white hair fluffed around her wrinkled face and faded green eyes alive with excitement. Marty's imagination picked up where her memory stopped.

Granny Lois got out of the car, came into the house, put her purse on the hall table. Then had she turned on the hall light or gone upstairs in the dark? Her eyes would have been accustomed to the dark, and she knew every inch of the house. Marty could almost see Rahab running to greet her human. Had the Siamese twined around Granny Lois's legs or had the old woman simply missed her footing?

"Oh, Granny," whispered Marty. "I should have agreed to go to dinner with you."

None of this would have happened. They would have started to get to know each other right then. Lois could have stayed a few extra days. Marty could have asked all the questions she needed answers to.

Should've, would've, could've. None of it mattered now. It was all in the past. Now was what was important. Marty sat cross-legged on the floor and started on Lois's collection of fiction. It was an eclectic mix of contemporary and older books. Twenty-three Agatha Christie, four Colleen Coble, six Maeve Binchy, two Susan Meisner, six Madeleine L'Engle.

Three books on the bottom shelf made her catch her breath: *Goodnight Moon, Bartholomew and the Oobleck,* and *The Wind in the Willows.* She remembered sitting in the soft bed on one side of Granny with Ruthie on the other side. A gentle voice murmured words she could sometimes recite as Granny Lois read.

Marty scrambled to her feet and followed the memory into the big bedroom at the other end of the hall. The same brass bed, but instead of the red and yellow Texas Star quilt, it was covered with a pink and blue double wedding ring quilt. Of course, Granny Lois wasn't there. Marty sat in a delicate lady's wingback chair upholstered in pink and blue floral chintz. A memory of a bentwood rocker stirred, but maybe that rocker was the one she'd remembered in the little girls' bedroom. Closing her eyes, she tried to release the memories. Not memories of any night, of one particular night, the night before that terrible day.

Nothing.

Marty moved to the bed. After only a moment's hesitation, she took the pillows and leaned them against the headboard. Then she sat where Granny Lois always sat. She closed her eyes again, willed herself back in time.

A different memory slipped into her mind.

She stood in the doorway watching Granny Lois write in a little yellow book. "What are you doing, Granny?"

"I'm writing in my diary. Come see."

She crawled up on the bed, leaned against Granny, and watched the pen make graceful, blue curves on the white paper. "What does it say?"

"Today it tells about our visit to the Phoenix zoo."

"Did you write about the black bird that wanted my lunch?"

"I didn't. I'll write it now. Tell me what to say, honey."

The diary! Sofia had said she might find answers in Lois's diary. Marty found it literally at her fingertips, on the bedside table with Lois's Bible. She opened a pink paisley volume and flipped through it. January 1 to June 7, page after page filled with small, carefully formed script. Lois had written at least once a week, occasionally every day. Marty began to read, skimming for references to the search for Martha Baker. Most of the entries contained a phrase like "prayed today to find Martha" or "prayed for more patience for my search." The first entry in April caught her attention.

> *April 4*
>
> *Martha is twenty-eight today. I still don't know where she is, what she's doing, whether she's healthy or sick, happy or sad, married or single. Some days I feel as though I'm close to finding her. Other days I feel as though I'll never see her again. Every morning, all through the day, at night when I'm ready to fall asleep I remember Philippians 4:13. "I can do all things in him who strengthens me." All things. I can find my precious granddaughter or never see her again. No matter what happens with my search, I will continue to pray for her, especially that she knows the grace and peace of our Lord Jesus.*

Marty couldn't name the feeling that gripped her as she read. Surprise, gratitude, longing, sorrow. None of those. All of those. But whatever the feeling, in that moment she remembered Granny Lois. More than the fleeting picture that had comforted her at the hotel, this time Marty remembered the presence made of love and laughter, hope and encouragement, persistence even in sorrow, the Granny Lois who could do all things through Christ.

Tears filled Marty's eyes, but instead of wanting to weep, she wanted to sing.

Granny Lois still loved her. Surely that meant she hadn't killed Ruthie! Surely it was safe to remember her sister's death. *Please, dear God, let me remember.*

Marty closed her eyes and waited. Counted to a hundred. Counted to a thousand.

Nothing.

Marty could no more make herself remember than she could bring her grandmother back from the dead. Bring Granny Lois back. The thought struck her that in a way the diary brought Granny Lois back to her. She opened it again. Later, when she had the answers she needed, she would read carefully to soak up the details of Lois's life.

Now she needed clues to what Lois wanted to explain to her granddaughter. As she skimmed, the important themes of her grandmother's life surfaced: friends, church, books, Bible study. And always the prayers. Mostly they were her own, sometimes a page or more, sometimes just a phrase. Occasionally Lois had copied a prayer from a book or transcribed one she heard at church.

Then in May Marty saw her own name. It practically leapt off the page.

> *May 11*
>
> *Progress! The detective Brad recommended has discovered the name of the family that adopted my little Martha. Greenlaw. They lived in the Washington, D.C. area back then. Unfortunately, there are a great many Greenlaws in Virginia.*

> *May 14*
>
> *I'm so impatient now. It's as if the encouragement of finding the name has robbed me of my ability to wait. I finally called Mr. Roberts. He's very kind, nothing like the detectives on television. He did his best to reassure me while*

trying to communicate the real problems we still face. He said it looks like the family moved from D.C. which will complicate his search. He reminded me Martha might be married and have a different last name. He even told me she might be dead! He's a gloomy Gus, but I refuse to be discouraged. God knows exactly where my little Martha is.

May 24

Something happened today I'm sure will lead me straight to Martha.

Carly called it coincidence. (I call it providence.) Carly's a sweet little thing and so interested in antiques! I think she sees me as a substitute grandmother, and I'm sure she would like me to see her as a substitute granddaughter. She doesn't understand as long as I have hope of finding Martha, no one can substitute for her. But none of that matters. The important thing about today's visit is Carly recognized the name Greenlaw! When I told her I hired a detective to find the Greenlaws, she got very excited. She said, "I know someone named Greenlaw. Marty Greenlaw." My heart almost stopped. Marty could so easily be a nickname for Martha! Carly told me she thinks this woman is about the right age. She's an antiques expert in Virginia who wrote a handbook Carly bought: "A Beginner's First Book of Antique Repair." Carly said it's a mixture of history, antique identification tips, and practical advice about repair. She says there's a photo on the back of the book. She promised to bring it tomorrow!

May 25

I'm so excited my hand is shaking so I can barely write. Carly gave me the book, so I'm looking at the photo as I write. Marty Greenlaw is as beautiful as I always knew my Martha would be. I could be looking at a picture of Ellie when my James married her. She has the same shining auburn hair her mother had and the same hazel eyes. I wonder if hers have the flecks of copper I remember in my Martha's eyes. Is this coincidence? Or is this God's Perfect Timing? I'm excited, but I'm also afraid. What if this young woman isn't my Martha? What if she is? I claim the promise of Philippians 4:13. I will go to Virginia next week.

Marty skimmed the last eight entries. Surely Lois had written out what she wanted to say to her granddaughter.

Nothing.

Marty closed the diary and put it back on the table. Philippians 4:13. She picked up the Bible, found the passage and read it slowly, trying to find the determination Granny Lois had found. "I can do all things through Christ, who strengthens me."

All things. Even find the explanation Granny Lois took to her grave? All things.

∼⌣∽

"Mingus High School. This is Monica. May I help you?" The voice was female. Not young enough to be a student worker.

"I need to speak to Mr. Ramos," Paul said. "Is he available?"

"He's in his office. May I tell him who's calling?"

Paul hesitated. Call himself doctor or not? He was calling as a parent, not as a professional. "Paul Russell. I'm the father of a new ninth grader." Or should he have said freshman? Linda had always been the liaison with Scott's school, one more ball he had dropped since her death.

A rich baritone voice came. "Mr. Russell? Anthony Ramos. Is your son Scott?"

"Yes, but how on earth do you know that?"

Mr. Ramos chuckled. "I've been assigning lockers this morning. I just finished the Rs. There was only one Russell."

"For a minute I was afraid Scott was in trouble before he ever got to your campus."

"Not at all. In fact, didn't I see Scott's name on the junior high debate club?"

Debate club? Paul was feeling guiltier by the second.

"How can I help you this afternoon, Mr. Russell?"

"I'm trying to find out the name of a boy who goes by the nickname of B.T."

A slight pause, but Paul realized Mr. Ramos might very well consider the information to be none of his business. Paul said, "Let me back up. I need to reach Scott, and I think he's with B.T." As soon as he said it, he thought how ridiculous it sounded. What kind of father didn't know the names of his son's friends? More to the point, what kind of father couldn't reach his son by cell phone? "I know it sounds like I'm a terrible parent . . ." Like the irresponsible father he'd become.

"I think you're a concerned parent, Mr. Russell."

"Please, call me Paul. Scott left home yesterday with an older boy who rides around on a motorcycle. Scott told me the kids call him 'B.T.' I'm sure that's a nickname. The boy has tattoos on every inch of visible skin." Now he sounded like a bigoted, irresponsible parent. He stopped talking before he got in any deeper.

"I know the boy you're describing. I assume Scott isn't answering his cell phone."

Paul debated how much of the story to tell. Why in heaven's name hadn't he thought through the conversation ahead of time? He slowed down, feeling his way. "Scott knew I didn't want him to go with B.T." Mention his concern about drugs or not?

Not. Paul wasn't ready to discuss marijuana with the assistant principal of the high school. For all he knew, Mr. Ramos was required to report any mention of drugs.

"The teenager you've described is named Lloyd Harper. I think 'B.T.' stands for 'Bat tattoo.' I haven't seen it, but some of the kids claim he's got a life-sized bat tattooed on his back. I'm not at liberty to discuss the details, but your instinct to keep Scott away from B.T. is good.

"Do you have B.T.'s address?"

"I'd like to help you, but I can't give out that information."

Did he detect a hint in the careful statement? "What information can you give me?"

"About all I can tell you is his name, Lloyd Harper, Jr."

And Lloyd Harper, Sr. must have a land line. "Thank you, Mr. Ramos."

"Tony. You're welcome. I'm the advisor for the debate team. I hope to see Scott at try-outs for Junior Varsity."

"I'll certainly encourage him. Thanks for your help, Tony."

Paul cut the connection and went to the internet. The first combination he tried in The White Pages was Lloyd Harper in Jerome. Nothing. Next, he tried Lloyd Harper in Cottonwood. Again, nothing. That left Clarkdale. This time he hit the jackpot. He punched in the first three numbers and then stopped. His call to the high school had been awkward because he had jumped in with both feet. This time he needed to plan what he was going to say.

Paul closed his phone and leaned back in his chair. For starters, even if Scott was at the Harper house, it was unlikely he would come to the phone. So planning a conversation was a waste of time. What he needed was an address. If he showed up at the house, he couldn't imagine Scott refusing to talk to him. His son might not be willing to come home, but at least he could reassure himself Scott was safe.

He couldn't find the address on the internet, but if he could find a paper phone book, he could look it up. He had a phone book at the house in Cottonwood, but here in Jerome he was relying on his cell. But he was willing to bet he could find a phone book at the Baker house. Marty wouldn't mind. He was down the stairs and almost to the front door before he thought about that conversation.

Did he want to ask to borrow the phone book, look up the information he needed, and rush away? That scenario felt awkward. If not that, was he willing to explain the situation with Scott to Marty? She probably already had a theory. They had tiptoed around the elephant that was Scott's absence from home. He'd felt good about spending time together without having to factor in his son. Now he wondered if she thought Scott had been her poltergeist.

The idea unsettled Paul. It couldn't be. Or could it? Vandalism wasn't like Scott, but what about B.T.? Scott had admitted being in the house when Marty first arrived. He had hotly denied locking Marty in the attic, but now Paul wondered if he could trust his son. If he hadn't seen the marijuana with his own eyes, he would have said Scott would never even touch the stuff, much less bring it home.

But standing here ruminating on the possibilities was a waste of time. He couldn't put the puzzle together without all the pieces. The next thing was to talk to Scott. As he headed out of the house, he knew he'd made up his mind about one thing. He wasn't ready to talk to Marty about his son. The fire station should have a phone book. He climbed in his Land Cruiser.

The fire station not only had a phone book, but also José was too distracted by the latest reports on the Prescott Fire to be curious. Paul scribbled the address on a pink phone message pad and hurried out with only a brief exchange of greetings, unusual with the talkative fire chief.

Paul drove the switchbacks faster than usual, but the highway was surprisingly empty and he could use the center of the road to make the sharp turns. At the bottom of the hill a heavy mixer from the cement plant lumbered across the road. As he waited at the stop sign, he caught himself drumming his fingers on the steering wheel. Paul shifted the Land Cruiser into neutral and quieted his hands.

Not so easy to quiet his mind.

The truck cleared the intersection. Paul shifted into low and drove more slowly into Clarkdale. It didn't take long to find the address, a small square house from the 1930s with a dusty yard surrounded by a rusted chain link fence. A shiny red Ford pickup sat in the driveway, but there was no sign of a motorcycle. The house didn't have a garage, but Paul told himself the bike might be around back.

A dog started to bark as soon as he turned off the engine. From the sound of it, a very large dog, no doubt kept to discourage visitors. But it was going to take more than a vicious dog to keep Paul from his son. Hoping to alert the owner of the pickup to his presence, he slammed his door. The dog barked even more furiously. Paul opened the torn screen door and knocked. Inside the house, the dog began to growl deep in its throat.

If Lloyd Harper, Sr. turned the dog loose on him, Paul knew he could run. It might be more years than he wanted to count since those college football fields, but he was still fast for his size. And if running didn't work, he remembered how to rope a calf and throw it to the ground. He didn't have a rope, but no dog could be as big as a calf. But a calf didn't have sharp teeth. He should have kept up with his jogging. The joy had gone out of it without Linda by his side.

Paul knocked again. No answer except renewed barking. Paul struck the door with the flat of his hand and shouted, "Mr. Harper?"

The barking ended in a sharp yip. Paul let go of the screen as the inside door banged open. A man about Paul's age with a hairy chest and a beer belly stood there zipping his jeans. A large Doberman snarled at his side. Not quite as big as a calf.

"What?"

Never show a dog you're afraid. Never ever show two dogs you're afraid. "Mr. Harper? Lloyd Harper?"

"This is my house, ain't it?" As if to emphasize the point, the dog started barking again. Harper hit the dog. "Shut up, Demon!" The dog quieted, but Harper kept shouting. "Who else would open the door of my house?"

Paul ignored the question as rhetorical. "Is your son here?"

"You from the school? Why can't you leave the kid alone?"

Paul looked down at his own faded t-shirt and frayed jeans. Hard to imagine Harper would think he was from the school. "My name is Paul Russell. I'm looking for my son, Scott."

"This ain't no home for runaway kids."

The man started to close the door, but Paul stopped it with his foot. "Scott left home yesterday with your son, and he hasn't been back. Are the boys here?"

All the bluster suddenly went out of Lloyd Harper. "Do I look like a babysitter? Man, I work nights. I can't keep tabs on Junior. By the time I was his age, I was working to take up the slack for my deadbeat father."

Paul recognized a rehearsed excuse. "Mr. Harper, my son is fourteen years old. If you can't, or won't, tell me where he is, I'm going to call the police and report these boys as missing."

"Whoa! You just slow down. If you want to keep your precious little boy out of juvie, you don't want to call the cops. I don't know where they are, but I pay for Junior's cell phone, and he knows when I call him, he'd better answer."

Finally, he was getting somewhere. "What if I come in and wait while you call your son?"

Demon snarled as if he understood.

"Wait outside." Harper slammed the door.

Paul went to the Land Cruiser to wait. Five minutes. Ten. Nothing. Losing patience, Paul strode back to the house, pounded on the door and shouted, "Open up, Harper, or I'm calling the police!"

Demon started barking, but after a moment, the door opened. Harper shouted, "Junior's at a buddy's house. Scottie's not with them. He took off last night."

Chapter Eighteen

Marty knew it was a measure of her desperation that she was considering calling her parents to ask why Lois Baker had given her granddaughter up for adoption. She didn't think they knew. And if they did, would they tell her?

A memory tumbled out of the attic, a memory from Before.

A box of clothes, not a suitcase, a box. Ruthie in the closet.

She called, "Come out, Ruthie."

"No!"

"I'll help you. We'll make a game out of it. You guess what's next."

"No!"

"Okay. I'll guess what's next."

"No!"

"We have to unpack, Ruthie."

"I don't want to live with Granny Lois," wailed Ruthie.

"Mommy and Daddy are in heaven. We can't live with them until after we die."

"Then I want to die!"

Ruthie had gotten what she wanted.

Feeling sick, Marty got up from Lois's bedroom chair and went back into the little study for her cell phone. She settled into the recliner and punched the speed dial for her parents' landline. The phone in the white stucco house just north of Orlando began to ring.

Once. Twice. Three times.

The clock on Lois's desk told her it was 5:30 or 8:30 in Florida. Her parents should be home on a Thursday evening. The phone rang a fourth time. On the next ring, it would go to voice mail.

"Marty, honey! I'm so glad to hear from you." Her mother sounded out of breath.

Normally Marty would have made small talk, asking what her mother was doing, how her father was, what they had heard from Ron. But nothing was normal. She blurted, "Why was I adopted?"

The silence on the other end was so complete Marty wondered if the call had dropped. Just as she was about to ask, her mother said, "What's happened?"

Marty wanted to say, "Nothing. Just answer my question." Of course, that wasn't true. So much had happened, too much to explain.

Suddenly Marty was sorry she had called. How to tell her mother why she needed to know without having to put words to an experience that hardly seemed real?

"Marty, honey, are you there?"

"Yes. It's a long story, and I don't want to go into it right now. I promise I'll explain in a day or two." Or a month or two, maybe a year or two. "Please, Mother, just answer my question. I really need to know."

"But you know the answer, sweetie. We adopted you because we wanted a daughter. We chose you."

"That's your side of the adoption. Why did my birth family give me up?"

This time the silence stretched out even longer, but Marty knew the call hadn't dropped. Finally, she said, "Please, Mom. I need to know."

Her mother sighed. "I can't tell you, honey."

"Can't or won't?"

"Can't. I don't know."

"But you have to know something! Surely you didn't take me without knowing something. Dad wouldn't have taken a chance without knowing what he was getting into."

"That's exactly what we did. In fact, that's why we took you. The social worker knew we wanted to adopt, but I was too old to be a good fit for an infant. She was watching for an older child for us. You were seven. Ron was nine. It seemed natural."

"But why me? Is the story you always told about having more than one choice and picking me a fabrication you told a child to make her feel special?"

"I need to let your father answer that question."

"Don't . . ." But it was too late. Marty heard the receiver being put down and then her mother calling, "Gene!" The old frustration welled up in her. Whenever anything was the least bit difficult, her mother deferred to her father, the psychologist. Marty knew what her father would say. He would give her the adult version of the adopted-child-as-chosen-child legend, complete with footnotes. She considered cutting the connection and turning off her phone. Later she could claim a dropped call and loss of signal.

"Hello, Marty." Her father's deep voice came in her ear, calm, carefully modulated, and at the moment her only source of information. "Tell me what's going on."

Tell me. The therapist's prompt, not a father's concern. Suppressing a sigh, Marty modulated her voice to match his. "I need information about the circumstances of my adoption."

"Give me a little context."

She very nearly cut the connection then. It was a measure of how badly she needed information that she didn't. "An elderly woman named Lois Baker tracked me down. She told me she was my grandmother. I need to know what you know about my birth family."

"What have you remembered?"

"Dad! Please tell me what you know."

He didn't answer at first. She had stepped out of the lines of the conversation, and she could imagine him trying to figure out how to get her back inside the lines. She waited.

"Tell me what you've remembered first."

"Why? Why can't you just give me the information I'm asking for?"

"Because I need to know more about your state of mind. Tell me what you've remembered. I promise I'll fill in the gaps as best as I can."

She couldn't see an alternative. As always, she gave in. But this time she would edit. She could tell him what she remembered without telling him about her grandmother's death. She didn't even have to tell him she was in Arizona.

"I have hazy memories of a Granny Lois. I've started to remember my birth parents and a sister. I need to know what happened to them and why Granny Lois put me up for adoption." As she said it, she realized her blunder. What to say if her father replied, "Why don't you ask her?"

"I imagine it was because of your state of mind."

"What do you mean?"

"You were seven. Most children remember quite a bit starting at the age of four or five."

Marty pushed away her annoyance. Experience had taught her getting angry at her father only resulted in a cross-examination about the source of her antagonism. She had to follow his example and remove herself emotionally from the conversation. Getting to her feet, she went to the French doors and out onto the upper porch. Paul's Land Cruiser was gone. She wondered if he had gone to get Scott.

"Please, Dad. Tell me what happened. I need to know."

"You were in a state of repression. The trauma of losing your family was too much to process, so you simply separated yourself from it all. You did fine in the present. You were cheerful and eager to please, but you functioned as though you had no past at all. As a lay person, your grandmother couldn't have known how to cope. The social worker knew of my training, and she thought your mother and I might be able to provide you the kind of safe environment you needed."

"You mean I blocked it all out."

"That explanation is over simplistic, but essentially correct."

"I think the block is beginning to lift or crack or dissolve or whatever blocks do. I remember my parents died in a car wreck. I've tried, but I can't remember what happened to my sister. Please, Dad. Tell me."

He was silent again. She could almost see his frown. She stopped breathing. He had to tell her!

"I'm sorry, Marty. I can't tell you that."

"Can't or won't?"

"Really, Marty. Why would I keep information like that from you? The social worker didn't tell us. She may not have known. We, your mother and I, assumed you were the only survivor of the car accident. I know absolutely nothing about a sister. I never did."

"Did you know I was living with my grandmother before you adopted me?"

"Yes. We never met her, but we were aware she stepped in when your parents died."

"Why did she give me up for adoption?"

"We were never told directly, but I believe there was a handicapped son, Down syndrome, if I remember correctly."

184

"Tommy. I remember him. I remember the car wreck. Why can't I remember about Ruthie?"

She heard the desperation in her voice, so she wasn't surprised when her father said, "Calm down, Marty. You're suppressing the memory of your sister's death. Your conscious mind can't force your subconscious to do its bidding."

"What could be more traumatic than the death of my parents?"

He didn't answer right away. When he finally spoke, his tone was almost gentle. "In situations like this, it's best not to speculate."

∿

To the accompaniment of the dog's barking, Paul got in the Land Cruiser and put the keys in the ignition. But before he started the engine, he checked his cell phone for a message from Scott. He knew he was wasting time. Scott had ditched B.T. without calling home, which meant his withdrawal was more than a moment of rebellion.

Still, Paul checked. He had a text message from Scott. Heart picking up speed, he opened it.

Got your messages. I'm fine. Not ready to talk.

No indication of where he was or when he would come home. No "Love, Scott."

But the message was something, an acknowledgment of the connection between them. Evidence enough of his son's safety to keep him from calling 911 and reporting the disappearance of a minor. Paul backed out and headed home. At the four-way stop where he'd waited for the cement mixer, he considered turning down the hill toward Cottonwood. To do what? To drive the streets of the little town looking for his son the way he might look for a dog that had wandered off?

He vetoed the impulse and headed back up the mountain toward Jerome. The afternoon was gone, and the switchbacks were a study in dusk and daylight, almost as confusing as his internal state. One moment he wanted to wash his hands of Scott and invite Marty to dinner. The next he wanted to explain everything to her and ask for input. But when he reached the turn that would take him home and to Lois's house, he drove on by. With no clear destination in mind, he simply kept going, past the Catholic church, beneath the Jerome Grand Hotel, and out of town. Into the smoke.

At the first overlook, he pulled off the road and got out. Cottonwood lay a couple of thousand feet directly below where he stood, but the lights were hardly more than pinpricks in the smoke-laden dusk that had settled in the valley. All he could think was his son was somewhere down there.

Doing what? Paul knew he hadn't picked up on the warning signs with Scott soon enough. Then when he finally got his head out of the sand, he'd let his temper get the better of him and practically invited Scott to run away. He still missed Linda enough to try to talk to her occasionally, yet he was thinking about a woman ten years younger who didn't deserve to be saddled with a troubled teenager. No question about it. He'd made a total mess of things.

"The devil only has one arrow in his quiver. Discouragement." Paul could almost hear his grandmother's voice. Over the years, he'd experienced the truth of her words again and again. But devil's arrow or not, tonight he was discouraged.

That was when Sofia Lopez came into his mind. More than anyone he knew, she possessed the gift of encouragement. And she could often discern the source of discouragement. In her early sixties, Sofia had been the third person in the prayer group with Linda and Lois. "We're three generations," Linda used to say, "grandmother, mother, and daughter in Christ." Now only Sofia, the middle generation, was left. She had to be grieving Lois as much, if not more, than he was. Still, as surely as Paul knew he needed to talk to Sofia, he knew she would welcome him.

Paul got back in the Land Cruiser and turned around. Dusk had faded into night, cloaking Cleopatra Hill in black velvet. He drove in darkness until he reached Main Street. At the corner, bright light and country-western music spilled out of the Spirit Room Bar onto the street.

Paul looped through town, turning up Hull Avenue, every bit as dark as the highway had been higher up on the mountain. Long ago the House of Joy and the smaller establishments of the red-light district would have been as busy as the Spirit Room was tonight. Now craft shops, art galleries, and jewelry stores were closed and dark.

He pulled into the dirt parking lot and got out. As he put the keys in his pocket, he realized he should have cleaned up. Crossing the street, he told himself he should have called. As he climbed the steps to the door, he almost turned around and went home. Just in time, he recognized the impulse for what it was, an excuse to avoid admitting to the mess he'd made of things. Paul pushed the doorbell.

A coyote howled in the distance, laughter floated down the hill, and then light came on in the gallery. The door opened, and Sofia stood there. She hardly came up to his shoulder, yet she was the strongest person he knew. "Paul! What a nice surprise."

"I'm sorry to show up like this." How many times had he made the ritual apology the first few months after Linda's death? He wasn't sorry. He longed to unburden himself to Sofia.

From long experience, he knew she understood, but she murmured the ritual response. "Don't be silly. Come in."

As he stepped from the dark street into the lighted entry-way, her smile turned to a look of concern. "What's happened?"

He had no idea where to begin. With Scott, with Marty, with his own stupidity? "I'm not sure."

She put a hand on his arm and looked up, studying his face. "Lois's death is a terrible loss to both of us, but I think it's more than that."

He hadn't been thinking of Lois's death, but now he realized it was key to his current problems, not a cause of them, a catalyst to their surfacing. "It's Scott," he said, choosing the problem that was easiest to articulate.

"I'll make coffee, and you can tell me."

Paul followed Sofia through her gallery into her studio and past a worktable covered with a riot of colorful silks. As she led the way into her miniscule kitchen, he said, "What are you creating these days?" The question was a way to get the focus off himself, but it was more than that. Sometimes he envied artists. If he could paint or sculpt, he might not have to knock down walls with a sledge hammer.

"Something new. I'm not quite sure what it's going to be yet. Maybe a silk mosaic." Sofia took coffee from a cupboard and filled a glass pot with water.

"An abstract design?"

"Maybe. I'm still auditioning colors to see what they want to do." She dumped the water into the coffee maker and turned it on. "You didn't come to talk art, Pablo. Sit down and tell me what's troubling you."

As he had so many times before, Paul moved the little table out from the wall and squeezed himself into one of the two chairs. "I wish I knew."

"So tell me what you do know."

"I know I'm a fool."

Sofia made a disapproving sound. "We're commanded not to call anyone a fool. You don't think that applies to self-talk?"

"In this case, it happens to be true. I practically invited Scott to run away."

"Tell me what happened."

He almost said, "Linda died, and I didn't deal with it well." But, with the possible exception of Scott, Sofia knew that better than anyone else. Besides, it was useless to start that far back. "The last few days have been a nightmare, the upshot of which is I evidently don't know my son at all."

Sofia took pottery mugs out of a cupboard. "Do parents ever know teenagers?"

"Probably not, but I've been so caught up in my own grief I was completely blind to what was happening to Scott. I thought I was paying attention. I tried to get him the help he needed, but when nothing worked, I gave up. I told myself I was giving him space, but I was giving myself space."

"Not so far back." She poured coffee. "Tell me about today."

"Today was a culmination. I need to start on Monday."

Sofia nodded and handed Paul a mug.

Paul cupped the steaming mug in both hands. "I thought spending the summer working on the house in Jerome would bring Scott and me closer. Monday I found out I was wrong." Sofia listened intently without interrupting while Paul told her about Scott's rebellion, about his reaction to Lois's death, about the accusations Brad and Marty had made, about the confrontation over the motorcycle, about his fruitless search for his son.

Sofia patted his hand and murmured, "Tell me the rest now, amigo."

Paul drank his coffee. It had cooled, but it was strong and black. "Marijuana. I found it in his backpack."

"You think he's on drugs?"

Paul considered. He was afraid for Scott, but did he think his son was on drugs? "No. Maybe I'm in denial, but Sofia, I swear I would have noticed if he ever came home high."

Sofia reached for the coffee pot, refilled his mug. "I agree. I don't think Scott is taking drugs."

"So, you think I don't have anything to worry about, beyond the fact that I've had my head in the sand for almost two years."

"I think Scott is struggling with something quite different than drugs. The heart of your story is his cry that he doesn't believe in fairy tales."

"Scott has lost his faith."

"You know faith is a process, Pablo. A continual dance of doubt and faith. Scott is in a period of doubt."

"You think he's old enough for that?"

"Of course. Scott has faith, but it must mature to trust God in the face of death."

"I wasn't strong enough to help him when Linda died. I didn't even talk to him about death until Lois died. By then it was too late."

Sofia made a soft clucking sound. "Don't be so hard on yourself. You didn't give up. I saw the two of you in church Sunday after Sunday."

"Habit. Not some mature faith."

"Sometimes it's the same thing."

"But now? Sofia, I don't know how to reach Scott." Or Marty. It was frustrating how she was never far from his thoughts, even when he should only be focused on his son. "He blames me for Linda's death."

"Because you blame yourself."

"No. It was an accident, physics. Wheels rolling on a slick surface."

Sofia shook her head gently. "If Scott blames you, it's because he's following your lead. What haven't you forgiven yourself for?"

Paul ran his hands through his hair, surprised by how long it was. "Snow was forecast for that night, but not until later. Linda did her best to convince me to cancel my class. She reminded me how unpredictable weather is on the mountain. When I wouldn't listen to her, she insisted on riding up to Flagstaff with me. God forgive me, I put my work ahead of my wife."

"God has already forgiven you."

"I know, but I can't forgive myself."

Sofia reached for his hand, took it in her two smaller ones, brown and gnarled like roots. "That's blasphemy."

"What?"

"You're putting yourself above God. God has forgiven you, but evidently you have higher standards than God does."

The room suddenly came into focus. Paul saw how much coffee was left in the carafe, where the light reflected off the window, the pale shadows cast by their coffee mugs. He saw every strand of silver in Sofia's dark hair so clearly he knew he could count them. Lifting Sofia's hands to his mouth, he kissed them.

She smiled, and he saw the young woman she had been. "I have a verse for you, amigo." Sofia drew her hands from his and reached for the Bible that always sat on her kitchen table. She opened it to the New Testament. "The Apostle Paul for Paul Russell." She turned a few pages, found the verse with her finger. "His letter to the church at Philippi." But instead of reading, she looked into Paul's eyes and murmured, "This one thing I do: forgetting what lies behind and straining forward to what lies ahead, I press on toward the goal." She paused. "You have to forget Linda's death."

"I'll never forget, Sofia. Not as long as I live."

"You won't erase it from your mind. That's not the kind of forgetting the Apostle Paul is talking about. I'm sure he carried the images of Stephen's death with him to the grave. When he says forget, he means to let go of the emotions, allow them to fade into memory."

"I've done that."

She shook her head. "Scott's accusation wouldn't have hurt if you had."

"I don't know what you mean."

"Think about it this way. I know you have a younger brother. You hit him?"

Paul shrugged. "More than once."

"Does it hurt when I accuse you?"

"Of course not. That was a long time ago. Pete and I are good friends now."

She didn't reply.

Gradually he understood, and the understanding took his breath away. "If I forget like that, I lose my last connection with Linda."

"You put her behind and do your best to reach what's ahead."

Marty, but he didn't have anything to offer her. Paul pushed Marty into the back of his mind and focused on his son. "How does this help me with Scott?"

"If you put the accident behind, you give him permission to do the same thing."

"I don't understand."

"Your son is watching you. He can't go forward until you show him how."

Chapter Nineteen

"Glass. Diameter 3 inches. Patterned millefiori on a lace filigree ground." Marty wrote the description in the column for paperweights. She didn't know much about antique paperweights, only that the valuable ones came from France from a brief period in the mid-1800s. She slid the ballpoint pen behind her ear and carefully lifted the next one out of the black velvet display case. Smooth in her hand, almost silky. As small as it was, smaller even than the millefiori, its cool weight was oddly comforting. In the center a yellow chamomile flower with two red buds was so lifelike she thought it must be real. Of course, it wasn't. She held it up to the light and tried to remember what she had learned of the Victorian language of flowers. Chamomile: something to do with adversity. Encouragement in adversity, something like that. Almost a message from Lois.

If only she could get the conversation with her father out of her mind, she could enjoy this part of the inventory. Where the ever-changing kaleidoscopes in Krystal's shop had left her uneasy, these glass paperweights fascinated her. But her father's words kept going around in her head: "Best not to speculate." She couldn't help speculating. What had she done, or not done, that might have led to her sister's death?

A faint knock interrupted the endless circle of her thoughts. Perhaps Rahab pushing something off the kitchen counter, but the Siamese hadn't reappeared since the chaos of the so-called poltergeist. Another knock, louder this time. Maybe the front door knocker. A third knock settled it. Someone was definitely at the front door.

"Marty?" A woman's voice. Whoever it was had opened the door and stuck in her head. Didn't anyone in this town honor a closed door at the Baker house?

"Marty, I know you're here!"

Marty put the paperweight back in the case and went downstairs, flipping on lights as she went. Sometime between when she had finished her conversation with her father and now, it had gotten dark. Krystal Cho stood in the entryway. She was dressed in an ankle-length black silk sheath embroidered with silver moons. A small beaded bag hung from her left shoulder, and a hard-sided bag slightly larger than a brief case sat on the floor at her feet.

"You didn't come back," Krystal said.

"Come back?"

"I asked you to come back tonight."

"I don't believe in ghosts or in your haunted kaleidoscope."

"Not haunted, enchanted."

"Haunted, enchanted. Use any word you like, Krystal. I don't believe in the occult, and I'm not interested in a confrontation with you over ghosts or kaleidoscopes."

Krystal smiled. "I don't want a confrontation any more than you do. So how about a cup of tea and a chat? Surely you believe in those things." Holding out her hands, she closed the distance between them. "Lois and I were friends. I want us to be friends too."

Marty hesitated. She wanted to refuse, but she suspected that being ungracious would only intensify Krystal's efforts to break down her resistance. She forced a smile and took the outstretched hands. As long as the conversation didn't turn to ghosts, Krystal might distract her from her own morbid train of thoughts. "A cup of tea does sound good."

In the kitchen, Krystal in her black silk looked so wildly out of place Marty felt herself relax. Krystal's power, if in fact she had any, depended on her setting. At the solid oak table without her mirrors and crystals, she seemed no more substantial than an exotic butterfly.

"Have you found the answers you came for?"

The question caught Marty off-guard. But Krystal was only articulating the obvious. She shrugged.

"You came to fill in the gaps from your lost years. Now Lois is out of reach, and you'll never know. A shame."

Why else would she have come halfway across the country? Maybe because she loved her grandmother. The thought came out of nowhere, making Marty ashamed of herself. Her trip had been entirely selfish, and she was still in selfish mode, caring only that Lois had died without leaving her the answers she needed. "You make me sound so calculating."

The other woman shook her head, releasing a wisp of ebony hair from the tight twist. "I don't mean it that way. All I want is to let you know I understand."

The kettle began to whistle, saving Marty from having to reply. She busied herself with cups and saucers, loose tea, and a silver strainer.

When they had cups in front of them and the tea was steeping in a china pot painted with delicate blue flowers, Krystal spoke again. "I can help you. That's why I wanted you to return tonight. Since you didn't come to me, I came to you."

Marty started to object, but Krystal went on in a casual tone, as if what she said was the most natural thing in the world. "I can help you contact Lois. We can ask her some of the questions you need answers to. I'm sure she's still here, watching you. She needed to see you as much as you needed to see her, you know."

"Lois is dead, Krystal. She's gone to be with the Lord."

"Not yet. I can feel her in the house."

"I don't believe---"

"Stop! I'm not asking you to believe. All I'm asking you to do is watch and listen. If Lois is gone, as you believe, nothing will happen. I'll be talking to myself in an empty room. But if Lois is still here, I can ask her the questions you need answered."

"I don't want answers this way."

Krystal seemed not to hear. "Lois and I didn't agree on everything, but we were friends. She had the rare gift of being able to look beyond agreements and disagreements to the person. She told me you were her last grandchild. The way she said it, made me wonder. There was another grandchild, I think. A little girl who died."

Marty's heart began to beat faster. "She told you what happened."

"No. Lois would never talk about it. But now that she's beyond her own pain and sees your need, she'll tell you."

Marty hesitated. Dabbling in the supernatural was wrong, but what Krystal was proposing wasn't witchcraft. And she wanted, needed, to know so badly.

Krystal didn't wait for Marty to decide. The tea forgotten, she stood and headed for the hall. "Upstairs, I think." She didn't tell Marty to come, but the silent command hung in the air.

Marty sat where she was. She told herself sternly to stay where she was, to refuse to go upstairs. But she had to know. As Krystal said, it wouldn't hurt anything. With trembling hands, Marty poured herself a cup of tea. She meant to sip, but she gulped. The hot tea was strong to the point of being bitter. She choked.

It was enough. Determined to tell the woman to leave, Marty went in search of Krystal.

She was in Lois's bedroom. The hard-sided case sat open on the bed, and Marty saw a kaleidoscope, different from any she'd seen in the shop. Krystal was busy clearing the bedside table, placing the Bible and the diary on the floor.

Marty picked up the Bible and the diary. "I want you to leave. Now."

"Are you so afraid of the truth?"

"That's not the point."

Krystal shrugged, an elegant movement in the silk kimono. "And the point is?"

"This is silly. I don't want to participate."

"Just watch then." Krystal shoved the bedside table to the center of the room. "You have nothing to lose. If I'm right, and Lois answers your questions, you find out the truth. If you're right, and there's nothing to my methods, you're no worse off than you are right now." Taking a three-legged brass stand out of the case, she set it up on the little table.

Marty knew she should repeat her demand that Krystal leave, but as she watched the preparations, her resolve weakened. Nothing was going to happen. It wouldn't hurt to watch for a few minutes. She sat on the bed and put the Bible and diary beside her.

Krystal placed a brass tube like a small telescope on the stand and pointed it toward the heavy brocade curtains that covered the French doors that looked out on the backyard. At the end of the tube she placed a heavy piece of glass, octagonal with each section a different color.

The kaleidoscope where she wanted it, Krystal moved the bench from Lois's vanity to behind the impromptu viewing stand. Then she turned off the lights and, going to the French doors, opened the draperies. Metal rings rattled as they slid over a metal drapery rod. Night entered the room.

Still reluctant to take part in the charade, Marty stood uncertainly by the kaleidoscope.

"Come here, Marty. You know you want answers."

The pull of her need to know was stronger than her resistance. Marty moved from the bed to the bench.

"Now," Krystal said, leaning so close Marty caught the scent of spices she couldn't identify. "Look into the eyepiece. Rotate the glass slowly and wait."

"Wait for what?"

"You'll know. I'm going to strike up a conversation with Lois. What questions do you want me to ask her?"

Marty didn't intend to play the game. The question seemed to speak itself. "Did I kill Ruthie?"

For once Krystal was silent, and Marty wondered what she was thinking. After a moment, the other woman let out a long breath and said, "Look into the kaleidoscope. Turn the wheel. Concentrate on the colors, particularly the blue."

Just silliness, but Marty obeyed.

Krystal murmured, "Lois Baker. We know you're still here. We know you want to help your granddaughter find peace from this terrible question that haunts her. Show yourself. Reassure Martha."

Just silliness, but through the eyepiece, the glass doors seemed to shimmer. Red stained the floor like blood. Yellow like a linen suit. The green of grass that grew on a grave. Blue like a summer sky that went on forever. The colors slid across the hardwood floor and danced on the door. Krystal's voice became a soft chant. "Lois Baker, a terrible question, peace." Over and over. "Reassure Martha."

Just silliness. Marty waited, but nothing happened. Just when she was about to declare the one-sided conversation at an end, Krystal said, "Lois isn't here."

"Of course not. This is just silliness."

198

"A child." Krystal cocked her head as if she were listening. "Not in this room." She moved toward the hall. "Come with me, Marty."

There was a command in Krystal's voice Marty couldn't resist, or maybe she didn't want to resist. In any case, Marty followed the other woman down the hall to the little study. Krystal crossed the room and stood beside the French doors. "Out here, I think."

No. Marty stopped in the doorway. "No."

"Yes." Krystal moved to take her arm. "You can ask her what happened."

Not Granny Lois. Marty knew, but she asked anyway. "Who?"

"You know who." Krystal flung the French doors open and went out onto the upper porch.

Marty meant to turn around and leave the room. Instead she stepped through the French doors. Into a night restless with a smoke-tainted breeze. Misty half-light from a lopsided moon, interspersed with total darkness when clouds smothered the light. Reproach washed over her, or maybe it welled up inside. Either way, wherever she turned reproach for what she had done surrounded her.

"She's waiting," Krystal said.

Marty knew, but she refused to believe it. "Who?"

"Your little dead sister."

"I don't believe in ghosts! I won't believe in ghosts!" Marty ran back into the bedroom, slammed the French doors shut. Heart pounding, she leaned against them and tried to catch her breath. For one blessed moment, everything was quiet.

Then Krystal's voice came. "Let me in, Marty. She's gone now. You're safe."

❧

Paul pulled into what was left of the driveway when the hovel had been a Jerome second story home, what could one day be a driveway again if he stayed to finish the reconstruction. He turned off the engine, but instead of getting out, he sat in the dark, gathering his thoughts. His visit with Sofia had left him with too much to think about. Though she hadn't told him what to do about Scott or Marty or his grief, she had prayed the questions.

The drive home had been a bridge from the past into the present, covering a distance so great he wished it had taken fifteen days rather than fifteen minutes. He didn't get out immediately. Just sat, letting his mind come out of the past, return from the future, settle into the present. He was sitting in the battered, blue Land Cruiser on a June night two years after Linda's death, powerless to do anything for Scott until his son came to him, across the road from a woman he was drawn to by feelings he thought he had buried with his wife.

It was time to forget the past, reach for whatever God had in mind for his future. Paul didn't know if Marty would be part of his future, but she was part of his present. He got out of the Land Cruiser and headed for the Baker house. Light from the entryway spilled from the leaded glass panels on either side of the front door, painting two yellow bands on the porch. Otherwise the house was dark.

Marty's car sat in the driveway, so she was probably at home unless she was out with Lockridge. He told himself not to be a kid. He wasn't in competition with Brad. As he mounted the steps, he heard the squeak of the porch swing.

"Hello, Paul."

Her voice was hardly more than a whisper, so he modulated the volume of his own voice. "May I join you?"

She didn't reply, but the swing creaked as she moved over to make room for him.

"What are you doing sitting here in the dark?"

"Probably the same thing you were doing sitting in your Land Cruiser."

"Yeah. Sometimes things are clearer in my head in the dark. What's on your mind, Marty?"

"I'm thinking about going home."

"When?"

"Tomorrow. Right after the funeral."

"You're going to turn over the inventory to Carly?"

"I suppose."

Something had happened. He wondered what. Stretching out his legs, he put his arm along the back of the swing, careful not to touch her. He wanted her to know he had all the time she needed.

After a moment, she sighed. "I shouldn't have come here."

"Lois would still have fallen. Someone else would have found her."

"I know. The only way Lois would still be alive is if I had spent time with her when she found me. I'm looking at it from a very selfish perspective, the way I've looked at this whole thing. What I mean when I say I shouldn't have come is I should have kept with my initial reaction to leave my childhood locked away in the attic of my mind."

Something about Marty's past had come to light, something more than her adoption. He wanted to say, "Start from the beginning," but he could almost hear Linda saying, "I'm not thinking about the beginning, I need to tell you about now!" He said, "Something happened today. Want to tell me about it?"

"You'll think I'm silly, gullible."

"Try me."

"You know Krystal Cho."

"Sure. She owns a little glass shop and claims to be an expert on Jerome's ghosts."

"She came to the house this evening."

Paul kept the surprise out of his voice. "What did she want?"

It took Marty a moment to answer. "She wanted to contact my grandmother."

"As in a séance?"

"Not exactly. She has these special kaleidoscopes. She claims they're enchanted."

Paul moved his foot to put the swing in motion. "So, she brought an enchanted kaleidoscope here to try to contact Lois. Did you let her in?"

"She just walked in. Does everyone in Jerome walk into other people's houses, or is it just this house?"

"A little of both. Lois made everyone feel this house was home."

Marty didn't reply.

Paul waited.

Finally, she sighed. "Krystal was trying to help me."

Paul wasn't sure how to respond. They were on tricky ground. Contacting the dead wasn't exactly a neutral topic. After a moment, he said, "Why did she think contacting Lois would help you?"

"That first day I told you I came to Jerome because Lois's visit triggered an old nightmare."

"Yes. You hoped your grandmother would explain it to you."

"I don't believe Krystal is psychic, but she's intuitive. She guessed I had unfinished business from my childhood. She offered to contact Lois and ask her the questions I need answers to."

"What questions?"

"Only one question." She took a shaky breath. "Did I kill my little sister?"

Paul felt as though a sinkhole had opened at his feet. For several moments, the only sound was the squeak of the chain as the swing moved gently. The moments lengthened into minutes. When it was clear Marty wasn't going to say more without prompting, Paul said, "Tell me about your dream."

"The details vary, but the basics are always the same. Ruthie, my little sister, dances and laughs. Then she runs away from me. She screams and disappears."

Paul considered. "All right. Let's pretend I'm Joseph. I'll interpret your dream."

"If you're Joseph, does that make me Potiphar? Or maybe I'm the baker who dies."

Paul moved his arm to her shoulders and pulled her close. "Neither one. You stay Marty Greenlaw."

"Or Martha Baker."

"Both. Your dream seems straight forward enough. You remember your little sister as happy, so she's laughing and dancing. When she died, she left you behind, so she runs away and disappears."

Marty shook her head. "It's more than that. As soon as I recognized Lois, I knew I had done something terrible, something so dreadful she sent me away. What if the awful thing was killing my little sister?"

"You're making a lot of assumptions based on the fact your grandmother put you up for adoption. I believe there were other circumstances."

"I haven't told you the rest of it. The nightmares are getting more detailed, and as they do, memories are starting to come back. In the first nightmare Ruthie just ran away from me. The next time she was chasing a clear plastic ball filled with butterflies. I remembered that ball when I was going through the toy box. I wondered why it wasn't there. Now I know. It was because Ruthie was playing with that ball when I . . . when I pushed her."

"Where did you push her?"

"It must have been off the porch over our heads."

"What makes you think that?"

"She screams and disappears! Almost as if the earth swallows her up."

Paul decided to try an end-around. "You still haven't told me what happened with Krystal and her kaleidoscope. Does she claim to have contacted Lois?"

"Not Lois. Ruthie. My little sister."

Paul felt his temper flare. He was about to tell Marty exactly what he thought of Krystal when she put her feet flat on the porch.

The swing lurched sideways and stopped. "She was there, Paul. On the porch. Ruthie is the reason I have to leave Jerome. She's in this house, and she hates me."

Chapter Twenty

Paul shifted his tool box to his left hand and reached for the screen door. Then he hesitated. He was about to walk into Lois's house without knocking. A habit. But the old Victorian with the lavender trim didn't belong to Lois anymore. It was Marty's house now. But for how long? If she stayed a few more days he might be able to help her find the copper box she was looking for. Or was it like Pandora's box? Better not to open. A gap in the memory of a casual acquaintance shouldn't bother him. But the feelings that fueled his concern for Marty lay at the edge of his known world. Beyond lay dragons. Or the future.

Paul reined in his thoughts and focused on now. This day. This moment. The reason he was on the front porch. The front door stood open, but he stuck his head in and called out. "Marty? It's Paul!"

No answer. He hesitated, called a second time. When he still didn't get an answer, he went in. Downstairs was quiet. As he walked soundlessly on the thick Aubusson, he wondered where Rahab was. Had the cat found a new home or had she decided she was through with humans for a while and was enjoying the freedom of the fending for herself?

At the bottom of the stairs, he called again. "Marty? It's Paul. Are you here?"

"Upstairs!"

He thought she sounded glad, but he waited until she came to the top of the stairs. She looked tired. More than tired, maybe a little desperate. But she was here. This one moment.

He smiled, willing her to return the smile. She did, though a little tentatively. He hoped she wasn't embarrassed by her revelations of the night before.

He hadn't ridiculed or scolded. Had done his best to accept her belief she had encountered her long-dead sister without agreeing it was possible. Had assured her she wasn't alone with whatever was happening in this house. Had offered his room for a second night. When she refused, had made sure she put his number into her cell phone. He'd made tea and told her Lois stories, happy stories, the only kind he knew about Lois. By the time he left, she had seemed genuinely calm, and she hadn't called during the night.

Still, it had all been pretty intense. He decided not to refer to it. If she wanted to tell him what she was thinking about the ghost of her sister, she would. He said, "I'm as bad as everyone else in this town. I just walked in."

"Sofia's already here. She's helping me go through Lois's personal things."

That was good. It didn't sound like she was packing to go back to Virginia, and Paul couldn't think of anyone he'd rather entrust Marty to than Sofia. He started up the stairs, more light-hearted than the situation warranted.

"With the memorial service this afternoon, I'd decided not to work this morning. But when Sofia came, she suggested we sort through Lois's clothes while we talked. What's the tool box for?"

She was talking too fast, filling the silence between them. He wanted to put down the tool box, pull her into his arms, and hold her until she relaxed. He wondered what she would do if he did just that. The thought took him to the edge of his known world. "I want to check the railing on the balcony over the front porch. See if it looks like it's ever been repaired or replaced."

She looked surprised, so surprised he was afraid he'd communicated his skepticism the night before. He didn't doubt Ruthie had died in a way that shocked her sister. He didn't doubt the little girl could have fallen from the balcony. It was the ghost Krystal claimed to have contacted that he rejected. For the second time, he decided not to refer to their conversation the night before. "You don't mind, do you?"

She shook her head. "Thank you."

She was thanking him for more than the toolbox. Shifting into older brother mode, he winked and tousled her hair. Ever so slightly. When what he wanted was to run his fingers through those long, coppery curls. "I'll let you know what I find. Tell Sofia I'll come say hello in a few minutes."

The little study was bright with sunlight. Now that he knew it had been a bedroom for Lois's two granddaughters, he looked at it through different eyes, wondered why Lois had chosen it for her private retreat. Whatever the reason, that choice argued against it being a room where one little girl had pushed another to her death.

Of course, there was another upstairs porch in the house, off Lois's bedroom. But this porch was the one where Krystal claimed to have encountered the little girl's ghost. He opened the French doors and stepped outside. The wind had dropped this morning so there was less smoke in the air up here on Cleopatra Hill. Below, the Verde Valley looked like Phoenix during a summer inversion, choked with smog. Was Scott down there? *Father . . .*

For the second time, Paul brought his mind back to the present, to the reason he was here. He put the toolbox in the middle of the small porch in easy reach. Then he got down on hands and knees and began to examine the railing inch by inch, spindles as well. It was close, tedious work. He wouldn't allow himself to obsess over Scott. He didn't have any new thoughts to add to that subject.

So, he thought about Marty. He knew she was genuinely frightened. As he ran through everything that had happened to her since coming to Jerome three days ago, he didn't blame her. Any sane person would be ready to go home.

Her grandmother's dead body.

Being locked in the attic by an unknown person with an unknown motive. Surely not Scott.

Wanton destruction in the house. Not a poltergeist, again an unknown person with an unknown motive. Surely not Scott.

Krystal's séance. The person was known, her motive unknown.

A crack in the top handrail of the porch caught his attention, but it was nothing more than a hairline split in dry wood. He moved to the next section.

Perhaps a single motivation lurked behind all three incidents. Maybe it was as simple as someone trying to scare Marty away. Or more than one person. Krystal's kaleidoscope show didn't really fit with the other two incidents where the house itself was the adversary. Looked at that way Lois's deadly fall down the stairs might fit the developing pattern.

But Lois's death was an accident. Wasn't it?

Paul sat back on his heels and looked through the spindles at his project, the house Scott called the hovel. Was this the view Scott had of their grand project, a jail? *Father* . . .

Paul got to his feet and picked up the toolbox. He was satisfied little Ruthie Baker hadn't fallen to her death from this porch. But even as he drew that conclusion, he wondered what he would find if he examined the main staircase where Marty found Lois. As he walked down the hall, he heard the murmur of the women's voices. He couldn't make out the words, but the tone sounded serious. Paul hoped Marty was telling her ghost fears to Sofia. He kept walking.

At the bottom of the stairs, he stopped and looked back up. The sheriff's theory was that Lois had come home late at night, started up the staircase in the dark, stepped on the red and white cat ball, and fallen backwards to her death. What else could have happened? Leaving the question open, Paul concentrated on the newel post at the bottom. He shook it, or tried to. It was solid. The carpet runner was tacked in place. No scratches on the wall. He moved up a step. Checked the spindle, the carpet, the wall.

On the fourth step from the top he found what he was looking for, or rather, what he hadn't wanted to find. The spindle was broken in the middle, a jagged break as if it had given way under too much weight. The two pieces had been so carefully put back together he would never have seen the break if he hadn't been looking for something not quite right. The house was old, the spindles original. A break wasn't surprising. What concerned Paul was that the break hadn't been mended or tagged as a hazard. The detail-conscious Lois would have made sure it was fixed as soon as it happened. Even if it broke in her rush to leave for Virginia, she'd have called him to fix the problem before she got home.

The next spindle was broken and put back together the same way. A section of stair runner missing a tack was held in place by a wad of scotch tape underneath the carpet. Like the spindle, someone had been at work to make sure the damage wasn't noticed. If Lois's fall had torn the carpet, it wouldn't have been repaired. Just beyond the torn carpet, superficial scratches ran along the wall at the place where Paul estimated Lois's hands would have been when she first toppled backwards.

Paul sat down on the step and put his head in his hands. *Father.*

～〃〜

Marty swallowed the ridiculous lump in her throat and placed the soft nightgown in the pile of clothes to give away. "You don't know how much I appreciate your help with this job."

Sofia smiled at her over a stack of neatly folded blouses. "Sorting through the belongings of someone who has passed away is never easy. All sorts of emotions bubble to the surface. It's good to have company."

"This shouldn't bother me."

"Why ever not?"

"For the last twenty-two years, I didn't know Lois existed. After she found me, I talked to her once. And that wasn't a very long conversation."

"You knew she existed, honey. I imagine you missed her every day if not in your mind, in your heart. Now, just after you found her again, she's gone. Leaving all those questions unanswered."

Only one question. "I don't want to believe in ghosts."

"But?"

Still holding three of Lois's slips, Marty sat on the vanity bench. "May I tell you what's been happening to me in this house?"

"Of course." Sofia positioned the delicate lady chair she was sitting in to face Marty.

"It started with finding Granny Lois's body."

"A terrible shock."

"Yes, but I wasn't frightened. I knew Granny was gone, that her body was an empty shell. It was what happened that night, very early the next morning really, that scared me."

"Here in this house?"

"Yes. I was at the Jerome Grand Hotel. I couldn't sleep. I had a nightmare." Not a ghost in a mirror. "So, I walked back here. I heard something upstairs." Not a ghost in the attic. "I went to investigate. I'm not sure exactly what happened, but something knocked me down and then locked me in the attic."

Marty paused, expecting Sofia to comment. When the other woman was silent, she went on. "The next evening I was up here when I heard a crash downstairs. The lights kept going off and back on. When I managed to investigate, I found all sorts of damage." Not a poltergeist. "Then last night Krystal Cho came here."

"Mm. I heard."

"You know about her visit?"

Sofia shrugged. "It's a tiny town. Krystal talks, especially when she can claim a ghost."

Marty's throat closed. She swallowed, tried to speak, cleared her throat. "I was ready to explain everything away until last night. I don't want to believe in ghosts."

"Tell me."

"Krystal's kaleidoscopes are just plain silly."

"Not 'silly.' 'Pathetic' is better, I think."

"What do you mean?"

"Krystal wants so badly to believe. But she resists faith."

"Why?"

"I don't know the details of her experience with the church, with a specific church, but something happened to hurt her. She's rejected faith and bought into an alternate spirituality she makes up as she goes along. I feel sad for Krystal. All that effort to invent her own religion, even to the clothes she wears."

"That's what I thought in her shop, even when she came here looking for Lois."

"But?"

"She admitted Lois wasn't here in the house. Then she told me Ruthie was on the porch off our bedroom, so I went outside." Suddenly Marty couldn't breathe as if someone, not a ghost, was pressing on her windpipe.

"Something happened on the porch," prompted Sofia.

Marty gulped air. "I didn't see anything, but I felt something, someone."

"Go on."

"It's hard to put into words. Fear, sorrow, anger, all confused into so much emotion I couldn't contain it all. In that moment, I knew Krystal was right. It was Ruthie. My little sister Ruthie! I knew it was her, just like I knew she was standing there hating me for what I did to her." Marty closed her eyes and tried to forget. Sorrow. Fury. The need for retribution.

"Martha Baker Greenlaw! Open your eyes and look at me."

Marty shuddered and obeyed.

Sofia took her hands and held them. "You didn't encounter a ghost last night, cariña. No matter what Krystal told you or what you felt, you didn't encounter a ghost."

"But Krystal felt something, not in this room where she expected it, but on the balcony outside of our bedroom. How is that possible?"

"Are you sure you didn't tell Krystal about your fears? Maybe just a hint."

Only one question. Did I kill Ruthie? "I suppose I did, but I didn't say anything about the balcony."

"Krystal has been in this house many times. She either knows or guesses the study was once a little girl's bedroom."

"But there was something out there."

Sofia squeezed Marty's hands. "It wasn't a ghost. When people talk about a ghost, they mean a disembodied spirit that lingers on earth after death. As Christians, we believe when people die, their spirits go to be with God, or not, depending on their relationship with Jesus. Ruthie was a tiny child when she died. There's no question in my mind she went to be with her heavenly Father. Whatever happened to cause her death, she's at peace."

"The hatred was real. I know it was."

"From yourself, cariña. Ruthie is at peace. You're the one who is in turmoil. You've got to give the process time. You came to Lois for healing. She's gone, but even if she were here, she's not the Source. You know Who is. Ask for healing and then trust it."

"Don't you mean I should ask for forgiveness?"

Sofia shook her head gently. "Your sister's death was a puncture wound deep in your heart. It healed on the outside, but deep inside it's still bleeding." Sofia turned Marty's palms up and kissed each one lightly. "Now we need to reclaim this house from confusion and fear. Come on, cariña."

Sofia got to her feet and drew Marty up beside her. In her sneakers, Marty was 5'2"; Sofia wasn't quite as tall. The older woman linked arms with Marty. "Where shall we go?"

Shoulder to shoulder. "The study. The balcony."

Paul was coming up the stairs as they started down the hall. "Join us," Sofia said. "We're going to ask God to put this house to rights."

"If you mean an exorcism . . ."

Sofia shook her head vigorously. "Not at all. Marty hasn't encountered ghosts or demons. What she needs is a blessing on her work here."

"Where two or more are gathered," murmured Paul.

"Exactly."

When they reached the little study, Sofia went to the French doors and opened them. Morning sunlight streamed in, momentarily undiluted by smoke. The three of them joined hands.

Sofia said, "Marty, tell us what you need to accomplish in this room."

A private quest, circumscribed not by distance but by time. She had become so enmeshed in her chaotic feelings, she had lost sight of the goal. But Sofia saw. Marty said, "I think this room was a happy place. I think Ruthie used to dance on this balcony." Memory or nightmare?

"I imagine she did," Paul said. "I couldn't find any evidence of repair in that railing."

Marty wanted to believe him, but her doubt must have showed because he opened the hand that was holding hers and threaded their fingers. "I don't see how Ruthie could have fallen from that balcony. Whatever happened to her didn't happen out there."

It was the touch as much as the confidence in his voice, but suddenly she knew he was right. She said, "I need to be able to remember the happy times in this room." As she said it, the words became true. She needed to recover the whole truth of her childhood, not just the horror of a single day.

"Let's pray," Sofia said. "Father, banish the fear from this house. Let it become a place of happy memories for Marty." She let go of Marty's hand and said briskly, "Where to next?"

Paul gave Marty a look she couldn't interpret: equal parts apprehension, sympathy, and something very like a warning. "The stairway."

Chapter Twenty-one

Paul reached up to adjust the tie he wasn't wearing, the tie that was at the house in Cottonwood with his suit, his dress shirts and leather shoes. He was surprised he'd brought the blazer up the mountain, except it was the one that hung on the back of his office door ready for unexpected formality. Like a summons to the dean's office. Not a funeral.

The tie usually stayed in the pocket of the blazer. But, for some reason he couldn't recall, he'd taken the tie out of the pocket and hung it in the closet with the rest of its kindred. No one at the service would notice what he was wearing, but he wondered what Marty would think of his dark red polo shirt and jeans.

He should have gotten his hair cut, should have shaved off the beard that was starting to look like more than a five o'clock shadow. But maybe Marty liked beards. She'd never commented one way of the other. A funeral, he told himself sternly, not a fashion show. Still he wished he at least had chinos. But he was clean.

Paul pushed away his ridiculous angst and knocked on the lavender door. Marty answered it so quickly he was afraid he might be late.

"Hi, Paul. I'm glad you're early. Thanks for offering to go with me to the service. I'm glad you walked over. I thought it might be easier if we took my car. It's not that I mind riding in your Land Cruiser, but ---"

She was talking too fast, more nervous than he was, no doubt for very different reasons. Suddenly he felt ridiculous. This wasn't junior high, and it certainly wasn't a date. "Great minds running in the same channel," he said, holding out his hand for her car keys. Too late, he realized he was making an assumption.

She didn't seem to notice, just gave him the keys. "You don't mind driving?"

"Not at all."

"You know the way and where to park." She stopped abruptly and looked up at him.

She was wearing high-heeled sandals, but she was still several inches shorter than Linda. He felt awkward, too large.

"I'm a mess," she said. "In case you hadn't noticed."

He had noticed, and she definitely didn't look a mess. Her curls shone copper in the early afternoon sun. Her black sheath fit nicely, and the cutout sleeves revealed slender arms. But he knew what she meant, so he said, "If I were in your position, I'd be a mess too."

"You would?"

"You bet." He slid his hands under a silky iridescent shawl and began to massage her shoulders. She went very still, but she didn't pull away. "You're in a strange town with people you don't know from Adam, or Eve, going to the funeral of a grandmother you didn't know existed until three days ago."

She rotated her head slowly, stretching her neck against his hands.

"And that's not factoring in the insanity of the last few days. I'd say you're holding up very well, Ms. Greenlaw. You're pressed, dressed, and ready to impress."

She laughed. He felt the tension go out of her shoulders, and it took willpower not to put his arms around her and kiss her. In reality, he would have had to grab her quickly as she slid out from under his hands and clicked down the stairs of the porch.

Marveling at the way she moved in the high heels without losing her balance, he followed her to the white car in the driveway. He pressed the unlock button on the car key and went to open her door. Again, she was too quick for him. Retreating or just in a hurry?

They rode in silence as he backed the car out onto the road and headed for the highway. They were in town passing Mystic Glass when she spoke. "I've been thinking about the broken spindles and the scratches you found on the wall of the stairwell. I can't seem to think about anything else. Who on earth would push an old lady down the stairs? And why?"

"Those are the questions."

"When I was in town yesterday, I was trying to figure out who might have been the poltergeist."

"And who locked you in the attic. The tricks being played on you are getting progressively more dangerous. Whoever is behind all of this wants you out of that house."

"Because he or she killed Granny Lois."

"Probably."

They lapsed into silence again. Like Marty, he couldn't get the scene on the stairs out of his head. The fragile old woman dressed in yellow, exhausted emotionally and physically, grateful to be home, climbing the stairs, possibly in the dark, but not necessarily now they knew she hadn't missed her footing. Someone surprised by her unexpected arrival, trapped upstairs with no way out except by the old woman.

"What's in Granny Lois's house that's worth killing for?"

Paul glanced at Marty.

She was staring out the window, but he didn't think she saw the metal sculpture moving in the wind in front of the artists' co-op. She was talking, but more to herself than to him. She didn't wait for him to reply. "The furniture is worth a small fortune, but it's hard to imagine someone planning to carry off a chair or a table in the middle of the night."

They started down the switchbacks, and as easy as the car was to drive, he had to keep his attention on the road. "Something upstairs," he suggested. "Something small but valuable."

"The paperweights? I don't know enough about them to know how much they would bring, but some of them are very unusual, things I've never seen before."

"Jewelry would be more likely."

"I suppose. I haven't started to inventory her jewelry, but if we can go by the quality of everything else in the house, she probably collected some very valuable pieces."

"We have a start on why then. Now we turn to who." Even with his eyes on the road, Paul felt her tense up. She had to be thinking of Scott and the stamp album.

Trying to keep his tone level, he said, "I know it must look to you as though my son is a good suspect, but I'll vouch for him. I absolutely believe him when he says Lois told him she wanted him to have the stamp album."

"I never . . ."

"It's okay. Let me have my say. I heard Lockridge when he accused Scott of stealing things to sell for drug money, but I don't believe Scott's a thief. Furthermore, I reject the idea my son could be using drugs and I wouldn't know it." Despite the marijuana. If he could just find Scott, he was sure there was another explanation.

"What about Carly? She needs money. We only have her word for it that my grandmother was ready to start selling some of her pieces or that she was planning to work with Carly. Or Krystal. It's not hard to imagine her stealing the glass paperweights."

Paul was grateful she hadn't argued about Scott. Because no matter what else he might be wrong about, even the drugs, Paul was certain Scott had loved Lois. No matter what she might have caught him doing, he would never push her down the stairs. An accident? Scott scared, Lois surprised, the Siamese caught between them.

Marty's words echoed his thought. "Maybe it was an accident. Maybe someone was trying to get around her on the stairs. Maybe she lost her balance and fell."

"If it was an accident, why didn't the person call for help?"

"I can't bear talking like this! Whatever the reason, I can't imagine anyone killing a helpless old lady."

"We have to talk like this, Marty. Whoever it was evidently isn't finished in that house. And that person is trying to get you to leave."

She was quiet for so long he wondered if she was fighting tears. A quick glance reassured him. She was frowning, not crying. Finally, she said softly, "I came pretty close to packing up last night. But after we talked, I thought about it for a long time." She paused, then added hesitantly, "I prayed about it. I decided if I'm going live with myself, I have to find out what happened to Ruthie, whether it was my fault or not."

"I agree with you in principle, but I retract the advice I gave you last night. I urged you to stay before I had any idea you might be in a killer's way. Go home, Marty. After the service, I'll drive you back to the house. I'll wait downstairs while you pack. Then I'll follow you to the airport in Phoenix and stay with you until I see you safely on the next plane back to Virginia." The passion in his voice surprised him, but he wasn't sorry. It was time to start dealing with his feelings for this woman.

She was quiet for a long time. He was about to ask her what she was thinking when she turned toward him and touched his arm. "Thank you, Paul. I may take you up on that offer in a day or two. But not today. Even if I could live without understanding my sister's death, now I have to find out what happened to Granny Lois. Who pushed her. And why."

∽ა

Marty spotted the tall metal cross a block before Paul turned into the sprawling gravel parking lot. A sign at the road announced "Good Shepherd," but the only building was a large metal structure like a warehouse.

"We've almost got enough money to start construction," Paul said. "We plan to pave the parking lot before winter and break ground on the sanctuary in the spring."

He parked between a late model BMW and a Chevrolet that had been driven hard for many years. He released his seatbelt but made no move to get out of the car. "I want to let you know Scott may be riding home with us. At least I hope that's what happens."

Marty heard the longing in his voice. So the teenager hadn't been home for two nights, and evidently Paul didn't know where he was. She didn't know what to say. Finally she murmured, "I hope so too." And she did. No matter what Brad said, she liked Scott. She believed his story about the stamp album, and if he had been the one to lock her in the attic, he'd probably thought of it as no more than a prank. He couldn't have known how hard she'd hit her head.

"Scott and I parted on pretty bad terms. I'm not positive he's going to show up for the funeral. If he does, I have no idea what sort of mood he'll be in. Scott's going through a rough patch right now."

"It's okay, Paul. Really it is. It's been a few years since I was a teenager, but I remember the moods and the flares of resentment at my folks." Unexpressed feelings because she was always a little afraid Mother and Dad, particularly Dad, might send her back. To where she didn't know. Just back. The thought startled Marty. Never once had she let that fear enter her consciousness. Not until this moment. What else was locked in the attic of her mind?

That was the past. Now was now. Paul's door was open. ". . . understanding . . ." He got out, giving her a moment to reorient.

Paul. Had he almost kissed her there on the porch, and had she almost reached up to touch the beard that was starting to look soft? Had she hurried to the car because he was too old for her? Not that, not exactly anyway. It was his teenaged son. Scott was too old for her.

Marty smiled at the thought just as Paul opened her door. He studied her for a moment, then offered her his hand. As she put her hand in his, he smiled, a smile that lit up his warm brown eyes. Was he reading her mind again?

Marty ignored the heat she could feel rising from her neck to her face and got out of the car.

He didn't make any comment, but he tucked her hand in the crook of his arm as if it belonged there. Funeral or not, at that moment Marty wanted to sing. She started to push the sudden joy away, then relented. She would let it stay if it promised to stay unexpressed. Now was not the time, not the place.

She changed the unspoken subject before one of them blundered. "We're early. I'm surprised at how many cars are here."

He took a moment to reply, and for one crazy moment she thought he was going to laugh. He cleared his throat, said, "Your grandmother was a founding member of this congregation. It started as a Bible study she led in the school cafeteria twenty years ago."

Two years after . . . Marty refused to go down that rabbit trail. "She knew everyone."

221

"You bet. Over the years, I believe she taught Sunday School, ran the nursery, organized women's circles, baked cakes, delivered casseroles, absolutely anything and everything that needed doing. She did it all in a way that made you feel as though you'd done her a favor by giving her the opportunity to help."

"Brad told me she was one of the first people he met when he came here."

A tiny pause. Something about Brad?

Then Paul said, "I don't think Lois ever met a stranger" and turned onto a white stone path that ran alongside of the building.

"We're not going in?"

"No. The service is going to be in the prayer garden. Lois had the vision for the garden even before we purchased this property. She planted the first roses and involved all of us in the construction. It became a real community effort, and people were coming here to pray long before we put up the temporary building that's here now." He was silent for a moment, then added, "We had Linda's service here."

Marty felt a pang of guilt. She had no business thinking like a giddy teenager about this man who had lost his wife. He was supposed to be her brother. She was saved from having to sort out her confusion by a casual crowd gathered on the path. Suddenly people were ahead, behind, and on both sides of them.

A few yards before they reached the entrance to the prayer garden, Paul stepped off the path. "Linda helped build the labyrinth in the center. She and I used to go out looking for stones. I never quite caught on because there was more than size to what she needed. Lois wanted to capture the mood of a labyrinth she walked in France, but she wasn't up to the physical labor. Linda found the stones, and Lois directed the youth group where to lay them."

"How long ago?"

"A little over three years. The project grew out of a trip to Europe Lois made right after Tommy died. She went on a tour of great cathedrals and came home with some beautiful slides and the vision for the prayer garden." He gave her an apologetic smile. "Sorry. I don't imagine you're interested in my trip down memory lane."

But she was interested, maybe more than she should be, certainly more than she could tell him. "Please," she said, "don't apologize."

She thought he was about to say something more, but then he turned away and stepped back into the flow of people.

The garden was larger than Marty expected it to be. Not just a single garden, several smaller gardens made up the whole. White stone benches defined the space, many of them shaded by scrub oak trees that must have been there for years. Narrow paths led from each of the small gardens to the center where pink, red, and yellow roses outlined the circular path that created the labyrinth.

In the center of the labyrinth a white stone monument of an open Bible held a decorative urn, Granny Lois's ashes. Flower arrangements in a rainbow of colors covered the ground all around the monument. Folding chairs had been set up in a semicircle facing the little table.

"It's lovely," Marty said.

"The folding chairs rather spoil the effect. When Lois planned her memorial service, I don't imagine she had any idea how many people would want to be here."

"Afternoon, Paul, Miss Baker." A heavy-set, middle-aged man held out two single sheets of stiff white paper to Paul.

Not Baker. Marty started to correct the usher, but then she remembered the old lady dressed in yellow linen standing in the doorway of her workshop. "You're Martha Baker. I'm

223

your grandmother Lois." Granny Lois. Suddenly Marty wanted to weep.

"Afternoon, Jack," Paul said.

Jack gave Marty a solemn smile. "As family, you should sit up front."

Family. Marty was all the family Lois Baker had left. And Granny Lois was all the family Martha Baker had left. A new thought, or another of the thoughts she was finally allowing into her conscious mind?

Caught up in her musings, Marty took the arm Jack offered her automatically and walked with him to the front row of the circle of chairs.

"Are you okay?"

Paul's voice brought her back to the present, to the garden, to the memorial service, to surprising sorrow. Marty nodded, and Paul handed her a program. They took the chairs Jack indicated, she on the aisle, Paul on her left.

"Are you sure you're okay, Marty? You look pale."

Like I've seen a ghost? The ghost of Martha Baker, the child who banished too much, not realizing she was banishing herself with it. "I think it's all catching up with me."

He took her hand, placed it on his arm, and covered it with his own. "It was bound to."

Marty wasn't so sure. The past was only catching up because she'd finally stopped running. But she wasn't the only one with a past. "How are you?"

He nodded. "I'm okay. Good actually."

"Hello, Marty."

She looked up. Brad Lockridge stood in the aisle, smiling down at her. Dressed in a slim gray suit, pale blue shirt and matching plaid tie, he looked his part, the successful young lawyer on a solemn occasion. "The back rows are filling up," he said. "I'm not family, but I wondered if I might join you."

Marty didn't really want to make it a threesome, but this wasn't a date. She gave Brad what she hoped was a welcoming smile. "Sure. As far as family goes, I think I'm it."

"Afternoon, Paul," Brad said. "Is anyone sitting next to you?"

"No. It's all yours."

Paul released Marty's hand and stood to let the other man by. Had he tensed up? Something about Brad. She wondered what.

People filled in behind them, chair after chair, row after row. Every few minutes Paul stood and scanned the crowd. Probably looking for Scott. Once Brad looked across Paul's empty seat and winked at her. Marty looked away, annoyed at Brad and then annoyed at herself. Everyone must know Paul was looking for his son.

Pastor Ray, a slender man of middle height in his early forties, stepped to the little table and picked up a cordless microphone. Unlike so many of the men sitting around her, he had a full head of dark hair. When he'd come to the house to discuss Lois's instructions for the service, he'd apologized profusely for not coming sooner. Someone, Marty couldn't remember who, had suffered a massive heart attack. As Marty looked at the growing crowd, she marveled that one pastor could meet all the needs. But maybe there was an associate pastor.

"Welcome, friends. For those of you who don't know me, I'm Pastor Ray. I was privileged to be Lois's pastor for the last three years, and I know she would greet each one of you with a smile if she could. Maybe in some way we don't understand, she's doing just that right now." Marty wondered how this service compared to Linda's. Were these the same words this pastor had spoken two years ago?

They stood to sing *In the Garden*, an old song Pastor Ray told them Lois had specifically requested. Probably not a song

Linda would have wanted. With a start, Marty realized Linda probably hadn't planned her service. People in their thirties rarely left funeral plans. Paul must have been left with the task as he grieved for his wife.

The sudden pang was so strong she had to swallow hard to keep back the tears. What was wrong with her? She couldn't weep over an imaginary funeral now. She had to remember where she was and the role she needed to fill. Whether she remembered them or not, she represented Lois Baker's family, especially her son. Daddy. Again those tears threatened. This time tears she hadn't shed when she was six and had to be strong for Ruthie.

With an effort, Marty focused on the little table that held the urn. A woman about her own age took the microphone from the pastor. In a clear alto voice, she read Luke's account of the women coming to Jesus' tomb early in the morning.

As Pastor Ray accepted the mike from her, he looked directly at Marty. "The women were dismayed to find Jesus' body gone. Just as you must have been dismayed to find Lois gone, Marty. Just as we are all dismayed to realize Lois is gone from our midst. But listen to what the angel said. 'Why do you seek the living among the dead?'"

Releasing Marty from the grip of his gaze, he looked out at the congregation. "Make no mistake, friends. Lois Baker, while not with us here in body, is nevertheless among the living."

"No, she's not!"

With everyone else, Marty turned to look for the source of the cry. Scott. Paul groaned and got to his feet, but the entire prayer garden separated him from his son.

"Lois is dead! Just like Mom is dead! Why don't you tell the truth? Dead is dead!"

By the time Scott quit shouting, Paul had worked his way through the rows of chairs to the perimeter of the garden.

But the teenager was quicker than his father. Pushing across the people in his row, Scott sprinted around the side of the building. Paul started after his son. The look on his face made Marty's throat ache.

Others had seen it as well because a voice behind her murmured, "Poor man."

"Amen," whispered Brad.

"Congregation," Pastor Ray said into the microphone, "let's take a moment to pray for Scott. As most of you remember, two years ago, we held a service very much like this one for Scott's mother Linda in this very garden. Join me, please." He bowed his head. "Father, we know you care about this young man and the burden of grief he bears."

Marty closed her eyes. *The burden of grief, so heavy he needs drugs?*

Maybe Scott was attempting to dull the ache of his mother's loss. Maybe he was too old to bury the memories as she had done when Mommy and Daddy and then Ruthie died. If Scott was dealing with the same confusion and pain that was surfacing in her own nightmares, he might be too young to handle his emotions. He might turn to drugs. Marty shuddered. *Dear God.*

Chapter Twenty-two

Paul followed Scott around the side of the building and down the path toward the parking lot. The teenager was running, but Paul waited until he was out of sight of the prayer garden before he broke into a full run. As much as he needed to catch up with his son, he didn't want to disrupt the memorial service any more than the two them already had. His restraint gave Scott, younger and quicker, even more advantage. The boy was halfway across the parking lot by the time Paul reached it. Paul knew he couldn't catch Scott, but he kept running.

Then the unexpected happened: Scott stopped and looked back. Paul waved and kept running. Scott took his cell phone out of his pocket and turned his back, but he stayed where he was. By the time Paul got there, his breath was coming in gasps and his heart was pounding. No matter he swam three times a week and had been doing manual labor the last three weeks, he wasn't fourteen and hadn't been for many years.

Scott was listening to whomever he'd called, so Paul turned toward the San Francisco Peaks that marked Flagstaff. In the late afternoon, they dominated the northern horizon, a jagged indigo tear in an azure sky. As his breathing slowly returned to normal, Paul tried to decide what to say. I lift up my eyes to the hills, from where will my help come?

"Dad?"

Scott, clutching his cell phone, looked ready to run again. Refusing to make eye contact, he blurted, "I know, Dad! I shouldn't have interrupted the service. I should have had more respect for Mrs. Baker and the people who were there to tell her good-bye. It wasn't the appropriate time to voice my feelings."

"If you already knew what I was going to say, why did you wait for me?"

Scott shrugged. "I guess I was surprised. I didn't think you'd come after me."

A myriad of responses rushed into Paul's head: I've been looking for you for two days! Why wouldn't I come after you? I know you're hurting. I want to help. Why didn't you come to me with all this pain? Instead, he said the truest thing he knew. "I love you, son."

"I know."

"But it doesn't help?"

"No."

Where to go from here? My help comes from the Lord. "Let's walk."

Paul's impulse was to drop an arm on his son's shoulders, but instinctively he knew it would be wrong. He set a brisk pace across the parking lot toward the street. His legs were longer, so walking gave him the advantage. Scott had to hurry to keep up. And that was fine.

The afternoon shadows were beginning to lengthen. A light pole made a dark stripe across the gravel that crunched under their feet, and out on the street a semi dragged its shadow along the pavement. A light breeze stirred the warm dry air. Automatically, Paul checked the sky in the southwest, but if the smoke cloud was still there, it wasn't visible from the valley.

"I'm sorry, Dad."

"Okay."

"That doesn't help either, does it?"

"No." Paul looked down at his son's blonde head, not so far down as he was used to looking. So much like Linda. But that kind of thinking wasn't going to get them anywhere. He had to start viewing Scott as a separate human being. Linda's son, his son, but a person in his own right, someone who wasn't like either one of them. A new thought, more than a thought, a new perspective. A paradigm shift so great it stopped his feet.

"Dad?"

"Sorry." Paul started walking again. They reached the street and stepped onto the sidewalk. "I think we start with the truth."

"I'm not lying! I really am sorry."

"I know you are. That's not the truth I'm talking about." How to explain this concept he had just stumbled across? How to explain to a person too young to imagine what it was like to have a child, much less what it was like to realize you had been going about parenting all wrong?

Sofia could explain it, Sofia who had recognized a fellow Christian moving through a season of doubt, even though that fellow Christian was only fourteen. But Sofia wasn't here. He was on his own.

"What, Dad? What lies do you think I've told?"

"Not lies. Truth. There's a big difference. The truth we need to start with is who you are, who you've become the last two years."

"I'm the same as I always was."

"No. Not possible. Life keeps shaping us. For the last two years, grief has shaped you, just as it's shaped me. We've both been grieving for the same person, but I've been grieving for my wife, and you've been grieving for your mother. Those losses are very different."

Scott was silent for the rest of the block. When they reached the intersection, Paul pushed the button for the cross-walk. Across the street in an empty lot a dust devil sucked up a tumbleweed, spun it three times, and released it. It bounced twice before the breeze rolled it up against a fence.

"I don't know what you want me to say, Dad."

Too complicated for a fourteen-year-old, maybe even too complicated for a thirty-eight-year-old.

If Scott asked him to put into words what the two years had done to him, what would he say? I was ripped into two pieces, and half of me burned to ashes with your mother's body? I was frozen inside. It was the only way I could keep going? I went to the edge of death and God was there? But those were descriptions of what had happened to him, not how those experiences had shaped him.

"I guess I'm not sure what I want you to say either. Maybe I've asked you an impossible question." The light changed, gave them their "Walk" signal. They crossed in silence.

When they reached the other side, Paul said, "Let's go to Mimi's. It's not far. We can get a piece of pie." He shouldn't assume, shouldn't tell this young man what he wanted to eat. "Or ice cream. Or whatever you want."

"Okay."

They lapsed into silence again, and Paul left it alone.

The tiny café was almost empty, too late for lunch and too early for supper. The waitress, a faded wisp of a gray woman, nodded at a table by the window and brought them menus and water.

"Just pie for me," Paul said. "What do you have back there?"

"Apple, blueberry, butterscotch, and maybe one piece of banana cream."

"I'll have apple and a cup of coffee. What about you, Scott?"

"Butterscotch."

"Are you sure you want pie, son? You can order something else."

"Pie's fine, Dad. I like butterscotch."

Of course he did. Paul told himself he was trying too hard. Better than not trying at all.

Scott looked up at the waitress. "Can I have a glass of milk?"

"Soon as I can pour it, hon."

Paul picked up the small glass of water and drained it in one long gulp. Scott drank almost as greedily.

Paul smiled. "Amazing how good a glass of water can be."

"I guess we were both thirsty."

I guess we're both feeling awkward. But Paul didn't say it. Instead he made a tentative start toward the conversation he wanted to have. "A while ago I got tangled up in abstractions neither one of us could put into words. Are you willing to answer a few concrete questions?"

"Yes, sir."

Paul studied his son's face for signs of sarcasm, but Scott looked perfectly serious. A little nervous but that was appropriate. He was nervous too.

The waitress approached their table, carrying a tray with their pie and a glass of milk. She served Scott first. He thanked her as he took his first bite.

She smiled. "Butterscotch is my favorite too." As she handed Paul his apple pie, she added, "Back in a jiff with your coffee. And it looks like you two could use more water."

"Yes, thanks."

When the waitress was out of earshot, Paul said calmly, "Are you using marijuana?"

Scott looked up, as startled as if Paul had reached across the table and slapped him. Then he looked down, stood his fork on one tine, and twirled it slowly. "Not exactly."

"I asked a yes/no question. You'll have to explain 'not exactly.'"

"I've never smoked it, Dad. Honest."

"But . . ."

"But I've been with B.T. when he was smoking."

"And . . ."

Scott put the fork down and looked out the window.

Paul realized he was holding his breath and let it out slowly. He hated the idea of a direct confrontation. If Scott would confess of his own free will, they would at least have a chance at building trust. "And . . ."

Scott looked Paul in the eye. "I let B.T. talk me into trying it. But I told him I wanted to be alone the first time. I brought some home with me. I never smoked it, Dad. It's still in my backpack."

Paul shook his head. "I flushed it."

"You went through my things!"

"Yes."

"That's not fair! If I ever went through your things, you'd kill me."

"You live in my house, son. I don't need permission to go through things you keep in my house. When you didn't come home and when you wouldn't answer your cell phone, I did some calling. I learned quite a bit about your friend Lloyd Harper, Jr. The more I heard, the more worried I got. So I looked. Unfortunately, I found what I was looking for."

"You tricked me."

"No. I wanted to give you the chance to tell me yourself. Thank you for explaining." For a moment, Paul was afraid he'd lost the tentative connection. Very deliberately, he cut a bite of pie with his fork.

Scott let out an explosive breath. "I'm glad you know, Dad. I'm glad you flushed it."

"What will you tell B.T.?"

"The truth."

"Which is?" Paul forced himself to eat the bite of pie he'd cut, but it might as well have been sawdust for all he tasted.

"My dad found it, and I'm glad because I never wanted to try the stuff in the first place." Scott picked up his fork and took another bite of his pie. When he looked up, the expression of world-weariness on his face made Paul's stomach clench. "I started out being friends with B.T. because I wanted to help him, but he almost pulled me down. I'm such a weakling!"

"No. You're a human being who can be tempted. Like all of us."

Scott looked toward the clock on the wall behind the cash register. "I gotta go back."

"Now?"

Scott nodded. "After my meltdown, I called Dan. I asked him if he could come get me. He said he'd come after peewee soccer practice. He's coaching, and he can't leave until all the parents come for their kids. He said it would be about 5:00."

Paul looked at the clock. 4:48. "What's your plan?"

With his fork, Scott pushed a lone piece of pie crust around his plate. "I want to go up to Flagstaff to his family's cabin. I need to be by myself for a while. I've got some things to think about."

Paul took a deep breath and fought to regain his objectivity. This young man named Scott Russell had his own agenda. "Can you tell me a little more?"

"I'll tell you after I come back, Dad. Promise. Can I go?"

At least Scott was asking. "If it's all right with Dan's parents and if Dan can spare the time, then it's all right with me."

"Thanks, Dad." Scott started to push back his chair.

"Just a minute. I need you to call Dan and ask him to pick you up here. I still have a few questions."

"Okay." A puzzled expression on his face, the teenager got out his cell phone and punched in the number.

Paul looked out the window. Puzzled was good. Better than guilty or resentful. Still he didn't look forward to continuing the grilling. Traffic was getting heavier, not heavy enough to qualify as rush hour in a big city, but enough to make crossing the street on foot a bit more difficult.

"It's fine," Scott said. "He's on his way."

Not much time. Paul considered letting the rest of it go for the moment. They were on a good footing. It would be nice to part that way. But he needed the truth, the rest of it. "Have you been back to Mrs. Baker's house since Mr. Lockridge took the stamp album away from you?"

"Why would I?"

"You tell me. Did you sneak out that night and go back to the attic?"

"No, Dad."

"You didn't lock Marty in?"

Scott stared. "You mean Mrs. Baker's granddaughter?"

"That's who I mean."

"No way, Dad! Why would I do that?"

"I have no idea. Did you go over to Mrs. Baker's house Wednesday night and throw a lot of breakable things around downstairs?"

"Dad, you're the one who's smoking dope."

"This is serious, Scott. I'm not kidding around. If you've been doing these things or know anything about what's going on at that house, you have to level with me. Now."

Scott shook his head emphatically. "No, sir. I have not gone back to Mrs. Baker's house. Not once. I swear!"

"And you don't know anyone who might have done those things?"

The resentment Paul had hoped to avoid flared in Scott's eyes. "You mean B.T."

Paul refused to be drawn into a side issue. "I made no accusations, son. I asked you a simple question. Please give me a simple answer."

"I don't know a single thing about any of this. Is that simple enough?" Scott looked out the window and then jumped to his feet. "Dan's here. I gotta go."

Paul wanted to shout, "Sit down! We're not done." But that reaction wouldn't do any more good now than it had three days ago. He watched through the window as his son got into Dan's rebuilt Jeep.

"Excuse me, sir. I thought maybe you'd want your coffee now." The waitress put a full cup in front of him. "Cream?"

Paul shook his head.

"I started to bring it sooner, but I didn't think I should interrupt."

"You have a teenager?"

"I had two. We got through those years, though some days I had my doubts. Thank the good Lord, they're both grown and settled. I'm a grandma now. It's a lot easier." She smiled. "Downright fun some days."

Paul returned the smile. "I'm glad to hear it."

"Let me know if you need a refill."

"Thanks." The kindness of a stranger. Paul was surprised at how encouraged he felt. Maybe they weren't strangers after all. Just members of the tribe of parents who hadn't been formally introduced.

He took a sip of the coffee. Hot and strong, the way he liked it. He was about to relax when he realized he'd missed a question. He hadn't asked Scott about the text. But as Scott had said about all the other questions, why would he? The text messages had to be part of the campaign to scare Marty away. The problem was, Paul had seen the number on Marty's phone. It was Scott's. No question.

～ِ

Just inside the door Marty stepped out of the stream of people heading for cake and coffee. Brad was still in the garden talking business with an old man, and she welcomed the moment of anonymity. She needed a chance to recover from the emotional roller coaster Scott's outburst had put her on. She also needed to prepare for the socializing she knew was ahead.

The metal building didn't look any more like a church inside than it did outside. An open space undivided into rooms, the building was obviously used for more purposes than worship. The floor was painted for a basketball court, a stage held a podium and a drum set, and wheeled bulletin boards defined a kitchen. At the moment, the purpose was fellowship.

Two long tables covered with white cloths sat in the center of the room. At one table a large woman dressed in a colorful Hawaiian muumuu was cutting a cake and placing pieces on small paper plates. At the other table, a man in a light blue suit was setting up a coffee pot while a gray-haired woman wearing a black lace dress filled paper cups with frothy liquid from a cut-glass punchbowl.

A tall, slender woman with chin-length, white hair detached herself from a chattering group and came toward Marty. "I'm Alice Worthington. I've been appointed your social director for this event. My first official duty is to set up a receiving line. Would you rather be introduced as Greenlaw or Baker?"

Not an either/or decision. "How about just 'Marty?'"

Alice smiled. "I told the girls that's what you'd say. I told them Lois wouldn't want to be called Mrs. Baker, and her granddaughter wouldn't want to be stiff and formal either."

The possibility people would expect her to act like her grandmother hadn't occurred to Marty. Suddenly she felt alone and inadequate. Where was Paul? With his son, of course. Right where a father should be.

"Pastor is waving at us," Alice said. "He wants us to stand by the refreshments so people won't be as inclined to stand and chat. They'll want to get to the cake before it's all gone."

She winked, and Marty's apprehension faded. She didn't need Paul. But the fact she had wanted him startled her. She pushed Paul firmly out of her mind and took her place beside Pastor Ray. As Alice predicted, the line of people offering condolences moved fairly quickly. At first, she tried to associate names with faces, but her mind kept wandering away. Had Paul caught up with Scott? Was Scott really on drugs? Would Paul come back to the reception?

The occasional stories were the worst. At any other time, she would have been eager to hear them, but now she couldn't keep focused. Partway through a detailed description of how much a miniature Schnauzer loved her grandmother, Marty wondered how she was going to last until the end of the line. The answer that came was so simple she was surprised she hadn't thought of it before. Most of the people shaking her hand were Lois's contemporaries. Surely one of them remembered Ruthie's death.

A middle-aged woman told Marty how sorry she was. A young mother hanging onto a squirmy toddler offered her condolences. The next person in line was a woman who looked to be in her seventies, easily old enough to remember the events of twenty-two years ago. "This is Maude Lewis," Pastor Ray said. "She and Lois were in the Dorcas Circle together."

"It's not going to be the same with her gone," Maude said. "I'm so sorry you missed her."

An odd way to refer to finding her grandmother's body, but Marty nodded agreement.

Then she blurted, "Do you remember my sister?"

Maude frowned. "I didn't know there was another grandchild."

"She died about twenty years ago, when we were visiting Jerome."

"How sad!"

"You don't remember?"

"Oh, no, honey. I retired to the Verde Valley from Minnesota six years ago."

It went on like that. Names and faces changed. The length of the friendship changed, but none reached back far enough. The answer to the question about Ruthie was always the same: "Lois never mentioned another grandchild. I thought you were the only one."

Then, at the very end of the line, a woman stooped almost double with osteoporosis said, "I don't know anything about your sister, but Luella Hodges might. She and Lois were best friends for forty years."

Marty's heart began to beat more quickly. "Will you point her out to me?"

"Luella doesn't get out anymore. But I'm sure she'd be glad of a visit from you."

"Does she live in Jerome?"

"Oh, no, honey. Luella moved to Living Waters a year ago. Or maybe it was two. I imagine you remember, Pastor."

"It was almost three years ago," Pastor Ray said. "Shortly after I came here."

Marty looked up at the pastor, who was accepting a cup of coffee from Alice. "Living Waters?"

"A very nice assisted-living facility."

Alice handed Marty a cup of punch, no doubt because Lois would have preferred it to coffee. Marty would have preferred coffee, but the punch was liquid, and she accepted it gratefully.

239

Alice leaned down to be at eye level with the old woman. "May I get you some punch, Maude?"

"That would be lovely."

"There's cake too." Alice took Maude's arm and helped the old woman move away.

Marty sipped her 7 up and lime sherbet. "Is Living Waters far from here, Pastor?"

"Between here and Sedona."

"I'd like to visit Mrs. Hodges."

"A good idea. I know she wanted to be here today. Please take her one of the flower arrangements." He beckoned to Alice and then turned back to Marty. "Luella will be glad to see you, but don't expect too much. Time doesn't mean much anymore."

"Ruthie died twenty-two years ago. She might remember."

"She might. Just don't get your hopes up too high."

But how high was too high? Luella Hodges represented the first real hope Marty had felt since finding her grandmother's body.

Chapter Twenty-three

Marty was out of the building before she remembered she didn't have the keys to the Camry. The parking lot was almost empty, and Paul nowhere in sight. Balancing the basket of yellow lilies and purple gladioli in her left hand, she reached into her bag for her cell phone.

The bag slipped off her shoulder, and she almost dropped the flowers. Setting the arrangement on the ground, she retrieved her phone and punched in Paul's number. It rang once, twice, three times.

"This is Paul Russell."

"Paul!"

"Sorry I missed your call. Please leave a message." Good news in a way. Evidently Paul had caught up to Scott. *Thank you, God.*

As she disconnected, Brad came out of the building. "Marty! I'm glad you're still here. I didn't get a chance to talk to you at the reception. Do you have a few minutes?"

"I have many minutes, many more minutes than I know what to do with actually. I don't have the keys to my car."

"Any idea where you dropped them?"

"In Paul Russell's pocket. We came together."

"I assume you tried calling him."

"His phone goes to voicemail."

"Maybe he found his son." Brad picked up the basket of flowers and started toward his Lexus, which sat in solitary splendor on the opposite side of the parking lot from the forlorn white Camry. "Let me take you to dinner. If Paul hasn't called by the time we're finished, I'll run you home."

A nice offer, but the only person Marty wanted to talk to was Luella Hodges. "If you've got the time, I'd rather go to Living Waters."

"The assisted-living facility?"

"Yes. Do you know it?"

He stopped beside his car, handed her the flowers, and opened the door for her. "It's almost to Sedona. Two clients live there."

As she slid in, he opened the back door and positioned the flower arrangement on the floor. "Who are we going to see?"

"Luella Hodges."

As Brad closed her door, Marty settled back against the soft leather seat. The strong scent of lilies filled the car, and she wondered if Mrs. Hodges knew Lois had died. She was trying to decide if it was her responsibility to break the news when her cell phone dinged.

A text message. Paul had realized he had the keys. She reached for her cell phone.

Beware Granny's fate.

Granny Lois had died. Was this a death threat? Marty wanted to dismiss the message, but Paul's suggestion someone had deliberately pushed Lois made that impossible.

Brad got in behind the wheel. "A message from Paul?"

Marty shook her head and handed him the phone.

"'Beware Granny's fate.' What does it mean?"

"Granny Lois died. I guess someone's trying to scare me."

Brad gave her phone back and started the car. "I don't understand."

"Neither do I! This is the third anonymous text message I've gotten, and not one of them makes sense. I got the first one in Georgetown right before Granny Lois walked into my workshop. 'Beware the wolf in disguise.'"

"As in Little Red Riding Hood? You're kidding."

Marty shook her head. "The second one came the morning after someone locked me in the attic. 'Beware the ghost in disguise.'"

"What do you mean 'the morning after someone locked you in the attic?' This is the first I've heard about that."

"I didn't think it was worth mentioning. I thought it was a combination of my overactive imagination and an old house."

Brad stopped at the intersection of the street and the highway. Suddenly sorry she'd brought the text messages to Brad's attention, Marty watched a tumbleweed skitter after a black pickup. Whatever the messages meant, they were all connected to the frightening experiences she'd had in the Baker house. It was one thing to talk with Paul about what had been happening; he'd seen the aftermath of her tormentor's work. It was something else to try to explain to an attorney who was sure to cross-examine her.

"Now you think different. What aren't you telling me, Marty?"

There it was, the first of the questions she didn't want to answer. "Paul thinks I heard someone in the attic. I thought I fell and hit my head, but Paul thinks whoever was up there hit me and then locked me in so he, or she, could get away."

Paul thinks. What did she think? Marty wasn't sure. The known-intruder theory suddenly seemed as outlandish as the ghost theory. She couldn't believe Krystal or Carly had pushed her grandmother down the stairs. Paul didn't believe Scott had done it, and frankly, neither did she.

Surely there was a third interpretation. Brad wasn't involved the way she and Paul were. Maybe his perspective was exactly what they needed.

Involved the way she and Paul were? How about she, Paul, and Scott? Marty pushed the thought away, concentrated on where she was. Now was now. Friday at 5:00 p.m., Brad's Lexus in surprisingly heavy traffic.

"When did this happen?"

Marty shifted her attention from the stream of cars to Brad. He was frowning slightly.

"Tuesday night, early Wednesday morning."

"The first night you were in Jerome? I left you at the hotel."

"I woke up and walked back to the house. It was a silly thing to do, but I was keyed up. I knew I'd never go back to sleep."

Brad pulled into an opening between a motorcycle and a green sedan. "I heard about your poltergeist."

"Who told you about that?"

"No idea. Jerome has an amazingly efficient grapevine." Brad passed the cutoff to the interstate and kept straight toward Sedona. "When I put the poltergeist with a ghost in disguise in your attic, it sounds like you've been having quite a time in your new home."

New home. Was that what the Victorian house was? An old home, maybe.

"You'd better give me details."

"It's a long story." Or maybe it wasn't a story at all. Maybe it was only a series of unrelated incidents. Maybe that's what Brad would see.

"We've got at least a thirty-minute drive. Probably forty-five minutes or an hour in this traffic."

So she told him: the details of the attic encounter, the poltergeist and the wanton destruction, Krystal's enchanted kaleidoscope and Ruthie's presence, her fears, Paul's suspicions, their list of suspects.

When she finally stopped, Marty expected Brad to tell her to look at the facts and quit being so fanciful. Instead he said, "I can add one piece of information. While I don't know how the text messages fit into the overall picture, I do know who's been sending them."

Something about his tone made Marty afraid to ask.

"Maybe you do too."

"No." But she could guess who he was going to name. "Scott Russell."

Marty's throat closed. Paul had seen the cell number when she showed him the second message, "Beware the ghost in disguise." He had to know his son's number. Were the questions about Krystal and Carly simply meant to protect his son? But why would he pretend to investigate? Why bring up the idea Lois had been purposely killed?

She cleared her throat. "How do you know?"

"I recognize the number."

"How?"

"Lois was possibly the most organized client I've ever had. She had contingency plans for every eventuality. When she gave me her power of attorney in case she ever became unable to make her own decisions, she designated Scott to take Rahab if she couldn't care for the cat. She gave me his cell phone number. I have a good memory for numbers and Scott's follows a predictable pattern: 928-982-2892."

Marty touched "recent calls" on the cell phone in her hand, checked the last one. Brad had recited it perfectly.

❧

Living Waters turned out to be a rambling white frame structure perched on a bluff above the Verde River. A white portico protected the front door from the elements. Brad pulled under the cover and shifted into neutral. "Take the flowers and check us in. I'll park and join you before you finish filling out our nametags."

Marty got out and retrieved the flowers from the back seat. A perfectly sensible plan, but it annoyed her. She didn't like having an agenda spelled out for her as though she were a secretary. But she could hardly object when Brad had rearranged his evening to bring her here.

She wasn't usually so touchy. She was just tense about meeting Mrs. Hodges, afraid the old lady wouldn't remember, afraid she would.

Marty maneuvered herself and the flowers through double glass doors into a large, airy room decorated in pale blue and mauve. Wingback chairs upholstered in coordinating florals were arranged in pairs on either side of small glass-topped tables. The reception desk, a large, polished oak semicircle, took up one side of the room.

The woman who sat there, "Nancy" according to her nametag, had mahogany skin and curly hair cut short. "May I help you?"

"I'd like to see Luella Hodges."

A look of consternation passed so quickly across the other woman's face, Marty wasn't sure she'd seen it. "Does Mrs. Hodges know you?"

"Not exactly. She knew my grandmother."

Nancy smiled. "You must be Mrs. Baker's granddaughter, Martha."

Marty returned the smile ruefully. The fact the receptionist knew the story shouldn't have surprised her, but it did.

Nancy explained. "Honey, Miss Lois came every week to see Miss Luella. For the entire last year, your grandma talked about finding you, how maybe you grew up in Massachusetts or maybe in Idaho. Maybe you were married with three precious kiddies. Maybe you were a career woman. I heard you turned out to be an author from Virginia."

Marty laughed. "Not exactly an author. I repair antique furniture. I wrote a simple handbook for beginners."

"Well whatever it was, Miss Lois was proud as punch of you. She was a sweet, sweet lady, and I was sorry to hear of her passing. I would've come to the funeral, but I was scheduled to work this afternoon. I imagine there was a large crowd."

Tears Marty hadn't cried at the funeral sprang to her eyes. Absurd how the phrase "proud as punch" affected her. More than the house, more than the diary even, those three words made her feel the loss of her grandmother. They would have been friends.

"The flowers are lovely, Miss Martha. I imagine you brought them from the funeral."

Marty took a breath and swallowed her tears. "Pastor Ray thought they might help Mrs. Hodges feel like she got to participate, at least a little bit."

"That sounds like Pastor Ray. He comes to see Miss Luella once a month. But I'm not sure that's such a good idea."

"What's not such a good idea?" Brad said, taking the flowers from Marty.

"Giving these to Mrs. Hodges."

"Evening, Mr. Lockridge. We haven't told Miss Luella Miss Lois passed."

"Why not? I'm sure she'd want to know."

Nancy picked up a telephone from the desk. "I'll let Kathy explain. She's in charge of resident care this evening."

Marty felt herself tensing up again. "Keep the flowers here or take them to the dining room. We don't need to talk about the funeral. I just want to visit."

Brad touched Marty's arm. "I know these people. Let me handle it."

"Hello! Welcome to Living Waters." A middle-aged woman dressed in navy slacks and a blue and white jacket crossed the lobby toward them.

Brad put the flowers on the reception desk and offered his hand. "Good to see you, Kathy. This is Marty Greenlaw, Lois Baker's granddaughter."

Kathy shook Brad's hand and then turned to Marty. "We all loved Lois, honey. We're so sorry for your loss."

"Thank you. I'd like to see Luella Hodges. I want to ask her about something that happened in Jerome when I was a little girl."

"She might be able to help you, or she might not. It's hard to say what she'll remember on any given day."

Brad put a hand under Marty's elbow. "I understand you haven't told her about Lois's death."

"As soon as Luella asks about Lois, we'll explain. Until then, we don't want to upset her unnecessarily."

"We understand," Marty said quickly. "I only need a few minutes with Mrs. Hodges, and I only want to talk with her about the past. Please put the flowers somewhere everyone can enjoy them."

Kathy looked relieved. "Luella is in the garden room on the second floor. The elevator is just past the dining room."

Walking down the hall with Brad, Marty fought a rising surge of panic. When they were on the elevator and starting up, Brad broke the silence. "Instinct tells me there's something at stake with this conversation. Mind telling me what it is?"

"You remember that first night at dinner I asked you if you knew why my grandmother put me up for adoption?"

"Yes."

"I have to find the answer to that question."

"Because?"

Marty took a deep breath. "Because I'm afraid my little sister's death was my fault. I'm afraid that's why my grandmother couldn't bear to have me around. I have to find out."

The elevator stopped, and the door slid open. Marty forced herself to look up and meet Brad's eyes.

"Pretty high stakes. I'm sure you're wrong. Lois would have told me about something that dramatic, but let's go see what Luella has to say."

They found the garden room at the end of the hall. The last rays of the June sun slanted through lowered venetian blinds, painting the beige carpet with stripes of light and shadow. The only occupant, her head dropped forward, dozed in a high-backed wicker chair. She had to be Luella Hodges.

Marty pushed an ottoman close to the old woman's chair and sat down. Brad went to the window and pulled up the blinds.

"Mrs. Hodges," Marty said. "May we talk to you?"

When the woman didn't stir, Marty tried a second time. After a third failed attempt to rouse the woman, Brad said, "Mind if I give it a try?"

"Go ahead."

"Wake up, Luella!"

The old woman stirred and raised her head. "What?"

Marty leaned close so the woman could see her face. "Mrs. Hodges. We're friends of Lois Baker. We'd like to talk to you for a few minutes."

The old woman patted Marty's cheek with a hand as dry as tissue paper. "You're teasing me, honey. Just like you always have. I know exactly who you are. You're Ellie Baker, Jimmy's wife."

Her mother. The old woman thought she was her mother. The thought took Marty's breath away. If she studied her reflection in the mirror, would she remember Mommy? "No," she began.

"Yes," Brad said. "That's right. May we talk to you for a few minutes?"

Marty looked up at Brad, but he was watching the old woman.

Luella ignored Brad, focused on Marty. "Where are the little girls? Martha and Ruth Ann. Didn't you bring them to see me?"

"No," Brad said. "Not this time."

"I suppose Lois wanted to keep them. She dotes on those two children."

Here they were in the past, where Marty wanted to be, but suddenly she was mute with dread. What if her fears were right?

Brad seemed to sense her reaction because he dropped his hands on her shoulders. "Martha's with Lois. But we haven't been able to find little Ruth Ann. We're hoping you know where she is."

Luella's hands went to her face. "Oh, no," she moaned. "Not today! We're always afraid for the children. All over town. We warn them and warn them, but the little ones don't understand."

"What don't they understand?" Brad said.

"The mine shafts. Everywhere underground, abandoned tunnels can give way. Poor Ruthie. Poor precious little Ruthie." Luella started to cry.

Marty couldn't breathe. "Be careful, girls," warned Granny Lois. "Don't go outside the fence."

Chapter Twenty-four

Marty walked out of Living Waters into a sunset as brilliant as the one she and Brad had watched from the Asylum restaurant. But down here on the valley floor, she walked through the sunset. Above, ahead, behind, right, left—red, magenta, orange, gold, copper—colors so vibrant they sucked the air from her lungs. The way smoke from a forest fire would. How many miles had the wind carried this sunset?

Brad was already in the Lexus. He'd taken off his suit jacket and tie. The neck of his shirt was open and the sleeves rolled up enough to show muscular forearms. Leaning across the seat, he opened her door and she got in. As she buckled her seatbelt, he said, "It's clear Mrs. Hodges knows what happened to your sister. What's not clear is whether she can ever articulate it. Did what she said jog your memory?"

Marty had had enough of the past for one day, but he deserved an answer. "A little. Not enough."

"And you don't want to talk about it."

"I'm sorry, Brad. I don't mean to be rude."

"Not a problem." He put his hands on the steering wheel but didn't start the car. "Any word from Paul?"

Marty dug through her bag for the phone and checked for messages. "Nothing." Not that she wanted to talk to Paul Russell. He could keep the car. She needed time to assimilate

251

the information Brad had given her about Scott. What the phone number might mean. She powered the phone off and dropped it in her bag.

"I'd like to take you to my house. It's not far and it has no connection with your past. I could throw a couple of steaks on the grill."

She didn't want to go. Her annoyance with Brad had dissipated, but she needed to be alone. "Thank you, but I'd really rather go home." Home. Suddenly Marty yearned for the safety of home. But where was home?

"I don't think the Baker house can feel much like home now. It sounds like an almost violent place. My house, on the other hand, is peaceful. It's in the red rocks overlooking a golf course. If you come, I'll run you back whenever you're ready."

Her resolve weakened. "On one condition."

"I promise I won't make a pass at you."

She smiled. "Actually, that wasn't what I was thinking. My condition is no steaks."

"How about pork chops? Ever had them on the grill?"

"No, but it sounds like a great idea."

He turned on the ignition. "Let me make sure I understand. As long as I don't offer you a bloody steak, it's okay to make a pass at you."

Marty laughed.

"I'm crushed. Women don't usually laugh at me!"

"They throw themselves in your arms, right?"

"You bet!"

She laughed again. It felt good to laugh, and for the first time all day, she relaxed.

As they left Living Waters behind, the long driveway dropped toward the Verde River and the last of the desert. Brad stopped at the junction of the two-lane highway that led to Sedona and then on to Flagstaff. "Mind if I put the top down?"

Marty looked curiously at the roof over her head, solid, not like a convertible top.

Brad laughed and pressed a button. "This roof looks like a hardtop because it is. This car is a hardtop convertible."

As the roof slid silently back, the wind streamed into the car, plucking at the scarf Sofia had given her, stroking her face, fondling her hair. Giving in to it, Marty took off the shawl and stuffed it in the bag at her feet. Grateful the wind made conversation impossible, she leaned back against the headrest and watched the canyon rush toward them.

And remembered the stories people had told about Lois at the funeral: a young mother who left her newborn with Lois while she searched for the best day care option; a widow who stayed with Lois for the first nights after her husband died; a young man who earned much needed money by doing odd jobs for Lois while he recuperated from chemotherapy; a fan who attended every Bible study Lois led. Stories that had nothing to do with her. Stories that made her miss the grandmother she had forgotten for twenty-two years.

Forgotten or refused to remember? Marty pushed the question away and concentrated on not thinking, on memorizing the way the gathering dusk deepened the salmon pink standing stones of the canyon ahead to rose and then to russet. Brad drove faster than the speed limit, skillfully passing the few cars on this stretch of highway. In a little while the road began to climb, not in switchbacks, in a long, lazy s-curve like a meandering river.

The Lexus slowed, and Brad switched on the headlights. "Not much farther."

Marty had the impression of the outskirts of town, a few structures scattered on the right side of the highway, then on both sides, and then closer and closer together. In the distance a traffic light glowed green. "Is this Sedona?"

"Legally, no. Functionally, yes." Brad slowed even more and made a quick left turn across oncoming traffic that made Marty catch her breath. "You're missing the full effect of this side canyon. You'll have to come back in daylight."

Marty wasn't sure why she didn't respond. Why wouldn't she want to come back?

Evidently Brad's invitation was rhetorical because he seemed not to notice her silence. "I have no idea how much you know about canyons, but often they're like rivers, a main canyon cut by the largest river and side canyons cut by tributaries. Enchanted Canyon is a side canyon that's large enough to accommodate a nine-hole golf course."

The Lexus followed a narrow road that twisted and turned between walls bleached of color by dusk as it eased into night. A red Humvee passed them, heading toward the road. Brad tapped his horn lightly, and the shadowy figure in the other vehicle did the same. The deeper they drove into the canyon, the narrower the space between the walls. When it seemed as though the road would dead-end at a wall, Marty saw a brightly lit guardhouse with metal arms stretched across the road on both sides.

Brad brought the car to a smooth stop and raised a hand in greeting. The guard, a bald man with a surprisingly deep voice, called out, "Good to see you, Mr. Lockridge." The metal arm on their side swung up.

Brad turned his head to look at her. "Twenty-four-hour guard service."

"I'm surprised. Do you have much crime?"

"No. It's pretty tame around here."

Except when someone pushes an old lady down a flight of stairs in her own home. But Brad hadn't commented on her story or the theory there was a pattern that added up to murder. His only response had been to suggest Scott was the author of the anonymous text messages. Did that mean he thought Scott was behind all of it, even Lois's death, or did it mean he considered the idea of murder too ridiculous to have an opinion on? They had arrived at Living Waters before she could ask his opinion of her story.

"Are you a golfer?"

The question, so out of step with her thoughts, startled her. "I took a few lessons once." To please Ted. Correction, to try to please Ted. "I wasn't exactly a natural."

"How about tennis?"

"I played a lot in college but not much the last few years."

"Ever played on a clay court?"

"Once or twice. Not enough to really get the hang of it, but I liked it."

"You'll have to come back and play here."

There it was again, an invitation or an order to come back? For the second time, Marty didn't respond. What was wrong with her? Brad was an attractive, interesting man. And Brad didn't have any children.

The canyon widened suddenly, and they emerged out of the shadows of the walls into the last of the dusk. Just ahead, the road divided in three directions. Brad took the left branch. Soon after they came to a Y. Again, Brad steered left. In a moment, the road began to climb steeply.

"My house is the last one on this road. Because it's built relatively close to the rim, it offers a unique view of the canyon."

The third story of Enchanted Canyon, where the rich people live. Somewhere in the attic of Marty's mind, Mommy laughed softly.

They passed two houses, one lighted, the other dark. Brad shifted into low. "It's a good thing we don't get snow down this far. Once in a while we get a dusting. Enough to create a photographer's paradise, but not enough to affect the road."

They climbed another quarter of a mile before he pulled into a driveway. "Here we are." He set the emergency brake and turned off the headlights. Uninterrupted darkness settled around them. No street lights, no neighbors with lighted windows, no lights on in Brad's house.

He opened the car door, but with the top down, no overhead light came on. As the shadowy figure beside her got out and came around the front of the car, Marty felt strangely vulnerable. Absurd. Still, she reached for her shawl. She didn't have time to do more than swing it around her shoulders before Brad opened her door.

Taking her hands, he helped her out. "The sensor light over the front door will come on in a second."

Silly to feel uneasy, but she didn't wait while he closed her door. She moved toward the house. It took three steps before the sensor caught her motion. Yellow light, the kind adopted by dark sky communities, illuminated the driveway with its hand-laid pink swirls, the tiny, xeriscaped front yard, the wide steps up to tall, double doors.

She was almost to the steps when he caught her. Putting his hands on her arms, he turned her towards him. He was about to kiss her when she pushed him away. "Brad Lockridge, you promised."

"I promised no bloody steaks."

"I mean it. I'm not in the mood for flirting tonight. We had a verbal contract."

He caught the scarf around her shoulders and pulled it off. "You've got a sense of humor, even when you're angry. I like that in a woman."

She held out her hand for the scarf. "I'm not kidding. If you won't honor our agreement, then take me back to Jerome right now."

Brad laughed. "All right. I was just testing to see where the boundaries were."

"Now you know."

"Now I know." He put the shawl around her shoulders and tied it loosely.

"Thank you."

"You're welcome." He kissed her lightly on the forehead and turned away.

Marty followed him up four stone steps to a wide landing not large enough to qualify as a porch. As he unlocked the double doors, carved figures in the surface of the wood caught her eye: saguaro, horses, quail, a roadrunner. With her finger, she traced a coyote howling at a moon only it could see.

"An artist named Roger Hill did these doors," Brad said as he swung the door open. "Sedona's an art community, three or four rungs up from what you find in Jerome."

He went in, and lights came on.

Marty's first impression of the house was space. There was a vaulted ceiling with exposed beams, an expanse of shining hardwood floor, glass on one side of a wide room, stone on the other, and arched doorways open to rooms beyond.

Brad pointed a remote control at an oak entertainment center, and the haunting sounds of a single flute filled the room. "Carlos Nakai. No one plays Native American flute better."

Not so much a melody as a bird's lonely cry. Or maybe the music just seemed lonely in the vast room.

Brad tossed his keys on a low table made from a polished slab of redwood and a twisted juniper pedestal. "I'll get started on dinner. Feel free to take the self-guided tour. This level is the living space. Bedrooms are downstairs."

"I'm glad to help in the kitchen."

"No need. I have it all under control." He disappeared through one of the arches into a shadowy room. In a moment, a light came on through another arch, and Marty caught a glimpse of the kitchen.

Glad to have a few minutes to herself, Marty let out a breath she hadn't realized she was holding. Hitching her bag on her shoulder, she began a leisurely circuit of the living room. To her right, floor-to-ceiling glass framed the last light above a massive rock wall that must be the end of the canyon.

She opened a sliding door and stepped out onto a wide redwood deck with an unobstructed view of the golf course below. The deck was furnished like an outdoor room with a gas grill, glass table, metal chairs, and a glider with aqua and rose cushions. The air was soft and cool, and Marty hoped Brad intended on eating out here. Curious to see the rest of the house, she went back in.

In the center of the living room, a leather sectional couch faced the entertainment center. A built-in shelf next to the entertainment center held a small bronze statue of a cowboy on a rearing horse. Another low redwood table, long enough to hold its own in front of the sofa, held several issues of *Arizona Highways*. Closely woven Navajo rugs in muted reds and browns were scattered across the floor.

Marty thought of Paul's house with its sagging floors and the wall Paul had knocked out to make the living room larger. Truly a hovel when compared to this opulence. But given a choice, at the moment she would rather be there. Absurd. She pushed Paul out of her mind.

The other end of the room wasn't a conventional wall but a double-sided stone fireplace that divided the living room from the dining room. Above the fireplace hung an oil painting of six or eight Indians on horseback. Rifles raised over their heads in defiance, they seemed to be riding through fog straight into the room. An odd image, strangely disturbing.

Marty turned away and headed for the stairs. Lights came on automatically as she moved through the house.

The master bedroom was directly under the living room. A king-sized bed covered with a brown velvet spread and salmon, rose and russet throw pillows seemed almost small in the oversized room. Double glass sliding doors looked out at the canyon, but down here the golf course dominated the view. A smaller deck held a large hot tub, covered now. Through an open door, she glimpsed a glass and Brazilian marble bathroom.

A second bedroom was set up as a home office with bookshelves, a large mahogany desk amazingly free of clutter and a closed laptop. The entire house was like the office, nothing out of place. Like her house. According to Ted, the house of a control freak. But she wasn't a control freak. She just couldn't think clearly in a muddle. She'd always been like that.

Always? In that place in the attic of her mind where the long-ago past was coming to life, Marty heard Granny Lois say, "Look, girls. I got you a toy box. Every evening, you pick everything up and put it in here. That way no one will trip at night." Surely that was what happened to Granny Lois. Surely Paul was wrong. Surely she tripped in the dark.

The third bedroom was a surprise. Set up like a museum, it housed a variety of collections. A tall set of narrow shelves held a dozen wooden figures identified by a label as "Hopi Kachina Effigies." The figures were dressed in a variety of costumes, only a few that Marty recognized. A clown, a wolf, an eagle. A display case contained a collection of antique guns. Three waist-high pedestals held small bronze statues of horses and riders in different poses.

She was looking at a coin collection displayed in a jewel case with black velvet shelves that turned slowly when Brad called down the stairs. "Five-minute warning!"

Marty left the little museum reluctantly, but she knew she wouldn't have to search for topics of conversation. She made a stop in the guest bathroom to freshen up and then went upstairs.

As she had hoped, Brad was outside. Yellow lights up under the eaves and along the railing created a soft glow that made it easy to see without overpowering the darkness beyond. The table was set with silverware rolled up in loosely woven napkins in the now-familiar shades of the red rocks. The plates were square, heavy pottery glazed a deep red-brown. A tall glass of iced tea sat at each place, and a basket of bread waited in the center of the table. The man was not only neat, he was organized.

As he pulled out a chair for her, Brad said, "So you found something interesting downstairs?"

"You know I did! I want you to tell me about your collections."

The grin he gave her made him look Scott's age. Scott Russell. Why couldn't she get father and son out of her mind this evening?

Brad handed her a plate with three pork chops on it. "My raison d'être."

Maybe Brad Lockridge had a more appealing side than she had seen. Maybe what she had seen of him so far was a part he played, the part of resourceful attorney, the go-to guy for all problems.

Marty chose a pork chop and set the plate beside the bread basket. Grilled corn was next, each cob already buttered and nestled in a specially molded plate. Last came a plate with thick slices of fresh pineapple grilled so the edges were crispy.

Suddenly she was hungry. "What a lovely meal. I didn't think I could eat after the cake and punch, but this looks delicious."

Brad sat directly across from her. "Not quite so sorry you didn't demand I take you home?"

"Was I that obvious?"

"You were. I don't blame you. I put the wrong foot forward. I hope you'll give me another chance."

"It depends."

He looked taken aback. "On what?"

"On what you have planned for dessert."

He laughed then, and Marty relaxed. Maybe this was just what she needed, a casual evening not focused on her problems or Paul's. Paul again. She cut a bite of the pork chop and thought about Brad, "Tell me about one of your collections."

"All different aspects of a single collection. Ghosts of the Wild West. We're not far from it here. Arizona was the last of the lower 48 to become a state in 1912."

"I see how the bronzes fit and the guns. And the Indians, especially the picture over the fireplace."

"One of a series the artist calls his 'ghost cycle.'"

Marty pushed delicate silver holders into each end of her corn. "What about the coins?"

"My first collection. Nothing to do with the Old West. Maybe the ghost of my childhood." He moved the last pork chop from the serving plate to his own.

She waited for him to explain. When he didn't, she said, "You can't end with a teaser."

He gave her that grin again. "I guess not. I was ten. My parents had just gotten divorced, the tired old story of an alcoholic father and an incompetent mother. The first summer after the divorce, my mother got us kicked out of our apartment for non-payment of rent. I stayed with my grandfather, her father, in Colorado while she found us a place to live.

"He took me to the Denver Mint and bought me a starter set of silver dollars from that year, 1992. He told me it was

261

worth the face value of the coins, about $10, but it would be worth a lot more if I kept them until I was an old man like him. Especially if history repeated itself."

"I don't know what you mean."

"A piece of coin collector trivia. In 1919, the U.S. government called in all silver dollars to melt them down for the war effort." He snorted. "Of course, not everyone cooperated. The hoarders were eventually rewarded handsomely for their civil disobedience."

"Silver dollars from before 1919 became a rare commodity."

"Scarce as hen's teeth but considerably more valuable."

"Do you have any in your collection?"

"A few. They don't show up on the market very often."

"What about the silver dollars your grandfather bought you. Do you still have them?"

"Yes, ma'am. They became valuable without the government's help."

Marty raised her eyebrows and waited for the punch line.

"My grandfather died three years ago and left me all his money, contingent on my ability to produce the 1992 proof set. It was a small fortune, enough to buy this house with some left over."

Marty contemplated the golf course and the dark wall of rock that brooded over it. She wasn't sure exactly why, but the story personalized the magazine layout setting and the interior decorator's dream house she had just toured. "Thank you, Brad."

"For the meal? You're welcome."

"For the story."

"Rags to riches, always a popular theme."

"I mean it, Brad. I feel like I know you a lot better now than I did ten minutes ago."

"Good. It's your turn. Tell me about a life-shaping incident from your childhood."

The copper box.

Chapter Twenty-five

Paul watched the headlights waver as the invisible car negotiated the dirt road and wondered what time it was. Ten or eleven. Marty wasn't exactly out past curfew.

With fits and starts, the moon struggled out from behind a cloud. Or smoke. Either way the pale light caught the car as it approached, a silver Lexus with the top down. Brad Lockridge's car. Of course.

The Lexus made the sharp turn into Lois's driveway smoothly and glided to a stop behind the white Camry. Lockridge got out. Marty opened her door a split second later. She was out of the car and had her door closed before he reached her. Paul couldn't see Brad's reaction from this distance, but he imagined the other man shrugging.

Marty pointed at the Camry, and Lockridge moved to the driver's side. The interior light glowed briefly, a firefly on the dark hillside. For a moment, Paul wished he hadn't left the keys in it. Marty would have had to come to him to get in the house. Or send Lockridge over.

Disgusted with himself, Paul got up and went inside. Fine to give himself permission to be attracted to Marty. Ridiculous to act Scott's age.

What now? He could always work on his book. He should work on his book. Three weeks into the summer and he was already significantly behind his writing schedule. He went upstairs to his study, turned on the laptop, opened the file, and tried to remember what was supposed to come next.

Fifteen minutes later, Paul put the laptop to sleep and went back downstairs to the kitchen. He took a bottle of water out of the refrigerator and opened it. Where was Scott now? At the Kenyon cabin? Wherever he was, Paul prayed he was safe.

He took a long drink and went back out on the porch. Had he allowed hope to get the better of good sense when he gave permission for Scott to go to Flagstaff? Would Scott have come home if he'd refused permission?

The Lexus was gone. She had sent Lockridge away. Would she do the same to him if he knocked on her door? He should apologize for leaving her waiting at the church.

He noticed the pun, and it was enough to break his mood. So what if she sent him away? So what if she slammed the door in his face? He finished his water and started for the Baker house. He was across the road at the bottom of the driveway when he heard a sound that didn't belong, a sound like bells. Not church bells, wind chimes. But he was sure Lois didn't have a set of wind chimes. "The wind blows too hard on this mountain," she said when he offered her a set Linda had loved. "I'd be forever taking them down." Had Marty bought some? Unlikely.

The sound came again. Pitched lower than wind chimes. And louder. As if someone hit copper pipes tuned to each other. It came from behind the house. Not from the back porch, the house would have absorbed the sound. Curious, he followed the tones.

As he came around the side of the house, the chimes tolled again, a ball of light bounced along the ground, and a scrap of white fluttered in the breeze out by the old mine shaft. Someone was playing tricks again, deadly tricks this time. He only hoped Marty wouldn't see. Or if she saw wouldn't come out to investigate.

Too late. Almost at the instant he thought of her, he heard her shout, "Scott Russell! Stop trying to scare me!"

Not Scott. Scott was in Flagstaff. No matter who was out there, it was time to catch the culprit. Paul sprinted around the fenced-in backyard. Whatever was going on was happening out on the open hillside. The incline was slight, but it was enough to confuse his stride. Paul's right foot landed on a rock, sharp through the thin sole of his worn-out tennis shoes. He lurched, lost momentum, pushed harder.

The gibbous moon peeked out to reveal someone else running toward the mine, someone much closer than he was. "Marty!" he bellowed. "Go back!"

Too late again. He saw her trip, stagger toward the old wooden fencing. He wanted to move faster, get there before what he dreaded happened. But he was moving in slow motion. His left foot caught on a kudzu vine at the same moment the fence around the collapsed mine shaft gave way.

Marty fell. For one chilling moment, he thought he was witnessing the very catastrophe he'd warned Scott about. Paul was afraid she'd gone into the sinkhole head first. The moon peeked out, illuminated the figure on the edge of the dark hole. As he watched, she tried to sit up.

"Don't move!" He stumbled, recovered his balance, kept moving.

He was close enough to hear her groan, but at least she stayed put. He kicked a rock, swayed, very nearly went down. Tottering like a drunken fool, he reached her. He should check her for broken bones, but there wasn't time. Doing more damage was the lesser of two evils. Any moment now, the edge of the shaft would give way. *Please, Father!*

He gathered her in his arms, breathed, "I have to move you. Don't try to help. Go limp if you can."

She cooperated. He half-carried, half-dragged her back from the edge. Not a second too soon. As they clung to each other, the earth parted where she had fallen, parted and disappeared into itself, sucking dirt, rocks, boards, anything and everything within reach, sucking it all into the depths of a new sinkhole.

Marty stared at the gap that had opened at their feet, whispered "Ruthie." She turned her head, hid her face against his chest. "That's what happened to Ruthie. Here." She began to tremble.

He held her carefully, murmured, "You're safe. Ruthie was in the past. She's at peace. You're safe."

Marty clung to him, drew a ragged breath. Another. The third breath was better. She loosened her grasp, began to untangle herself from his arms.

Voice shaky, she said, "You keep reading my mind."

"A survival skill required of all teachers."

"So that's it. You can let me go now."

Reluctantly he loosened his grip on her. "I should call 911, get Glenn to come up and take a look at you."

"And have the fire truck scream all the way to my front door? I'm all right now."

"Can you wiggle your toes?"

"Yes."

"Stand on one foot, rotate your ankle."

"I'm okay, Paul."

"Humor me. Turn your head from side to side."

She shrugged, obeyed.

"Does that make you dizzy?"

"No. I'm fine. Honest."

He let her go, brushed the top of her head with his lips, so much less than he wanted to do. Now was not the time. But soon.

Paul put an arm around her shoulders, meant to support her, pulled her close, almost blurted "Thank the Lord, you're not hurt, darling." He took a deep breath. "Ready to go back?"

Sometime in the last few minutes, clouds had shrouded the moon, so he felt rather than saw her nod. But they had only gone a few steps when her knees buckled. Because he still had his arm around her, he was able to keep her from going down.

"Sorry," she said. "My left leg hurts."

He squatted and ran his hands along her leg. The knee of her sweat pants was wet, not damp, soaking wet. "You're bleeding!"

"A skinned knee."

He reached for his cell phone. He hardly had it out of his pocket when she snatched it. "No fire truck! I mean it, Paul. I've had all I can take."

He didn't argue with her, just picked her up and started for the house.

"Put me down!"

The moon chose that moment to emerge from the clouds, giving him just enough light to see the treacherous kudzu and steer around rocks larger than a baseball. Miracle or coincidence, Paul was grateful.

"I can walk."

"Hush. You're light as a feather, but I don't have enough breath to carry you and argue."

She laughed weakly and put her arm around his neck. For one crazy moment, he thought she might kiss him. Not that, but she let her head rest on his shoulder, almost as good.

The moon shared its meager light long enough for him to maneuver through the gate in the chain link fence and make his way across the yard. As he carried her up onto the back porch, it went back behind the clouds.

"You can put me down now."

"In a minute. Open the screen door."

He expected her to object again. Especially since he'd barked a command. When she simply complied, he knew she had to be in pain. He carried her into the bright kitchen. Blinking against the light, he went to the big oak table and set her down. Light as a feather, but he was out of breath.

Pale and shaky, Marty stared at the torn leg of her sweatpants. "Looks like more than a skinned knee."

He didn't bother to answer. "What do you have on under your joggers?"

"My pajamas."

About to climb over the railing upstairs and swing down a rope made of tattered sheets and threadbare drapes. Paul pushed the memory away. "Okay, then. Let's find out how deep that cut is."

He gave her the most encouraging smile he could summon. Whether she liked it or not, if she was still losing blood, he would call 911. "Let's get you out of those pants so we can look at your leg. It'll be easier to pull them down from your waist than try to cut the leg off. Agreed?"

She nodded.

"Can you stand on your right leg?"

She nodded.

"Okay. I'll hold you up while you get out of the sweatpants. Ready?"

She took a deep breath. "Ready."

He helped her stand, put his arm around her back, and braced her against his side. She took another deep breath and pulled at the sweatpants. Luckily the blood was still wet enough the fabric didn't stick too badly. Nonetheless, by the time she sat back down in the chair and he had the pants away from her feet, she was trembling.

"Okay?"

She nodded.

"All right. Let's take a look." The knee wasn't skinned, the flesh had been peeled away. A deep abrasion down the outside of her leg was bright with blood.

He caught her eye. "I really think we need to call Dr. Zimbelman. If you don't want the fire truck, I'll call him directly."

She shook her head. "Tomorrow. I promise. It looks worse than it is. Let's just clean it up."

He was about to refuse when she touched his arm. His resolve crumbled. She wasn't his child. She was a grown woman, not even his wife. "I don't suppose you know where we could find any first aid supplies."

Even to his own ears his voice sounded harsh, but she ignored the tone, accepted the words. "I noticed some things under the sink in the hall bathroom upstairs."

"All right, ma'am. Up you go." Against her protestations, he lifted her in his arms and carried her. She didn't comment as they climbed past the broken spindles, but he could almost hear her thoughts echo his: Why would someone push an old lady?

He found antibacterial soap, gauze, and an elastic bandage. Clean-up and disinfecting took about fifteen minutes. By the end of the process, she was even paler than she had been. "Where to, ma'am?"

"I've moved into Lois's room. I can walk."

"I'm sure you can, but why bother when you have a palanquin at your beck and call?" He picked her up, and this time she made no objection. He deposited her carefully on the bed.

She looked exhausted. "You're sweet, Paul. Thank you."

"How about a cup of warm milk?"

"I'd rather have a glass of water and two aspirin."

He chuckled. "Much more practical." He found them in Lois's bathroom. As she swallowed the aspirin, he said, "I want to go outside and look around a bit, but if you've got the energy, I'd like to hear what happened first."

She nodded toward the wingback chair. He sat. The chair was too small to be really comfortable, but he didn't expect to be there long. He stretched out his legs and gave her a questioning look.

She sighed and leaned back against the pillows. "I was in here getting ready for bed when I heard a sound like a bell. It came from somewhere outside, and it gave me an odd feeling, as though something was about to happen. I told myself I was imagining things, that I was overtired from the day. I ignored it.

"Then I heard it again. Curious, I went to the French doors to look out back. That's when I saw a light, a ball of light really. At first I couldn't tell if the light was reflecting on the glass of the door or if it was outside. I wasn't afraid, just puzzled.

"The light seemed to be on the porch, so I went out to see what was causing it. At first I thought it was gone, then I spotted it out in the yard. At the same time, something white danced at the edge of the mine.

"That made me mad. I knew someone was playing another ghost game with me. I pulled on my sweats and my sneakers and went downstairs. I was headed out the back door when I heard the bell again, except this time it kept ringing."

"Like wind chimes."

Marty nodded. "I thought it must be . . ."

"Scott," he finished for her. "I heard you shout his name."

"I thought he was out there, trying to scare me again." She paused. "I guess that's when I got confused. All I could think was Ruthie was out there and she was about to fall into the mine. I had to save her.

"I started running. The light kept flashing. It got in my eyes, and I fell really hard." She took a long shuddering breath.

271

"That's when I heard you shout my name. I don't know what would have happened if you hadn't called out just then." Her voice trailed off.

Paul didn't want to think about the near miss any more than she wanted to verbalize it. Getting to his feet, he closed the distance between them. "Never mind." This time he didn't fight his feelings. He leaned down and kissed her gently, just to let her know he was grateful he'd been there at the right moment.

She didn't seem surprised, returned the kiss in the spirit it was given. Her lips were soft, and he wanted more. But it was enough for now. "You get some sleep. I'm going to see what I can find out about this intruder."

"Be careful."

He smiled and brushed her cheek with the back of his hand. She blushed a soft pink. Was it too much to hope she returned his feelings, at least a little? Abruptly he turned off the lamp and headed for the door.

"There's a flashlight in the pantry."

"Don't worry about me. Sleep." He caught the "darling" and managed to swallow it. Not now. But soon.

He found the flashlight, a heavy-duty model with a powerful bulb that was just what he would have expected in Lois's pantry, sufficient for any serious power outage. He switched it on and let himself quietly out the back door. No doubt the perpetrator was long gone. Paul didn't know what he was looking for, but he was ready to confront whoever was playing this deadly game. After tonight's near escape, he knew they were dealing with someone who wouldn't hesitate to kill again. He just wished he knew what the faceless figure wanted. Something in the house. Something more valuable than human life to the culprit.

The clouds were still playing cat and mouse with the moon, giving the scene a restless feel. Paul swept the area with his light. The chain link fence reflected briefly, then he was out of the gate and checking the hillside. Kudzu, rocks, broken wooden fencing, the sinkhole. Nothing to give him a clue to how the trick, if "trick" was the right word, had been accomplished.

Higher on the hill, his light caught another wooden fence. The mine entrance. Of course. A perfect place to hide equipment. Following the strong beam of his light, he covered the ground reasonably quickly. Not that he expected to find the culprit lurking in the mine. But he needed to walk off some of the tension. He was tired of puzzling out clues. He wanted to act.

He was almost to the fence around the mine entrance when his light picked out a small white sign. The black outline of skull and crossbones made the hair on Paul's neck stand up. More than anything he'd encountered so far, that symbol captured the essence of the person he was tracking. Because that's what he was doing. Tonight, he'd seen the danger first-hand, and he was sure the goal had been to kill. From here on out, he was on a collision course with the murderer.

His light skipped across a broken place in the rickety fence. Paul steadied the beam so he could step over. He moved with care, examining each inch of ground before taking a step. At the mine entrance, the ground was packed hard and smooth from years of use. He ducked to keep from hitting his head on the crossbeam, but inside the ceiling soared up into the dark hillside, and he was able to stand erect.

The flashlight swept the open area, essentially a man-made cave used as a staging area for the mine. The air was clammy, heavy with a musty odor, the walls glistened with moisture, and the floor was scattered with rusty tools. Two tunnels ran at right angles back into the mountain. Several yards from the entrance, a shaft went straight down.

Paul knew enough about the copper mines in the area to know the shaft connected this level with lower levels of tunnels where ore was dug or blasted out of the walls. He had no idea how many levels down this mine went, but he was sure there must be at least two more. The tunnel that had given way tonight showed signs of an earlier collapse.

What had triggered the two cave-ins? Years of dirt sifting from the roof, but some catalyst had been needed to cause the roof to finally collapse into a sinkhole. The first time there had probably been a natural cause, heavy rains or a fault line shifting. But he was sure tonight's collapse been engineered.

It didn't take him long to find the tools: blasting caps, a set of heavy wind bells, a small generator, a projector, and a child's white nightgown. Not Scott. Possibly Carly or Krystal. Or was it someone else, someone who had managed to stay so far back in the shadows they didn't even suspect him or her. And why? What of Lois's possessions could be worth all this?

∽

Marty woke in fits and starts. She was in Granny Lois's bed buried in quilts. Her left leg throbbed. Someone was snoring. Snoring? Marty turned toward the sound. Paul was draped across the delicate lady chair, legs splayed out in front of him, arms practically touching the floor. It was no wonder he was snoring. His head was in a position she was sure would cause a stiff neck when he woke up.

What was he doing? Sitting with her as if she was a sick child, as he might have done with Scott long ago. Or guarding her against an intruder. Whatever he'd been thinking was unnecessary. But sweet. She had to admit it was sweet.

She didn't know how to respond. They were casual acquaintances or maybe new friends, but they didn't have the kind of relationship that called for him to feel protective of her. But how she was going to respond was the least of her worries. At the moment, she needed to make a trip to the bathroom without waking him. Digging out of the quilts as quietly as she could, she slipped from the bed and tiptoed down the hall to the guest bathroom.

By the time she was finished washing her hands, she had a plan for dealing with Paul. First, she pulled two quilts and a pillow off the bed. Wrapping herself in one quilt, she dropped the other things beside the chair. Then she moved to the side of the chair just out of Paul's line of sight and said quietly, "Paul, it's time to trade places. You get in bed. I'll take the chair for a while."

He came partly awake. "Marty?"

She repeated her instructions.

"Are you okay?"

"I'm fine. It's your turn to sleep in the bed."

As she had hoped, he was groggy enough to follow instructions without arguing. The bed looked too small for him, but it was better than the chair. As he stretched out with a contented sigh, she untied his sneakers, so worn she wasn't sure they could still be classified as shoes. The socks weren't much better, but as soon as his feet were free, Paul turned on his side and went back to sleep. Marty retrieved the second quilt and covered him with it.

She considered going into Tommy's room, but the bunk bed didn't appeal. Besides, to keep from making herself a liar, she had to do at least a short stint in the chair. She pulled the bench from the dressing table around and put her legs up on it, being careful with her left leg. It had stopped bleeding, and she didn't think it would need stitches.

Using the pillow to prop her leg, Marty got as comfortable as she could. Then she studied Paul. Obligingly cooperative in sleep, he turned again, this time to face her. The scruffy beard was thicker along the line of his angular jaw. If he didn't want to look like Pa Kettle he'd have to trim it soon. His hair was a dark tangle she suspected would wave if cut properly. With his deep brown eyes closed, she noticed surprisingly long lashes.

He was too tall for her, or she was too short for him. Scott was already taller than she was. And it was naïve to think of Paul without considering Scott. A fourteen-year-old still had a lot of growing up to do, years at home, in college and finding an adult path. The ten years between her age and Paul's was insignificant when compared to the fourteen-year difference between her age and Scott's. Whether the teen was guilty of drug use and mayhem or innocent as a newborn babe, she couldn't imagine trying to be a mother to a teenager.

Mother? What was she thinking? Not thinking, feeling. Paul's kiss had been tender, soft on her lips. Certainly not the kiss of a brother. Another time, another place maybe. She could almost hear Vicki: "You're in love, Mart. Quit fighting it."

Marty closed her eyes to block out the figure on the bed that kept sending her mind on rabbit trails. Was she in love and fighting it? There was no doubt her feelings were different from any she'd experienced for Ted. Or for Brad. Less complicated. But what about Paul? Was he in love and fighting it?

Before she could decide about either of them, she drifted off to sleep.

Chapter Twenty-six

Now I'm angry. Marty has gone back on her word. She told everyone she would leave Jerome after Lois's funeral. The funeral is over, but I haven't heard so much as a rumor that she's bought a plane ticket. That's a problem.

Paul Russell is another problem. What was he doing at her house at midnight? If he hadn't showed up, my little show at the mine would have worked. It was the most carefully planned of my little charades. And it was coming off without a hitch until the white knight appeared to rescue the damsel in distress.

I've never liked Paul, but he had his life, and I had mine, and there was never any need to interact. But now, the more Marty listens to his theories, the bigger threat he becomes. He's smart. I've got to give the devil his due. But knowing what happened to Lois and proving it are two different things. I'm certain he understands that. Even if he shoots off his mouth, Sheriff Winston will see the futility of trying to rewrite history. Because that's what Lois is: history. An urn of ashes. Not that it would matter if there were a body to exhume. Lois Baker fell down the stairs. A sad accident.

But I've got to be careful about the rest of it. I can't make the mistake of underestimating the esteemed Dr. Russell, particularly not if he and Marty become a solid team. It's been amusing to watch the two of them dance around each other. Unfortunately, I'm afraid his rescue has cemented their relationship. They're running out of time for their star-crossed courtship.

Paul will be the next one to have an accident. This one will be for keeps. I don't have a firm plan yet, but I'm good at improvisation. Very good.

Chapter Twenty-seven

Paul stretched, slammed his hands into metal, explored the contours. A brass bedstead, not his air mattress. He opened his eyes to an elaborate white tin ceiling. Not the hovel, Lois Baker's house. Marty, the sinkhole. But how had he gotten into the bed? He remembered stretching out in the awkward little chair. He turned his head. Marty was curled in the chair, sound asleep. Sometime in the night they had changed places.

Paul stretched again, being careful where he flung his hands. He sat up, swung his legs to the floor, and realized his shoes weren't on his feet. They were beside the bed, lined up as neatly as if his mother had put them there. What must Marty think of him? He rubbed his face. It was time to decide whether he intended to grow some sort of real beard or shave. He also needed a haircut, clean clothes, and a shower. Not in that order. He should go home.

He pulled his shoes on, got up as quietly as he could, and studied the sleeping form. Auburn curls hung in disarray around a peaceful face. Swathed in the pink and blue quilt, she looked like a child wrapped in a favorite blanket. He knew what Marty would say if she could hear those thoughts. If he knew what was good for him, he'd never voice them. But it didn't keep them way.

He forced his thinking into a more productive channel and considered what action to take. Leave her where she was or transfer her to the bed? Remembering her leg, he winced at the idea of jarring it while she slept and decided to leave her where she was. Paul tiptoed out of the room and down the hall. He paused at the point where he imagined Lois grabbing the railing.

He had to find out who. And why. Or maybe he needed to look at the puzzle another way, figure out why, then determine who. But until he knew the identity of the killer and made sure he or she was locked up, he had to keep Marty safe. The only way he could think to do that was to stay close. He didn't expect a frontal attack in broad daylight, but he hurried.

As Paul mounted the stairs in the hovel, he wondered if he would ever think of this house as anything else. Maybe Scott was right. Maybe the best alternative was to tear it down. Or abandon it to the fate of so many tumbledown shacks in Jerome and start over somewhere else.

That brought him right back to Scott. And no cell phone service at the Kenyon cabin. There was nothing to do but wait for his son to come home. He suddenly understood the parable of the prodigal son from the father's point of view.

Fifteen minutes later, clean but still shaggy, Paul raided his refrigerator for the makings of French toast and loaded it all in a plastic grocery bag. Fifteen more minutes and he was frying sausage in Lois's cast iron skillet.

"I smell breakfast!"

Paul thought he'd admitted to himself how he felt about Marty, but he was surprised at the welter of emotions the sound of her voice stirred up. Relief, joy, excitement, love. Love? That surprised him. Of course, he was attracted to her, but love was an emotion that grew slowly. Or so he'd always believed. He turned the idea over in his mind, wondering if he should tell her. With a spatula in one hand and a paper towel in the other?

Paul cleared his throat, did his best to clear his mind. "I hope you're hungry this morning."

"Hungry enough to eat the entire pig that sausage came from. What else is on the menu?"

"How does French toast sound?"

She hesitated.

She didn't like French toast. He turned to face her. Her damp hair curled in dark ringlets that hung to her shoulders. "I can fry eggs or scramble them."

"No. French toast sounds perfect."

She was wearing white shorts and a green t-shirt embossed with a white rocking chair and the slogan "Antiques Rock." Her left leg was wrapped with an ace bandage. He focused on breakfast. "If you don't like French toast, it's not a problem."

"But I do! It's just that I suddenly remembered Granny Lois fixing French toast for Ruthie and me. On that day."

He didn't need to ask which day.

"With peanut butter. Do you suppose there's any around here?"

Peanut butter on French toast didn't sound like a gourmet item, but Paul knew that wasn't the point. "No idea. Check the pantry."

She opened the door and turned on the light. Paul focused on breakfast. Again. He was not a teenager with a crush on a pretty girl. He cracked eggs in the glass baking dish, added milk, and then put two pieces of bread in to soak. He heard the pantry door close. "Find any?"

"Real maple syrup. No peanut butter."

"I have some. I can run home and get it."

"Thanks, no. That combination doesn't actually appeal. I suppose I thought it might bring back more of that day."

"You're starting to remember."

"Bits and pieces."

"What about the copper box?"

"I haven't found it." Marty went to the silverware drawer, opened it, and started setting the table. "But I found someone who remembers what happened to Ruthie."

He flipped the French toast in the skillet, then put two more pieces of bread to soak in the egg. "Great! Who?"

"Not great, just good. Luella Hodges. Her story wasn't exactly coherent."

"If I'm thinking of the right person she lives out at Living Waters. I didn't see her at the funeral."

Marty opened a cupboard and took down plates. "No. Brad drove me out to see her."

He lifted the skillet off the burner, turning to face her. "About yesterday, Marty. I'm sorry I went off with your keys in my pocket."

"Scott is much more important than the keys to a rental car, to any car."

She gave him a smile that told him she was speaking the truth. He felt a weight lift off his shoulders, completely out of proportion to the minor offense.

"Did you have a good talk with Scott?"

"I'll know in a day or so." Paul wasn't ready to try to explain an interaction that was far from finished. He transferred two pieces of French toast to a plate. "I hope yesterday was one of Luella's good days. What did she tell you?"

"That Ruthie died when a mine shaft collapsed, the one out back."

Paul added a sausage patty to the plate and handed it to her. He was right about an earlier collapse of that tunnel. "Now you know you didn't push her, surely the nightmares will end."

"Not necessarily. Luella told me how Ruthie disappeared. But I still don't know why she was running away. I might have been chasing her, caught up, and pushed her into that sinkhole." She paused and took a shaking breath. "The copper box has something to do with it. I know it does. I remember hiding it, but I have no idea where."

"Tell you what. As soon as we've finished breakfast, I'll help you."

"Marty! Is Paul Russell here?" Lockridge's voice.

∿

Marty saw the color drain out of Paul's face, his jaw clench. He thought Brad had news of Scott. Her stomach did a flip.

"What's happened?"

"He's been arrested."

Marty took a deep breath. Not good, but at least the teen wasn't hurt.

The color came back into Paul's face, but he didn't look surprised. Marty wondered why. Then she realized she didn't know what he'd found out by the mine shaft. Evidence Scott was the culprit?

Paul put the skillet in the sink. "Where?"

"In Cottonwood."

Marty saw a muscle in the back of Paul's neck tighten, as if the information surprised him, though she couldn't imagine why.

"For?"

"Drug possession."

This time Paul's shoulders sagged ever so slightly. He must have been expecting the answer or something like it. Marty supposed she should feel relieved Paul had an idea of what was going on. Instead all she felt was sad.

Brad went on. "He's at Juvie."

Paul nodded and reached for a paper towel.

Marty said, "I'll go with you."

Avoiding her eyes, Paul wiped his hands. "No."

"We can take the Camry."

"No, Marty. Thank you."

"At least take the Camry. You'll make better time."

Paul looked at her then with an expression that made her want to pull him into a hug. "No, Marty. Thank you. Scott is my son. I need to deal with this in my own way."

So formal, she was surprised he didn't call her Ms. Greenlaw.

Paul gave Brad a stiff thank-you and left.

Marty realized she was still holding the plate of French toast. Putting it down, she started to go after him.

Brad caught her arm. "Let him go. He has to do this alone."

Of course, Brad was right. Had she misread Paul's feelings so badly? She'd thought something was happening between them, something that would have included her in this tragedy.

"I know this is upsetting," Brad said. "Scott seems like a good kid. But this is exactly what I've thought was going on from the very start."

Marty nodded numbly. Maybe she hadn't misread Paul; maybe she'd simply projected her own feelings on to him.

"It looks like you haven't had breakfast. Come on. I'll take you into town."

"I'm not hungry. I'll just clean up this mess and then I'll get to work on the inventory."

"Sit down, eat what's on your plate and tell me what happened to your leg."

Three commands in a single sentence. But Marty was too focused on Paul to do more than notice. She sat in the chair Brad held out for her and picked up her fork.

How to say, "The man I love rescued me?" But, of course, that truth was totally inappropriate. She gave herself an internal shake and took a bite of French toast that had all the appeal of cardboard. "I had another visit from my prankster last night."

Brad raised an eyebrow. "'Prankster'? You told me you and Paul had decided you were up against a murderer."

"We thought we were. But I can't believe Scott pushed Lois down the stairs! There must be another explanation for those broken spindles." She handed him her plate. "I really can't eat."

Brad took the plate and set it on the counter. "I won't argue with that. I've never believed Lois's death was anything but a sad accident. But we're talking about last night. What happened? What prank did Scott pull?"

Not a prank. But she didn't want to admit to anything that would make things look worse for Scott. "A light show with wind chimes for sound effects."

"That doesn't sound dangerous. How did you hurt your leg?"

"What he did wasn't dangerous. It was my reaction that got me hurt. I was running in the dark. Not surprisingly, I fell." She knew she was making light of a serious situation, but she felt protective of Scott. Or of Paul? Had he known all along Scott was the culprit? He must have recognized Scott's number as the source of the text messages. And those messages started it all.

"I don't understand. Where were you running in the dark?"

"Out back."

"In the back yard?"

"Out by the old mine."

"Pretty dangerous venue for a prank. If you'd fallen into that old sinkhole, you could have been badly hurt."

Or killed. But she didn't say it. "I fell on some rocks. This bandage makes my leg look worse than it is, but I couldn't find anything else to wrap it in. It'll be fine in a couple of days." She pushed back her chair and got to her feet. "I'm ready to get some work done. If you'll give me a hand with the dishes, we can make short work of the kitchen."

"Do them later. Let me help you. Maybe we can get the inventory finished."

Anything to get out of the kitchen. Anything to take her mind off Paul, off Paul and Scott. "I want to concentrate on finding the little copper box I told you about. I'm close to re-membering what happened, Brad. Really close, so close I can feel it."

"Sure. Where do we start?"

Marty shrugged. "Maybe in the attic. I've looked there, but Carly and I haven't done an actual inventory of the contents."

"Kill two birds with one stone. Look for the box and do the inventory. Where's your laptop?"

Marty shook her head. "We're doing the first step the old-fashioned way, with pencil and paper. I transcribe into a computer file every night. The notebook is on the dining room table."

He followed her down the hall. "Last night after I got home I remembered an interesting anecdote Lois told me about the copper box."

"I don't suppose she told you where I hid it?"

"No. She told me what makes it special. But maybe you already know."

"All I know is it's been in the family a long time."

"Since the 1890s."

"From about the time Jerome became a town?"

"Just about. Lois told me Henry's great-grandfather made the box as a gift for his first grandchild."

"Grandpa Henry's father?"

Brad nodded. "The family joke was Leo Baker was born, not with a silver spoon in his mouth, but a copper box in his fist."

Marty tried to smile. But nothing about the copper box seemed amusing. She opened the loose-leaf notebook and took out several sheets of blank paper. "It definitely qualifies as an antique then. But I need it for much more recent family history."

"You're sure you hid it the day Ruthie died?"

"Positive."

"All right. Instead of sifting through the attic, let's see if we can reconstruct your actions that day. Let's go up to the little study. Wasn't that the room you girls shared?"

Brad put his hand under her elbow and guided her toward the staircase. She looked up at him curiously. "That's actually a good idea. Did you major in psychology in college?"

"Nope. Pre-law all the way. But a good lawyer has to be able to read people."

As they climbed past the broken spindles, Marty thought of Paul's careful scrutiny of the staircase. A good teacher had to be attentive to details. And that probably included people. What about family?

When they were in the study, Brad said, "Sit in the recliner. Put your feet up. Relax."

"Do you do hypnosis as part of your practice?"

Brad grinned. "Sometimes I wish I did. It would save a lot of time sifting through the lies to get to the truth." He pulled the desk chair next to the recliner and positioned it to face her. When they were both settled, he said, "Do you remember anything specific to that day?"

"I think Granny Lois made French toast with peanut butter."

"Is that why Paul was making French toast?"

"The reverse. Smelling the French toast brought back the memory."

"Makes sense. So breakfast was French toast. What happened after breakfast?"

Marty closed her eyes. Ruthie ran away, screamed, and disappeared. She opened her eyes. "Maybe this isn't such a good idea, Brad. I'm not sure I'm ready." She wanted Paul to be here, but she didn't say it.

"You were six, Marty. No matter what you think you did, it couldn't be that bad. You're what now? Twenty-eight? Use your adult perspective. Tell yourself it's time to remember."

Brad was wrong, of course. Marty knew whatever she had done was so terrible it could never be forgiven. But he was right too. It was time to face it. She'd rather Paul was here, but at least she wasn't alone. And Brad wasn't distracted by a son in crisis.

Marty took a deep breath and closed her eyes. Again Ruthie ran away. But this time she looked back, laughing. Suddenly she screamed and disappeared. No doubt into the sinkhole Luella had told her about. But where was she as she watched Ruthie? Marty put her hands over her face. Before that! Before Ruthie ran away. "I think we had a fight."

"That's a start. What was the fight over?"

Marty opened her eyes, shrugged. "No idea. I think I had a short fuse when I was little."

"Okay. What did your grandmother do? Did she separate the two of you? Send you to your room?"

"She told us to go outside." The words came straight out of her memory without going through her conscious mind. "She said it was a pretty morning. Now the rain was finally over we should go outside to play."

"Let's go."

Marty got up, followed him down the stairs and out the back door onto the porch. The morning was cool, like it was twenty-two years ago. "The yard was muddy. Granny Lois told us to stay on the porch."

Brad pulled two Adirondack chairs out toward the edge of the porch. Marty shook her head and went to sit on the steps. "I need to do what I did then."

"Okay. What happened next?"

Marty closed her eyes. Ruthie, the little girl with a halo of golden hair from her dreams sat on the steps beside her. Marty reached in the copper box for a black button with a diamond in it. Probably glass, but they believed the buttons had diamond centers. She handed the first button to Ruthie, then reached in the box for a second one for herself.

"I had the copper box out here. I wasn't supposed to take it outside, but Granny Lois was busy with Uncle Tommy. Besides, the porch wasn't really outside. Not like the yard. I sneaked into the living room and pulled the ottoman to the fireplace. I was tall enough to reach the mantel if I stood on the ottoman.

"I was ashamed of myself. I knew I was breaking the rules, but I was bored. Besides, the copper box was mine. I was the oldest. I looked in the copper box again. Tiny seashells, no bigger than a penny. One seashell for Ruthie, one for me.

Brad's voice was a whisper in Marty's ear. "What happened next? Tell me, Martha."

Had she been remembering out loud? She wasn't sure. But she started using words. "Tommy was yelling to come out on the porch. Ruthie grabbed a shiny coin. I grabbed it back. I had to put everything in the box. Tommy was a tattletale, and I didn't want Granny Lois to get mad. Ruthie snatched another coin. I slapped her hand and took away the coins. She stuck out her tongue at me. Then she grabbed the ball with the pink and yellow butterflies in it and ran down the steps into the yard."

Her voice stopped working. The memory was so intense that she wasn't twenty-eight remembering what it was like to be six. She was six years old. And Tommy was yelling like he did sometimes. Granny Lois kept trying to get him to be quiet. Martha knew they were going to come out on the porch. She had to hide the copper box someplace safe from Tommy. Somewhere Ruthie couldn't find it.

Under the porch. Tommy was too big to crawl under there, and Ruthie was afraid of the dark. Martha picked up the copper box and jumped off the porch. She knew about the corner where the lattice that covered the crawl space had come loose. All she had to do was pull it back and get on her hands and knees.

It was dirty under the porch, but Martha knew the copper box would be safe there. As she tucked it in a cubbyhole she'd found the first time she explored under the porch, she heard Tommy's heavy shoes over her head. She had to get out quick. Granny Lois would be right behind Tommy. Martha was crawling out from under the porch when she heard Ruthie scream.

Chapter Twenty-eight

Paul downshifted the Land Cruiser. Traffic was light through town this early in the morning, but he needed to slow down. Not just his physical speed. His mind was racing, jumping from one out-of-context piece of data to the next. No matter how he looked at it, he didn't have sufficient information to draw a useful conclusion.

All he knew was what Brad had told him: Scott was at Juvie. In Cottonwood. His son had been arrested. For drug possession. He should have responded to Brad's information with questions: why Scott hadn't called him, who had contacted Brad, if Scott was with B.T., where Dan Kenyon was.

Instead he had allowed his dismay to catapult him into action before he understood the situation clearly. Paul had no reason to doubt Brad, but he still couldn't quite believe it. He had been so sure Scott wasn't using drugs, so sure his son was telling him the truth. He had accepted he was out of touch with Scott's feelings about the work on the house, had accepted he had emotionally abandoned Scott the last two years. He hadn't accepted, still didn't accept, that he couldn't tell when his son was lying to him.

Of course, there could be another explanation. Scott had said he was trying to help B.T. Maybe Scott had been in the wrong place at the wrong time. But that excuse wouldn't fly.

Scott had told him he was going to the Kenyon cabin. What was he doing getting arrested in Cottonwood?

Not that any of the answers to those questions mattered. No matter the reasons, or lies, behind the current crisis, Paul still would have headed down the mountain, still would have insisted Marty stay behind.

Why had Marty wanted to come with him? He was drawn to her, maybe even in love with her, but Scott was his problem. Marty didn't really even know Scott. Had she wanted to come to support not the son, but the father? That would mean . . .

On the passenger's seat, Paul's cell phone jingled, the tones that meant Scott was calling. Any other call he would have ignored. But not this call, not under these circumstances. He was on a straight stretch of road, passing the artists' co-op. Paul ran his finger across the face of the phone, touched the call icon, said, "Scott! Thank God."

"I love you, Dad."

"I love you too, Scott. No matter what's happened, remember I love you."

"I'm sorry I said it was your fault Mom died."

"It's okay, son. I understand why you said it."

"I don't think you do, Dad. Because I didn't understand, not until last night anyway. I've been blaming you because I was afraid to blame God."

Whatever Paul had expected Scott to say, it wasn't that. It took him a moment to rearrange his thoughts.

"Dad? Are you there?"

"I'm here. I was just surprised."

"I know. It sounds crazy to blame God."

"It doesn't sound crazy at all, son."

"I slept outside last night. You know how many stars you can see up here on the Peaks. The sky looks almost crowded. I started thinking about God, and then I started talking to him.

I haven't really prayed in a long time. It was like when Mom died, God died too. But He didn't. I'm not making sense, am I?"

"You're making perfect sense, son."

"I've always heard we can say anything to God. He knows what we're thinking anyway, but he wants us to be honest with him. I told him I didn't understand why he let Mom die, especially after how hard we all prayed."

"Did he give you an answer?"

Scott laughed shakily. "No. But it felt good to just go on and say it. Then I started looking at all those stars and I thought how little I am and how crazy it was to think God was actually listening to me. But I knew he was. I could feel him, like being in a dark room with someone. You can't see them, but you know they're there. I fell asleep thinking about that."

Paul started to say, "I've felt that sometimes too," but Scott wasn't finished.

"I woke up really early this morning and watched the sun come up. It was like a new day started in my heart too. I'm not mad at God anymore. I still miss Mom, but I know she's in the best place. And I know it wasn't your fault she died. I get it, Dad. We've both changed, and we need to get to know each other again. I want to do that, Dad."

Paul felt a surge of hope. *Thank you, Father.* But he was confused too. How did all of this fit with being arrested for drugs in Cottonwood? But there wasn't time for an explanation now. He was almost at the top of the switchbacks, and they would lose their signal as soon as he started down. "I want to do that too, son, no matter what's happened. I'll be at Juvie in thirty minutes, forty tops."

"Juvie? I'm in Flagstaff, Dad."

The road doubled back on itself, headed down the side of the mountain. Paul put his foot on the brake, but the Land Cruiser didn't slow.

He pumped the brakes. The Land Cruiser accelerated.

"Dad?" The cell phone slid to the floor.

The speedometer read fifty, too fast for the next turn. Paul pushed the brake pedal all the way to the floor. Nothing. He pulled the steering wheel hard, managed the left turn.

The road veered right. If he could just make it around this switchback, he could ram the Land Cruiser into the side of the mountain. A head-on collision with rock was preferable to a double or triple somersault to the canyon floor. Unless God chose that moment to work a miracle and suspend the laws of gravity, those were his options.

Even as he leaned on the steering wheel, Paul knew he wouldn't have time. The pieces of the puzzle dropped into place: Lockridge's car parked beside his Land Cruiser. Scott in Flagstaff. Marty …

～

Marty opened her eyes.

Brad was standing over her, frowning. "You've remembered. Tell me."

She blinked in the sunlight. It had been dark under the porch. "Ruthie was outside the fence. We were never allowed outside the fence. I should have been watching her."

"She was outside the fence. Where were you?"

But the narration, once begun, couldn't be interrupted. "Ruthie was running toward the sign with the skull and crossbones. I shouted."

"Where were you, Marty?"

"One minute Ruthie was running away and laughing. Then the dirt under her feet started to move. Ruthie screamed. The ground opened around her, sucked her down to where the fire is. She disappeared."

"The mine tunnel collapsed, created a sinkhole. Where were you, Marty?"

Marty blinked. "Didn't I say?"

"You did not. Where were you when you saw Ruthie disappear?"

"I was crawling out from under this porch. The corner. The lattice was loose."

"Is that where you hid the copper box? Under this porch?"

Marty nodded.

"Is it still there?"

"I guess so. You said my grandmother didn't know where it was. Unless she found it under the porch and then it was lost again."

"Unlikely." Brad exhaled noisily, as though he'd been holding his breath. He held out a hand.

Marty took it, let him pull her to her feet.

"Great!" He smiled. "I don't imagine it will be too hard to retrieve."

"There's no need. Now that I've remembered what happened, I don't need the box."

Marty looked out over the backyard, past the hollyhocks, beyond the gold fish pond they used to call "Granny Lois's folly," across the kudzu-covered hillside to the sinkhole, larger now than when Ruthie tumbled in.

"I didn't push Ruthie with my hands, but I pushed her away by refusing to play with her. If I'd been nicer to her or even just watched to make sure she stayed in the yard, she wouldn't have died." No wonder she'd buried the memory so far down, as far as Ruthie fell.

"You may not need the box for the memory, but it's quite a family heirloom. You don't want to leave it under the porch."

"It's been perfectly safe there for twenty-two years. One of these days I'll borrow a six-year-old who can crawl under there and retrieve it for me."

He grabbed her arm. "Let's do it now. I'll help you."

295

"For Pete's sake, Brad. It's not important."

"You don't understand. How far under the porch is it?"

She pulled loose from his grasp. "I have no idea."

A crackle of electricity like a radio signal gone awry filled the air. Then an echo: eeee—eeee—vaaa—eee—vaa—cuu—ayy— Finally they heard the voice: "Evacuate. Evacuate now. You are ordered to evacuate. Evacuate now. You are ordered to evacuate." Over and over, getting louder and then receding.

Marty looked at the dark sky. "We have to go."

He grabbed her arm again. "Not without the box."

"The box doesn't matter, Brad."

"Not the box itself. What it contains. Or don't you remember?"

"Buttons, seashells, coins."

"Five 1893 Carson City Mint silver dollars never circulated. Near proof like quality."

She stared at him. Brad? The copper box? "Tell me I'm wrong," she whispered. "Tell me your coin collection wasn't worth Granny Lois's life."

"Each one of those coins is worth something like $55,000. Multiply that by five, and you'll understand why I was interested in the copper box. When Lois told me the family joke about baby Leo and the copper box in his fist, she explained the silver for Leo's birth wasn't a silver spoon, but five silver dollars, I was afraid to believe it. But I did some research. Sure enough, baby Leo was born in 1893, the last year the Carson City Mint, the closest mint to Jerome, was in operation. I realized those coins had never been circulated. I did the math."

"Granted, $275,000 is a lot of money. But it's not as if you're destitute, Brad."

"You think I was after money?" He looked insulted. "Don't you see? Those silver dollars will be the crown jewels of my *Ghosts of the West* collection."

"But to murder an old woman."

"Like I've said all along, her fall was an accident. If Lois had stayed with her schedule, I wouldn't have been in the house when she came home."

"And the rest of it, locking me in the attic, the poltergeist, last night's light show?"

"You could have gone home, Marty. Instead you decided to stay."

"What about Krystal? Is she in this with you?"

"Let's just say Krystal is a friend, a suggestible friend."

"She's in love with you?"

Brad shrugged. "She wants this house."

"And Scott?"

"He didn't have anything to do with it, besides being a most convenient scapegoat."

"But the text messages from his phone."

"Accomplished with a trick of the internet any junior high kid, no doubt including Scott Russell, could explain to you."

"But why?"

"To scare you into staying out of this. It was better than even odds you would turn out to be the long-lost granddaughter. If you were, I hoped the message would keep you from coming to Jerome. If you didn't turn out to be Martha Baker, no harm done." Brad pulled a small pistol from his pocket and pointed it at Marty. "You realize you're forcing me into this. Get the box."

EEEE—VAAA—EEE—VAA—CUU—AYY—

Marty stared at the gun. Up until this moment, it had all been theoretical. Someone had pushed Granny Lois down the stairs. Now it was all real, much too real. Brad Lockridge had killed once for the silver dollars, and he would kill again. He would kill her. With the gun.

She went down the porch steps and walked to the corner where in her memory the lattice was loose. "The trellis has been repaired."

"So pull it off. You're a big girl now."

She put her fingers through the spaces in the woven wood, grasped, pulled. It gave but didn't come loose.

EEEE—VAAA—EEE—VAA—CUU—AYY—

"Give it a real tug," Brad said. "As if your life depended on it."

She pulled, tugged, pulled. When the nails finally let go, she staggered back.

"Now get the box."

Marty went down on her hands and knees, ignoring the sharp pain that shot down her left leg. The deck was just barely high enough for a six-year-old, certainly too low for an adult. Reaching under, she groped for the box. Nothing but dirt. "It's not here. Or else it's out of reach. I can't possibly get under there."

"There's a rechargeable flashlight in the kitchen by the back door. Get it. And get a broom or something to fish out the box."

"The box might not even be under there. Maybe I'm not remembering right."

"Quit stalling. If you're waiting for Dr. Russell to come to your rescue like he did last night, you're out of luck. In fact, we might have a double funeral for you and your boyfriend."

The smoke closed in. Marty could neither see nor breathe. "What do you mean?"

"It's pretty tough to go down the switchbacks without brakes, even in a classic Land Cruiser. He should have taken you up on your offer of the Camry."

Paul! "Scott?"

"Is fine as far as I know, for an orphan."

Paul.

"You know, Marty, it's a shame you preferred the professor to me. You and I could have done this the easy way. Too late now." He waved the pistol. "Get the flashlight. And don't get any ideas about making a run for it. I'll be with you every step of the way."

Marty moved mechanically. Up on the porch, open the door. She couldn't think. Paul. Marty knew she was in shock, but knowing didn't change anything. Brad might be lying. Paul! She had to think, had to get away.

The flashlight was where Brad said. She took it from its charger.

"Get a broom."

She didn't see a broom, remember a broom. "I don't know where it is."

"Find something else to use then, quickly."

"EVACUATE. EVACUATE NOW. YOU ARE ORDERED TO EVACUATE."

Someone was there, José with his fire truck. Maybe at the end of the road. But out there. Someone who could help.

If she could just think what to do! The pantry? Go in, close the door. It wasn't much of a plan, but it was better than nothing. She went to the pantry and opened the door. But before she could step inside, Brad was there, holding the door. "I'd hate for you to get trapped in the pantry. Lucky for you, I see a broom. Get it."

She couldn't think of anything else to do, so she obeyed. When they went back outside, the smoke was thicker. Marty coughed and looked up at the fringe of forest on the ridge behind the house. The tops of the pine trees were burning. What had she heard? A crown fire was impossible to stop.

Evidently Brad saw it too. "Hurry up, Marty."

She went back to where she had crawled out twenty-two years ago, dropped to her knees, swept the area under the porch with the yellow light. Rocks, dirt, bits of brick, rusted nails, no gleam of copper.

But the box had to be there. An adult couldn't have retrieved it. What other child would have gone under the porch? Tommy would have been too big.

"Do you see it?" She heard Brad come down the steps.

She didn't dare tell him no. She swept the light a second time. This time it showed her something square, back so far it was almost at the foundation of the house. Not the rich copper color she remembered, greenish blue, weathered from years of waiting.

He prodded her with his foot. "Is it there?"

"Yes." Marty sat back on her heels and coughed. "It's pretty far back. I'm not sure I can reach it, even with the broom."

"Try."

She did. Holding the wooden pole. Holding the straw. Crawling in so her shoulder was against the edge of the porch. The box was always just out of reach. One or two inches, but out of reach. No use.

"I can't get it, Brad. My arms aren't long enough. You might be able to reach it."

"Now there's an idea. You hold the gun while I get the box." He prodded her with his foot. "Get up. We'll just rearrange the agenda."

She didn't want to know, didn't ask. Just got to her feet and stumbled ahead of him into the house. Through the kitchen. Around the corner to the stairs. She saw him shift the gun in his hand so he was holding the barrel.

Now she had a pretty good idea of what he was thinking, but she couldn't for the life of her, literally for the life of her, figure out any way to stop him. Paul, I never told you . . .

Marty knew Brad was going to hit her with the gun. *Dear God, Father.* Pain exploded behind her eyes. She crumpled into darkness.

Chapter Twenty-nine

No angelic voices singing praise. No bright light. No Linda. Paul decided he must be alive. But not for long if he couldn't free himself of the suffocating airbags. Or the seatbelt that was pressing against his windpipe.

"Dr. Russell? Are you okay?"

A male voice. Young. A student? He was hallucinating.

"Dr. Russell?" The door in the ceiling squealed and opened. "Are you alive?"

Paul coughed, struggled to get his bearings. The door was overhead, so the Land Cruiser was on its side. God had decided on a miracle. *Thank you. Now for Marty, Father. She needs a miracle too.*

"Is Scott in there?"

Paul coughed again, located his arms, the steering wheel, pushed himself back from the airbag in his face. *Thank you. Tend to Marty, please!*

"Dr. Russell! Can you undo your seatbelt?"

Paul found the buckle, pushed. The pressure on his windpipe eased. *Thank you. Marty.*

"Is Scott in there?"

Scott. In Flagstaff. Not arrested. "No. I'm alone." *Thank you. Marty.* Paul studied the young face. Vaguely familiar, but he couldn't call the name. Not a student.

"Can you move your legs?"

Paul wiggled his toes. "Yes." *Thank you. Marty.*

"If you can move, I can help you get out."

For an answer, Paul untangled himself from the seatbelt, dragged his right arm out from under his body, and lifted his hands. The young man reached in through the open door, grabbed Paul under his arms, and pulled. Whoever he was, he was strong. Paul pushed, scrambled, and finally climbed out. *Thank you. Marty*. That was when he knew. This miracle was intended for both of them. He had to get to Marty.

Paul started to thank his rescuer, a young man with tattoos on both his arms. "B.T.?"

"Scott isn't answering his cell. I thought he might need help getting away from the fire. I saw your Land Cruiser flip and roll. It's some kind of miracle you're alive, Dr. Russell."

"Yes." But he had to get to Marty. Paul spotted the motorcycle, a Honda like Pete's. "It's a miracle you were here to help me. Will you let me use your bike?"

"You know how to ride? I thought you hated bikes."

Marty. "Later." Marty. "I've got to get up the mountain. Can I use it?" The request was automatic. Paul didn't plan to take no for an answer.

"They won't let you through. They're evacuating Jerome."

Paul was already moving toward the motorcycle. "I'll get through."

"You want me to go with you?"

Father, please! Paul swung his leg over the idling bike. "I'll make better time alone."

"Where's Scott?"

"Flagstaff. Call the sheriff. Tell him to come to the Baker house. Now!" Without waiting for another question, Paul kicked the stand and pressed the accelerator.

Fourteen years since he'd ridden a motorcycle, his promise to Linda when Scott was born. Anyone watching him wobble and weave the first mile of switchbacks would have wondered if he'd ever been on a bike at all. Marty.

The road was deserted, no doubt because the highway patrol had the road blocked at the bottom of the mountain. *Thank you, Father, for B.T. and his motorcycle.* A second miracle, a personal Good Samaritan rescue. Someday he would think it through, acknowledge the lesson. Someday.

Suddenly Paul regained his balance, as if he'd ridden every day of the intervening years.

Marty. No matter how fast he rode, it wasn't fast enough. Lockridge. Paul now knew who without an inkling of why.

A sharp right toward the mountain. Left toward the flimsy guardrail. Then two lanes of traffic coming down. The first wave of evacuees. Paul gritted his teeth, wove in and out, capitalized on every inch of roadway, made space where there wasn't any. Marty. Easy to let the roar of his engine drown out angry honks and shouts. Marty. He'd thought he'd never feel this deep desire to share everything with another woman again. In a way, he'd been right, what he felt for Marty wasn't the same as what he'd felt for Linda. Love, an inexact word for a range of emotion impossible to pin down. All of it intense, need as much as desire.

Then he was in town, and he no longer had even a portion of his mind to examine his feelings. Here the congestion was even more complicated, but here he had driveways and parking lots to add precious inches to the road. Marty. No time to wonder if he was in time. It took every ounce of concentration to avoid first one collision and then another.

Finally, Paul leaned in and turned up the old mine road. One house, a second house where an old man backed his battered pickup into the road. Paul swung around and pushed harder. The empty stretch, the old warehouse. Higher up Cleopatra Hill the old boardwalk was in flames.

Several hundred yards from the Baker house, Paul turned off the motor and laid the bike down. Surprise was the only advantage he had. Marty. *Father!*

Even as the plea took shape in his mind, a scrub oak not twenty feet away ignited. One chance in a million to get her out of here. About the same odds he had when the Land Cruiser took to the air. *Father!* Paul started to run.

Thirty minutes or thirty hours since he so willingly walked into Lockridge's trap? Marty. In spite of his desperate need for speed, pain in his right leg slowed him down. Paul pushed away the pain, pushed away the fear he might already be too late, pushed everything out of his mind except the need to find Marty.

The Lexus sat in front of the hovel in the spot that had been so convenient to the Land Cruiser's wheels. The work of ten minutes to puncture the brake line so the fluid would leak out slowly. The Lexus was hope of a sort. Lockridge was still here. Hope as insubstantial as the smoke seeping out around the attic window. Marty. *Father . . .*

Across the road, a tongue of fire licked the roof of the hovel and curled toward the window of his study. Paul turned away. He hunkered down, ran for the Baker house. Lois's porch, the screen, the front door. The knob turned easily. Paul pushed the door open a few inches, listened.

Down the mountain, José's voice came over the loud-speaker, "Evacuate. You are ordered to evacuate!"

Inside the house, silence.

Paul held his breath, then pushed the door open all the way. Lockridge's voice, a steady rant, a string of curses. Not inside the house. Around back, the porch.

Marty. *Father.* Paul went inside. Entry way, empty; living room, empty; parlor, empty. He was halfway down the hall when he heard the moan. Marty. *Father?*

He sprinted, negotiated the corner, and ran headlong into a nightmare. Marty lay at the bottom of the stairs where they'd found Lois. The difference was Marty was moaning. *Thank you.*

Oblivious to the pain in his leg, he squatted beside her. With gentle fingers, he explored her head, where he found a goose egg so large it made him wince. He explored her neck, felt the vertebrae lined up, put his mouth to her ear, and hissed, "Marty!"

Something crashed outside. Wood splintered. Lockridge cursed.

Paul had to get Marty away, now. *Father!* He slid his arm under her shoulders and lifted. Her eyes opened. For a moment, all he saw there was confusion. Then recognition.

"Paul!"

"Don't let him hear you."

She put her arms around his neck and raised her head until her lips were against his ear. "I love you, Paul."

He wanted to respond, shout he loved her too, crush her in an embrace until she squealed. Not the time. Not the place. "I love you too."

Another crash, this one just outside the back door. Paul wanted to scoop her up and make a run for the motorcycle. But he knew his leg would give out before he had her off the floor. "Can you stand up?"

She kept one arm around his neck, got her feet under her, and tried to stand. Hanging on to her, he struggled up. They clung together, swayed in a surreal potato sack race, and managed to get upright. Marty put her mouth to his ear. "He has a gun."

The knot in Paul's stomach tightened. One chance in two million now.

He felt Marty tense, heard her swallow a cough. Suddenly Paul realized he couldn't breathe, not just from fear, from smoke. Smoke drifted down the stairs, filled the hallway.

"Brad didn't want to wait for the forest fire."

Father . . . They had to get out, with even less time than he'd thought.

Marty swallowed another cough. "The mine. We'll be safe there."

Lockridge was in the back of the house. Out front was fire. Marty was right. They would be safe in the mine. Their chances rose to one in a million if they could get by Lockridge with his gun. They would have to go around the side of the house. But there wasn't a door on the side.

The windows in the living room. He didn't waste time explaining, just took her hand and limped back down the hall. She came without question as if she read his mind.

They made it to the living room, almost to the windows, when Lockridge roared from the hallway, "You won't get away, Marty!"

Paul let go of her hand, pushed her toward the window, and hissed, "Go!"

"Not without you!"

"He doesn't know I'm here. All he knows is you're not at the foot of the stairs. I'll get the gun and be right behind you. I've got surprise on my side."

That was all he had. The adrenaline that had gotten him this far was wearing off, and he was feeling every one of what must be a hundred injuries. One chance in three million now. *Father.* He brushed her cheek with his lips and then turned away.

As Paul limped back across the room, he felt blood ooze down his right leg. But he didn't have time to worry about an open wound. He stood to the left of the doorway just out of the line of sight. He was ready when Lockridge came through, ready for a gun, not for an ax. Just in time to keep from burying the blade in his own chest, he checked his leap.

"Russell?" For a split second the other man sounded genuinely bewildered.

That split second was all Paul needed. He grabbed Lockridge's right arm and twisted. The other man shouted in pain and dropped the ax. Before Lockridge could recover his balance, Paul pushed him to the floor. For a moment, he thought he had him, but then Lockridge rolled out of reach and scrambled to his feet. Paul braced himself, but the other man ran out of the room. It was Paul's turn to be bewildered.

"He's gone for the gun," Marty said from his elbow. "You get on one side of the door. I'll get on the other. If we both jump him, we can get it."

"You were supposed to ---"

"Don't argue! Get over there." She gave him a shove.

One chance in a thousand. He obeyed.

Lockridge was ready to be jumped on one side but not on both. Almost as if they'd planned it, Marty rammed her head into Lockridge's stomach and Paul grabbed his arm. As Lockridge dropped the gun, it went off, sending a wild shot somewhere much too close.

Before the other man could recover his balance, Paul forced him to the floor. Marty snatched up the gun and trained it on Lockridge. He wondered if she knew how to shoot it. Lockridge would have the same concern. Either way, she looked deadly serious.

"Marty," Paul said, "now will you go?"

"Not without you."

Out in the hall the ceiling burst into flames as the fire ate its way down from the attic. Paul hauled the other man to his feet. "We've got to get out of here, all of us. Right now!" He pushed Lockridge toward the window. "You first."

The other man turned back toward the doorway. "You're going to have to shoot me."

Marty looked at Paul.

"Let him go."

They ran.

The window frame was so hot, Paul felt his fingers blister. Gritting his teeth, he yanked it up. "Go! And this time don't argue. I'm right behind you."

At last, Marty climbed through. As he followed, his injured leg suddenly refused to move.

Marty was there, helping him through. "Your leg is bleeding!"

Before he could reassure her, she was on his left side, draping his arm around her shoulders, half-pulling him away from the house. Little but strong.

Fire was everywhere. The trees on the hill above the house were burning. Flames ran down the kudzu vines. In places, even the bare dirt smoldered.

Paul couldn't breathe, and Marty was coughing steadily. He stumbled once, but somehow, she kept him on his feet. He quit limping and started dragging his left leg. "Go, Marty!"

"Not without you."

At last they were there, just outside the mine entrance. Blocked by a sturdy wooden fence. If his leg had been even partially functional, he could have climbed it. "Go!" he said. "I'll be all right here."

This time she obeyed. She went over the fence, and he felt himself relax. At least she would be safe. He turned to face the fire. It was coming closer. He started to cough. If he was lucky, the smoke would get him first.

Then he heard it. Something crashing into the fence about ten feet away. Through the haze of smoke, he saw Marty attack a broken board with a long metal pole, a piece of rusty rebar. "Move!" she shouted. "I've almost got it."

He couldn't disappoint her, so he pulled himself up and clung to the fence. Hand over hand, he pulled, dragging the useless leg. He was almost there when she breached the fence. He stumbled through. She draped his arm over her shoulders again and practically carried him into the mine. Marty. Little but strong.

Cool, damp air filled his lungs, caressed his face, surrounded them.

Beside him, Marty drew in a sharp breath. "Brad. No!"

Lockridge was a dark silhouette on the porch of the glowing house. He flung the ax aside and dropped to his knees. As he reached for something only he could see, the roof of the porch exploded in flames and collapsed.

Epilogue

Marty almost missed it. Only a corner peeked out from inside the cement block that had been one of the porch supports. Even as she reached for it, she wasn't sure. Not red-gold, not blue-green, black with soot. But it was a metal box six inches by four inches.

She drew it out of its hiding place, but she didn't open it. Not yet. She left it on the ground, straightened, and looked up at the house, what was left of it. Not much had survived the fire. A few pieces of furniture she'd sent to Carly's shop. The stamp album in Brad's office. The paperweights. Some of the jewelry.

A week had passed since the fire fighters won their hard-fought battle. They'd halted the forest fire before it got to town, but the Baker house had burned to the ground. The hovel was gone, too, collateral damage of the fire Brad started in the attic of Granny Lois's house.

Two weeks since Brad's death. Ten days since she and Paul decided they really did love each other enough to figure out the distance between Virginia and Arizona, to create opportunities for Marty and Scott to forge a friendship, to decide what to do about their jobs.

She heard Paul coming, so she was ready when he put his arms around her waist, ready to meet the kiss he offered. When he let her go, he noticed the box on the ground.

"You found it. Are the silver dollars inside?"

"I haven't opened it."

"Come on. We'll do it together."

They went to the only place left to sit, the little wrought-iron bench beside Granny Lois's folly. The water had all evaporated from the tiny pond, leaving only the white rocks and the desiccated plants that had no business in Arizona anyway.

Marty handed Paul the copper box. It looked small in his large hands. "You open it."

He gave her a quizzical look.

She brushed a lock of unruly hair off his forehead. "I only wanted it for the memories I thought it held."

"You didn't need the copper box at all. You remembered when you were ready."

He had read her mind again, a habit she was getting used to. She stroked his smooth cheek with the back of her hand, traced the line of his mustache with her finger, scratched the carefully trimmed beard on his chin.

Paul put down the box and pulled her into his arms. "Ready to make some new memories?"

She kissed him then, hard. Mind-reader, father, professor, lover, soul mate.

Sometime later, Scott came whistling around the side of the ruined house. "Here you guys are!" He came to an abrupt halt twenty feet away. "Oh, sorry."

Marty let Paul go reluctantly. He took her hand, threaded their fingers together.

Marty smiled at Scott. "It's okay with us, if it's okay with you."

Scott's faced flamed. "Yeah. I mean, sure."

"What have you got there?" Paul said.

"Rahab," Scott said, holding out a slightly singed and much subdued cat. "She was sitting where the front porch used to be."

"We found something too," Marty said. "Come see."

Scott let the cat go and jogged over to the bench. Marty might have thought of his movement as "skipping," but she was learning.

"That's the copper box? It doesn't look like much."

Marty handed it to the teenager. "Open it."

Scott lifted the lid. Four black buttons, three tiny seashells not much bigger than the buttons. The silver dollars winked in the morning sun. He picked one up and turned it over so they could see Liberty's face on the back.

"I thought these might turn out to be nothing more than a family legend," Paul said.

Marty shook her head. "I remembered them. I just didn't know their value."

Scott took out the coins, then handed them one by one to Marty.

"Five bucks," Paul said.

"More like a cool quarter-mil," Scott said. "You going to rebuild the house, Marty?"

She hesitated. How to put half-formed feelings into words? "I don't think so. Maybe the three of us have had enough of the past. What would you think of helping your dad and me design something new? It will take time and patience. It might be interesting, maybe even fun."

Father and son responded almost at the same instant, two kisses for the price of one. Marty threw one arm around Paul's neck and the other around Scott's. Laughter bubbled up in Marty, exploded in Paul, burst from Scott, whispered on the air as if Lois Baker, little Ruthie and all the ghosts of Jerome joined in.

A Note on Setting

Jerome, Arizona is a real town. If it's possible to be in love with a town, I'm in love with Jerome. I've spent countless hours poking around in shops and art galleries. When I decided to take my desire to write fiction seriously, I went to Jerome. Many of the places in the novel exist pretty much as described: the three-stories of the town, the Jerome Grand Hotel, the Asylum Restaurant, the ice cream shop, and the handkerchief-sized park at the top of the long flight of stone stairs. Other places are purely imaginary. Mystic Glass, while its floorplan is loosely based on a delightful gift shop called Sky Fire and its collection of kaleidoscopes comes from my memories of an equally fascinating shop called Nellie Bly, doesn't exist. Neither do Granny Lois's house, the hovel, or Good Shepherd Church, though they wouldn't be out of place on Mingus Mountain or in the Verde Valley. If you've visited Jerome, I hope this story evokes memories of the largest ghost town in America. If you haven't yet been to Jerome, do your best to visit someday. You just might fall in love with a town.

The characters all came out of my imagination and are not based on any real person, living or dead.

You May Also Like

Adventrous Brooksie discovers a hidden room in her grandparent's house. She finds a doll sent from her grandfather to her mother long ago. A few days after showing it to her father, he is murdered and the doll becomes a memory. Could finding the doll have played a part in her dad's murder?

Deadly Doll by Brooke Cox

Patience McDonough heads to Verity College in Hades, Mississippi. She soon discovers secrets tying her family to the dark beginnings of Verity, founded on a slave plantation, and is forced to question the character of the people she has always trusted. Will the truth set her free?

Whitewashed by Amy C. Blake

Naomi Shetler has the perfect life – six lovely daughters and one son, a loving husband, a comfortable home in an impeccable community. All of it is threatened when she experiences a vivid dream that eerily comes to pass. Tragedy looms as she tries to stop the outcome of her latest dream.

Naomi's Sacrifice by Dr. Patrick Johnston

Mantle Rock Publishing

 Stay up-to-date on your favorite books and authors with our free e-newsletters. Sign up today at mantlerockpublishing.com.

 Find us on Facebook. facebook.com/mantlerockpbulishing/